"All I can tell you is...the truth."

"The truth?" Chase asked, sounding skeptical.

Marni nodded as she turned to face him. "The truth is...I'm in love with you."

For a moment, she thought he'd laugh in her face. "Cut your losses and give up this charade," he said, dropping his voice to a menacing softness as he leaned closer. "You are no more pregnant with my child than you are in love with me."

Before she could move, he took her face in his hands. In the depths of his gaze, she saw what he planned to do. He took her mouth with an intensity that stunned her. Her body ached; no one had ever kissed her like this.

He broke off the kiss and shoved himself away from her. "You and I have never kissed before," he said. "If we had, I would have remembered."

Dear Reader,

You've told us that stories about hidden identities are some of your favorites, so this month we're happy to bring you another, in the HIDDEN IDENTITY promotion. Join B. J. Daniels for a special Christmas HIDDEN IDENTITY mystery.

B.J. loves old houses, like the one in *Undercover Christmas*—set in her hometown of Bozeman, Montana—because they always have secrets of their own. So do families. Coming from a family that is rumored to have had a few horse thieves of its own, B.J.'s always been fascinated by family dynamics. She'd love to hear from her readers at P.O. Box 183, Bozeman, Montana 59771.

We hope you enjoy it—and all the HIDDEN IDENTITY books coming to you in the months ahead.

Regards,

Debra Matteucci

Senior Editor & Editorial Coordinator
Harlequin Books
300 East 42nd Street
New York, NY 10017

Undercover Christmas
B. J. Daniels

Harlequin Books

TORONTO • NEW YORK • LONDON
AMSTERDAM • PARIS • SYDNEY • HAMBURG
STOCKHOLM • ATHENS • TOKYO • MILAN
MADRID • WARSAW • BUDAPEST • AUCKLAND

To my daughter, Danielle Rosanne Smith.
Thanks for all the laughs, the love
and the encouragement.
You're the best.

ISBN 0-373-22446-X

UNDERCOVER CHRISTMAS

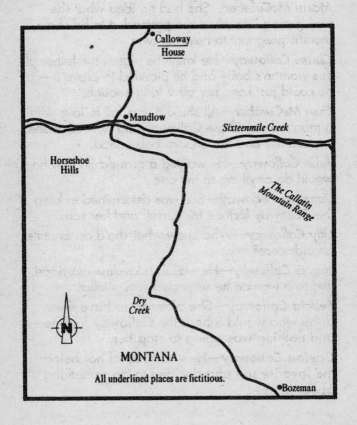

Calloway
House

• Maudlow

Sixteenmile Creek

Horseshoe
Hills

*The Gallatin
Mountain Range*

*Dry
Creek*

N

MONTANA

All underlined places are fictitious.

• Bozeman

CAST OF CHARACTERS

Marni McCumber—She had no idea what she was getting into when she pretended to be seven months pregnant to help her twin.

Chase Calloway—He knew he wasn't the father of this woman's baby and he planned to prove it—if he could just keep her alive long enough.

Elise McCumber—All she did was fall in love with a man named Chase Calloway and now someone wanted her and her unborn baby dead.

Jabe Calloway—He wanted a grandchild and he would do anything to get one.

Vanessa Calloway—She was determined to keep the Calloway fortune for herself and her sons.

Lilly Calloway—Who knew what she'd do to settle an old score?

Hayes Calloway—He was in a loveless marriage, tied to a woman he suspected was a killer.

Felicia Calloway—She planned to have the baby who would inherit the Calloway fortune—and nothing was going to stop her.

Dayton Calloway—He was tired of not being the favorite son and decided to do something about it.

Prologue

November 3

A biting cold wind stole down Main Street, sending the last of the shoppers scurrying. Chase pulled his coat around him and stepped to the curb in front of the old Bozeman Hotel to check again. It wasn't like his father to be late. But then Jabe Calloway had been doing a lot of unlikely things in the past few weeks.

Lights flickered off as downtown stores closed for the night. The traffic dwindled, exhausts cloudy and white as the vehicles passed. From the dark sky, snow sifted, covering the town in an icy layer of frost.

Worry stole Chase's thoughts the way the cold stole his body heat. He stomped his feet and rubbed his gloved hands together trying to stay warm. No, it wasn't like Jabe Calloway to be late nor to call his oldest son and ask him to meet him on a street corner.

The memory of something Chase thought he'd heard in his father's voice suddenly chilled him more than the weather. He hadn't been able to put a name to it. Probably because it was a word he'd never associated with his father. Fear. Chase glanced at his watch. Almost an hour late. Jabe had been explicit about the time. Nine sharp. Jabe had some papers he needed to sign at the family attorney's office and he wanted Chase to go with him. But at this late hour? No,

Jabe Calloway wasn't himself lately. Either something was terribly wrong or—

Chase turned at the sound of hurried footsteps slapping the snow-coated concrete. Jabe Calloway halted beneath the streetlamp across the intersection ten yards away and glanced upward as if waiting for the traffic light to change. He wore a gray Stetson hat on his salt-and-pepper hair, and a dark plaid shirt, jeans and boots beneath the long stockman duster that flapped open in the wind. At sixty-five, Jabe still stood six feet four and looked as solid as the lamppost next to him.

And yet for one ridiculous moment, Chase thought he saw his father stagger. Thought he saw frailty in those broad shoulders. And vulnerability.

The light changed. Jabe seemed to hesitate. Worried, Chase stepped off the curb and headed toward his father. He could feel Jabe's pale blue gaze. Eyes the same color as his own. Eyes always filled with a stubborn determination that brooked no interference.

Jabe nodded once and started across the street, all that usual arrogance and authority in his step. Chase almost laughed. Had he really thought Jabe Calloway might be in trouble? That this immovable rock of a man might need help?

The truck appeared out of nowhere. Headlights sliced through the snowfall as its engine revved and bore down on the tall cowboy in the street. Chase dived, hurling his father to the gutter as the truck's grill connected with Chase's left leg, the pavement with Chase's head. The lights went out. The truck kept going.

Chapter One

December 20

Marni pounded on the motel-room door, panicked by the hysterical phone call that had sent her racing across town on icy winter roads just days before Christmas.

"This'd better be good, Elise," she muttered as she waited impatiently for her sister to answer the door. This was so like Elise. After a five-month absence, a frantic phone call from a motel. And what was Elise doing staying at a motel anyway? She always stayed with Marni between adventures. So what had happened this time?

Only one answer presented itself, flashing on like one of the Christmas lights strung along the motel's eaves. It *had* to be man trouble, Marni thought with a groan. That was the only thing that rattled her sister's legendary composure.

Marni pounded on the door again, trying not to think about how many times she'd had to rescue her sister. Elise had a natural ability for getting into trouble but no talent for getting herself out. She also had a knack for the dramatic. Marni rolled her eyes. Of course Elise did. She was in the theater. It didn't matter that she designed sets rather than performed onstage; Elise loved the drama. All Marni could hope was that things weren't half as bad as her sister had made them out to be on the phone.

On the other side of the door, she could hear Elise fumbling with the lock.

The door opened a crack and El's tear-streaked face peeked around the edge. "Hi," she said with an apologetic smile.

Marni looked into the mirror image of her own face and felt instant relief that Elise appeared to be all right. Her twin sister had made it sound like the end of the world, as if this time she was in serious trouble. So serious that Marni had abandoned her employees at the boutique to come charging over here at two in the afternoon on one of the busiest shopping days of the year, to save her twin who appeared not to need saving at all, just a shoulder to cry on.

Elise opened the door a little wider and Marni pushed her way in, feeling a lecture coming as surely as her next breath.

"El, this better not be another one of your—" The word *stunts* never left her lips. Speechless, Marni stared at her twin.

Elise stood, pigeon-toed and timid, wearing a flannel nightgown and a pair of bunny slippers. She gave Marni another apologetic smile, her eyes filling with tears as she looked down at the source of Marni's speechlessness—her swollen belly.

"You're...pregnant?" Marni cried. "You're pregnant?" Frantically she tried to remember the last time she'd seen her twin. Summer. El had stopped by the boutique, slim and excited about the new man in her life. Admittedly, Marni hadn't been paying a lot of attention. A new man in Elise's life wasn't exactly earth-shattering news. Now, if it had been Marni with a new man—any man—*that* would have been news.

"You're pregnant," Marni repeated. She replayed what she could remember of Elise's phone call five months ago. Something about a theater tour in London. Marni had suspected the "tour" was also a romantic rendezvous but it had never crossed her mind that El might be— "Pregnant!"

Elise nodded. Tears began to trickle down her cheeks and Marni could see the dam about to break. She rushed to her sister, hugged her tightly, then took her hands in hers.

No wedding band. At least Elise hadn't eloped and forgotten to tell her. She'd just gotten pregnant and failed to mention it.

"A baby," Marni said brightly as she led Elise over to the bed. They sat on the edge. A zillion questions buzzed around in Marni's head. "How did this happen?"

A stupid question. And obviously the wrong one. Elise burst into a flood of tears. Marni grabbed a box of tissues from the night table—where already used ones were piled high—and handed several to her twin.

The story came out between sobs, sniffles and nose-blowing. Elise had met a man last summer, fallen head over heels in love and found herself pregnant—and him long gone. "His name is Chase Calloway."

Sounded like a made-up name, if Marni had ever heard one. "Where did you meet him?"

"Remember that fender bender I had last June in Bozeman? It was his truck I ran into." El smiled at the memory. "He bought me dinner because I was upset. He was so sweet and thoughtful."

Marni just bet he was.

"He was in town for a few days so we spent them together."

"In town?"

"He travels a lot, just like me."

Marni just bet he did. "How few days?"

"Four. And don't tell me someone can't fall in love in four days."

Heaven forbid Marni would even suggest such a thing. Elise could fall in love in four seconds. "He knows about the baby?"

Elise nodded. "He'd been out of town for a while and I was worried about him. When he called in August—" she sniffed "—he said he couldn't see me anymore. He couldn't explain. It was complicated, had to do with his father and his family and the way he was raised."

"So you told him about the baby," Marni interjected.

Elise shook her head. The waterworks started again and through the crying Marni pieced together the story as best she could. In August, El, heartbroken and feeling heroic, had decided to have the baby on her own and had taken off to London to live the tragic life of a romantic heroine. But her bravado started to fail when her belly started to grow, the play closed and her job ended. Now she was having complications and had flown back to the States where her doctor had prescribed bed rest until the baby was born.

"So when *did* you tell him about the baby?"

"Yesterday, when I got back. I called his family's ranch in the Horseshoe Hills. When he came to the phone, he sounded…strange." Elise chewed her lower lip for a moment. "He acted like he didn't know me and didn't know what I was talking about."

"So," Marni said, trying to figure out exactly what her sister wanted her to do about all this. "You want me to find you a place to live and someone to come in and stay with you until the baby is born?"

Elise shook her head.

"You want to move in with me?"

Elise shook her head.

Marni let out a silent sigh of relief. As much as she loved her twin, she couldn't imagine the two of them living under the same roof for more than a short visit. They were too…different.

"You want to go live with Mom?"

"Good heavens, no!" Elise cried.

"Maybe you'd better tell me what it is you want me to do."

"Take me to see him."

"Who?" she asked, wishing she didn't know.

"Chase."

"Did your doctor say you could go?" Marni asked and saw from El's expression that he'd said just the opposite.

"I have to talk to Chase," Elise cried. "He loves me. I know he does. He said he's always wanted a baby. Something is wrong or he wouldn't be acting like this now that he knows I'm pregnant. He's avoiding me because of his family. His father, Jabe Calloway."

Marni reminded herself of all the times since grade school her twin had involved her in "sticky situations," but at the same time she and Elise both knew that Marni McCumber was a registered, card-carrying sucker for anyone in trouble. And her twin was in classic trouble.

"Chase said his father rules the family like a dictator," Elise cried. "Chase wouldn't deny his own baby unless he was being forced to. I know if I could just talk to him—"

Marni looked at the lump on El's lap. All the other times, it had just been Elise in some dilemma. Now there was a baby. Marni's niece or nephew.

"I'll call this Chase Calloway and talk to him," she relented. What could that hurt?

Elise hugged her and provided the phone number at the Calloway Ranch. Marni reached for the phone on the night table and punched in the number.

A woman answered on the third ring. Marni asked for Chase.

"May I tell him what this is in regard to?" she inquired.

"Just tell him it's urgent that I speak with him. My name is Elise McCumber."

She could hear a man's voice in the background. "I'm sorry, Chase Calloway isn't taking calls," she said and hung up.

"Well?" Elise asked, eyes wide and hopeful.

"He isn't taking calls."

"See, I told you." Elise started tearing up again. "He's in terrible trouble. I have to go to him."

"You're not going anywhere," Marni reminded her. "You have to do what's best for the baby and the doctor said bed rest, right?"

"What am I going to do? I'm trapped here, and who knows what's happening to Chase."

Marni tried to assure her Chase was fine, but El wouldn't hear of it. "Surely this can wait until after Christmas." Maybe she could talk Elise out of pursuing this man by then. Or maybe Chase would have a change of heart over the holidays. Sure.

"Chase is in trouble," El cried, her hand going to her stomach. "I feel it."

Marni seriously doubted Chase was in any kind of trouble. The baby, however, was another matter. She knew her sister; she'd never been good at waiting for anything, especially a man. Elise couldn't sit still for a few days, let alone two months until the baby was born, before she knew what was going on with this Chase character.

"I'll go talk to him," Marni heard herself say. The thought of telling Chase Calloway what a lowdown louse he was definitely had its appeal. Maybe the boutique could survive for one afternoon without her being there. "Where's his ranch?"

El quit crying. "I'm sure you can find it, but you can't go there like you are."

"What?" Marni knew she wasn't going to like this.

"You have to pretend you're me, like we used to."

"What? Do I have to remind you how much trouble we got into, pretending to be each other?"

"But this time it's different," El cried. "You have to pretend you're pregnant or Jabe Calloway will take one look at you, think you're me and that I lied about being pregnant, and not even let you in the door."

The last thing Marni wanted to be was pregnant, pretend or otherwise. No thanks. "All I have to do is explain that

I'm your twin sister,'' Marni said reasonably. "You did tell Chase you have an identical twin, right?''

El looked chagrined. "It never came up.'' She gave Marni another apologetic glance through her tear-beaded lashes. "You won't be able to convince Jabe—or Chase—unless they see *you* like this. Once Chase admits his love for me, you can tell him the truth. He'll listen then. Oh, Marni, it will work. We look more alike now than we ever have.''

Marni studied her sister. While they were identical twins, Elise had always been the picky eater and the skinnier one; Marni had what she liked to think of as the more well-fed, "rounded'' look. Now that Elise was pregnant, grudgingly, Marni had to admit that her sister was right. They did look more alike than ever. Except for El's protruding stomach.

"Chase will break down when he sees the woman he loves that he thinks is me, pregnant, especially seven months along,'' Elise said with such confidence, Marni found herself almost believing it. Almost. And she couldn't see even an old ogre as awful as this Jabe Calloway sounded turning away a very pregnant woman. Especially right before Christmas.

All Marni needed was a chance to talk to Chase Calloway and decide for herself if he was avoiding Elise on his own—or because of his dictatorial father.

"El, what if I talk to Chase and he doesn't want a relationship with you or the baby?'' she asked gingerly.

"If Chase truly doesn't love me and doesn't want me or the baby, I'll accept it,'' Elise said with a dignity her bunny slippers belied. "But I know how he feels about kids. He said finding a woman to share his life with and having children was all he'd ever dreamed of.''

Marni turned away to roll her eyes. Geez, couldn't El tell a come-on when she heard one? "Okay. I'll go up there and talk to him. I'll give him one last chance.''

Elise nodded. "You'll see. He loves me.'' She patted her round belly. "And our baby.''

"I'll go on one condition," Marni said. "That you go to Mom's—at least temporarily." She expected an argument.

But El readily agreed. Marni stared at her sister. Until that moment, she'd had no idea how much Chase Calloway meant to her twin. Marni cursed the man's black heart.

MARNI COULDN'T BELIEVE what she'd volunteered for as she took Dry Creek Road out of town headed for the Horseshoe Hills north of Bozeman. She wound through the snowy foothills that lay in the shadows of the Bridger mountain range. Farmhouses became fewer and farther between, and the road narrowed as she left civilization behind.

Occasionally she'd catch her reflection in the rearview mirror, and do a startled double take at the woman who looked back at her. Elise had insisted on putting a russet rinse on Marni's normally dark-blond, curly, shoulder-length hair. Marni had drawn the line at chopping it off to look like El's short wedge.

"He'll just have to think I let my hair grow," she told her twin. "El, are you sure there's no chance that this guy really *doesn't* remember you?"

El laughed. "Not after the four days we spent together." Her eyes sparkled. "It was...magical."

Magical. Marni suspected that wasn't the way Chase Calloway would describe it, especially now that Elise was pregnant.

"Here, let's do something with your makeup," El had said. "Then we'll call my friend at the costume shop and get you a maternity form."

Elise had filled her in on how she and Chase had met, where they'd gone and what they'd done, just in case she needed those details to get past Jabe Calloway to Chase. Marni only hoped she could keep it all straight. The last thing she wanted was to get caught in this whopper of a lie.

The deejay on the radio cut into Marni's nervous

thoughts with more disturbing news. A winter-storm warning. Great, exactly what she needed. "White Christmas" began to play on the radio. How appropriate. Well, it was too late now, she thought, looking at the darkening sky. All she could hope was that she'd get finished with Chase Calloway before the storm hit. And that he'd have some reasonable explanation for his disappearing act, just as El believed.

But common sense told Marni that Chase's father wasn't keeping him away from Elise; he was just using the old man as an excuse. Even if Jabe Calloway had forbidden his son to acknowledge El and the baby, and Chase had conformed to his father's wishes, what kind of man did that make Chase?

No, Marni decided as she headed up the canyon, there was nothing about Chase Calloway she was going to like. She dropped down a hill through the snowy pines into Maudlow, an old railroad town with an abandoned clapboard hotel and gas station-grocery. Signs over the ancient fuel pumps outside listed gasoline at thirty-seven cents a gallon.

Marni hung a left at Maudlow, driving past the old schoolhouse on the hill up Sixteenmile Creek, and felt her first real trepidation.

The canyon narrowed in a thick fringe of snowcapped pine trees, rocky cliffs and creek bottom. She followed the winding frozen waters of the creek farther up the dead-end road and into the darkness of the approaching storm. She could feel the temperature plummeting outside her four-wheel-drive wagon and realized she hadn't seen another vehicle on the road since the Poison Hollow turnoff.

She cranked up the heater and rubbed her cold fingers as she looked anxiously to the snowy road ahead. A Montana native, she knew how quickly the weather could change. Especially in December. But it wasn't the cold or the storm that worried her. It was not knowing what lay ahead in this isolated part of the country.

She'd convinced herself that she'd missed the turnoff, when she saw the sign. Calloway Ranch. She shifted down, amazed at how cumbersome the maternity form was. How did pregnant women drive? She felt like a hippo out of water.

She turned up the road, feeling even more isolation as she crossed the creek on the narrow one-lane bridge and drove into another narrow dark canyon.

To her surprise the canyon opened up and in the middle of the small valley sat a huge, Gothic-looking house. It towered three stories. Nothing about it looked hospitable. No Christmas lights stretched across the eaves. Nor did any blink at the windows. Under the grayness of the approaching storm, the place looked dismal and downright sinister. Not that she'd expected a warm reception.

Marni pulled her car in front of it and cut the engine. She sat for a moment, rehearsing. She was Elise McCumber. She checked herself in the mirror. Nice eye shadow, El. She was seven months pregnant. She patted the maternity form. "How ya doin', 'Sam'?"

Then she shook her head in disbelief that she was doing such a fool thing and opened the car door.

It didn't look as if anyone was home. No dogs ran out to greet or bite her. What few vehicles were parked along the side of the house were snow-covered. What kind of ranch was this? Didn't El say they raised horses?

An uneasiness raised goose bumps on her skin. She looked up. A face peered out at her from a tiny window under the eave above the third floor. Then the face was gone. But the uneasy feeling remained.

"Well, *someone's* home," Marni muttered. "And the family now knows I'm here." She took a deep breath and mounted the steps.

An older woman answered the door with a dish towel in her free hand. "Yes?" she inquired, giving Marni a disdainful once-over.

"I'm Ma—Elise McCumber," Marni said. "I'm here to see Chase Calloway."

"And what may I say this is in regard to?" she asked, even more cool and reserved than before. Unless Marni missed her guess, this was the same woman she'd spoken with on the phone earlier.

"It's personal," Marni said meaningfully as she opened her coat and patted "Sam."

The woman rocked back on her sensible shoes.

"Would you please tell Mr. Calloway I'm here. Elise McCumber." Marni started to step into the foyer but the woman blocked her way.

"Mr. Calloway isn't seeing—"

"I'll take care of this, Hilda," called a male voice from some distance behind the woman.

The moment Hilda moved out of the doorway, Marni stepped in from the cold, breathing a sigh of relief. She'd gotten her foot in the door, so to speak.

Marni wasn't surprised to find the inside of the house as forbidding as the outside. The interior provided little warmth, from the dark hardwood floors and trim to the somber wallpaper and heavy dusky draperies. In the corner sat an artificial Christmas tree, flocked white and decorated with matching gold balls positioned perfectly around its uniform boughs. So different from the McCumber tree at the farm with its wild array of colorful ornaments, each homemade and placed on the tree by the McCumber kids.

At the sound of boots on the wooden floor, Marni turned to see a large older man in western clothing coming down the hall. He filled the hallway with his size alone—he had to be close to six foot six—but also with his imposing manner. Marni took a wild guess. Jabe Calloway.

"Yes?" he asked, assessing her with sharp, pale blue eyes. He seemed surprised by what he saw. "You're inquiring about my son?"

Marni watched the housekeeper scurry toward the back of the house as if the place were in flames.

"I'm Elise McCumber," she said, saying the name over and over in her head like a mantra. Or a curse. "And you're...?"

"Jabe Calloway," he said, plainly irritated. "What is it you want with my son?"

"I want to talk to him. What it's about is between Chase and me." A strange sound made Marni turn. She blinked in surprise as a younger man hobbled into view from down the same hallway Hilda had disappeared. Marni told herself this couldn't be Chase Calloway.

"Chase," his father said, also turning at the sound. "There's no reason to concern yourself with this. Ms. McCumber was just leaving."

"But this *is* my concern," Chase said.

Under normal circumstances, Marni would have reacted poorly to the fact that Jabe Calloway was trying to shuffle her off without even a chance to talk to his son. But what was normal about any of this?

She stared at Chase, too surprised to speak. She'd just assumed he'd be handsome, knowing El. But this man set new standards for the word, from his broad shoulders and slim hips to his long denim-clad legs. He had a thick cap of wild dark hair that fell over his forehead above a pair of blue eyes that put his father's to shame. The resemblance between the two men was remarkable. But while Chase had his father's strong, masterful features, his mouth was wider, his lips more sensual, even turned down as they were now. He was the kind of man women dreamed of. This explained a lot.

Chase's muscular shoulders were draped over a pair of crutches. He limped toward her, his jeans trimmed to allow for the cast on his broken left leg. Eyes downcast, he seemed intent on maneuvering the crutches across the slick floor. Or on avoiding looking at her. On closer inspection, Marni decided it was the latter. The coward.

A few feet from her, he stopped and looked up for the

first time, his pale blue eyes welding her feet to the floor.

Marni didn't move an eyelash as his gaze flicked over her. Would he recognize her for the impostor she was?

He frowned, those blue eyes intent on her face. She let out a silent oath. She knew this wouldn't work; any man who'd been intimate with a woman would know whether or not she was his lover when he saw her. One look at this man, and Marni knew she'd never be able to fool him. He made her feel as if he could see beyond the dye job and the eye shadow right into her deceitful soul.

"I wondered when you'd show up here," Chase said.

So much for that theory. "What did you expect?"

His gaze dropped to her swollen abdomen, then insolently moved back up to her face. His eyes iced over. "Not this."

She shot him a look that she hoped would give him frostbite. Had he thought Elise wasn't serious when she'd told him she was pregnant? Or maybe he thought by rejecting her she'd just go away.

"We need to talk about the baby," Marni said, putting a protective hand over "Sam."

Chase clenched his jaw, eyes narrowing. "The baby? I thought I told you on the phone, this wasn't going to work. What is it you want?"

"For you to own up to what you've done and accept some of the responsibility," Marni snapped.

Hushed voices drifted down from the second floor.

"For what *I've* done?" Chase demanded. He seemed to be fighting to keep his voice down. "What are you trying to pull here?"

The muffled voices silenced. Marni looked up to see a small crowd gathered at the top of the wide, circular staircase. All eyes stared down at her.

"This is not the place to discuss this," Jabe interjected abruptly. "Let's take it into the library."

"That won't be necessary," Chase said, locking his gaze with hers. "I don't know who you are or what you want. But I can assure you of one thing, that...baby...isn't mine."

Chapter Two

After that stunning declaration, Chase turned on his crutches and hobbled off without a backward glance.

Marni started after him, planning to use one of his crutches to help refresh his memory, but Jabe put a firm hand on her arm.

"I'd like a word with you in private," Jabe said. "Come this way."

She had a word for him—*and* his son. "Excuse me, I don't mean to be rude, but you and I have nothing to discuss. Your son, on the other hand, is a whole different matter." She heard a door slam in the direction from which Chase had disappeared. The group at the top of the stairs didn't even bother to pretend they weren't eavesdropping.

Jabe studied her with a look of mild surprise. "I think you're wrong about that, Ms. McCumber, I believe you and I might have a great deal to talk about." He motioned toward an open doorway down the opposite hall. "Please?"

Marni had a feeling the word didn't come easy to him. And although she suspected he planned to read her the riot act once they were behind closed doors, she also saw it as an opportunity to share a few choice words she had for him about his son.

"You might be right," she said to Jabe.

The group at the top of the stairs descended in a scurry of curiosity before Jabe and Marni could escape. The oldest

of the women broke free of the others and approached
them.

"Is there a problem?" she inquired, pretending to ignore
Marni. She had a diamond the size of Rhode Island on her
ring finger and wore her marital status like a badge of
honor. This had to be Mrs. Jabe Calloway.

"Nothing to concern yourself with, Vanessa," Jabe assured her. "Go on in to dinner. I'll be along shortly."

Vanessa looked as if she'd been dragged into her late
fifties kicking and screaming. From the bleached blond hair
of the perfect pageboy to her tightly stretched facial features, she looked like a woman at war with the aging process.

She gave Marni a disdainful look, hesitating on the protruding belly for one wrathful moment before she turned
and swept away. Over her shoulder she said, "Don't be
late, dear. You know how Hilda hates it when you're late."

Her words sounded hollow, lacking authority. It was obvious who ran this household, just as Elise had told her.

Marni took a calming breath as she followed Jabe Calloway down the hall. She reminded herself why she'd come
here. To talk to Chase. To give him a chance to explain, if
not rectify, the situation. To give Chase a chance, period.
Because Elise loved the man. Although at this moment,
good looks aside, Marni could not fathom why.

THE LIBRARY WAS as large and masculine as Jabe himself.
He motioned to a chestnut-colored leather couch that
spanned one wall. Built-in bookshelves bordered the room.
A huge rock fireplace stretched across the only open wall.
An oversize brown leather recliner hunkered in front of it.
Several other chairs were scattered around. Everything in
the room seemed to have been sized to one man—Jabe
Calloway.

Marni scanned the bookshelves as she headed for the
couch, curious if the books were for looks only or if someone in this family actually read them.

"Do you like to read?" Jabe asked from behind her.

She nodded as she spotted one of her favorites and pulled it from the shelf, surprised to find the cover worn.

"You're a Jane Austen fan, too?" Jabe asked.

Marni turned, the copy of *Pride and Prejudice* still in her hand. Jabe Calloway didn't seem to be someone who would enjoy Austen.

"She's one of Chase's favorites."

"Really?" Marni said, her surprised gaze momentarily connecting with his before she put the book back and went to the couch. "I didn't know that." She was beginning to realize how little she knew about Chase Calloway; she wondered how much Elise really knew.

"The subject of books probably never came up," Jabe said as he took a seat across from her.

She started to sit on the couch, forgot how awkward sitting was "pregnant" and basically fell into the soft, deep, low sofa.

"Did Chase tell you about this house?" Jabe asked, obviously making small talk, probably thinking he could mollify her once he had her alone. "It was built by a wealthy horse thief turned politician a hundred years ago."

She didn't comment, not half as impressed with the horse thief as he was. Nor was she interested in this house.

He must have realized that. He quit smiling and leaned back in his chair, studying her openly. "Tell me about my son."

Was he serious? "Has he always tried to avoid responsibility?" she asked instead, attempting to get comfortable in the deep couch in her present condition. She ended up resting her arms on Sam.

Jabe seemed to consider her question. "No, as a matter of fact, Chase has always taken his responsibilities very seriously. That's why I'm surprised by his attitude toward you."

"Me, too," Marni said. Although, in truth, she wasn't all that surprised. Furious, yes. Surprised, no.

"I have to be honest with you, Ms. McCumber, you aren't what I expected," Jabe said. "When I heard that a woman was calling here, claiming to be pregnant with Chase's child, well—" He waved a big hand through the air as if it went without saying what he thought. He settled his gaze on her, his look almost kind, but Marni feared he could spot her for the fraud she was.

"Tell me, if you wouldn't mind, how did the two of you meet," Jabe said.

Marni licked her dry lips and related to Jabe the story Elise had told her. But unlike El, Marni began at the beginning. "It started with a little fender bender in Bozeman last June."

"Really?" Jabe said. "In one of the ranch trucks or one of Chase's cars?"

Marni met his eyes. So this was a test. "The ranch's white truck, the three-quarter ton with the stock rack and the words Calloway Ranches printed in dark blue on the doors."

He nodded with an apologetic smile. "Please continue."

Marni told him everything El had told her. Fortunately or unfortunately, depending on how much time and patience a person had, Elise had a way of recounting the smallest, most insignificant details, often overlooking the big picture. It was the thespian in her.

"I felt so awful about running into him that he asked me to dinner. At dinner, something just clicked between us," Marni said, condensing Elise's account. "The rest is history, as they say."

"How long did you date?" Jabe asked.

Date? "We spent four days together."

He lifted an eyebrow at that. Marni couldn't say she blamed him. Only Elise could fall in love over dinner and think four days constituted a lifetime commitment.

"In August I realized I was pregnant."

"I'm surprised Chase wouldn't use protection," Jabe said.

Marni was surprised this conversation had taken such a personal turn, and had it been her who was pregnant she would have told him it was none of his business. But if there was a chance of getting Jabe on Elise's side— "We always did, except for one night in a hot-springs pool near Yellowstone," she said, lowering her gaze, wondering why she felt embarrassed when she hadn't even been there.

When he said nothing, she continued. "Chase called me in August to say he couldn't see me anymore. He said it had to do with his family and was very complicated."

Jabe looked confused. "Why didn't you confront him in person before this?"

Her chin went up defiantly. "I decided to have the baby on my own." Not unlike what Marni herself would have done in the same situation.

"What changed your mind?" Jabe asked.

"I wanted to be sure this was Chase's decision and not yours," she said truthfully. Well, as truthfully as she could, all things considered.

"I see. You think I have that kind of control over my son?"

"I don't know," she replied. After meeting Chase, Marni wondered just how much control anyone could wield over the man. "Do you?"

He shook his head ruefully. "Chase is his own man, I assure you. But I know my son. If you're carrying his child, he'll accept responsibility."

She wished she was as convinced of that as he seemed to be. Could Elise have been wrong about Jabe Calloway? Could he be an ally rather than the diabolical family patriarch? That would mean, though, that Chase was the louse Marni suspected he was. In her heart of hearts, she'd hoped there would be a good explanation for Chase's denial of Elise and her baby. Marni was a sucker for happy endings.

"When I called yesterday, Chase pretended not to know me and told me not to call again," Marni said. "That doesn't sound like a man who accepts responsibility."

"That doesn't sound like Chase." He frowned as he studied Marni openly. "I'm sure you're aware that Chase has had some…problems since the accident."

Accident? "When he broke his leg," Marni said with a silent groan as she realized her mistake. She should have shown more concern for his injury or at least asked about it. Elise would have. "It looks like he's getting around fine now. Did he break it skiing?"

"You haven't heard then?" Jabe asked, sounding surprised. "I just assumed that you had and that was why you were here."

He made her feel guilty. And that made her mad. "I would have sent a card, but Chase wasn't even taking my calls."

"That was my fault," Jabe said. "I was the one who told Hilda to turn away your calls. I was afraid you were trying to take advantage of my son because of his injury."

"Take advantage of his broken leg?" she asked.

"You don't know about Chase's memory loss?"

Memory loss?

"Chase suffered some temporary memory loss because of the accident."

"I'm sorry, what accident was this?" she asked, wondering if he really believed she was buying the memory loss.

"A hit-and-run driver," Jabe said. "Chase saved my life."

Marni felt a good shot of repentance. Chase had been injured saving his father's life and she'd thought Jabe was lying about Chase's memory loss.

"Right after the accident, he couldn't even remember his sisters-in-law," Jabe said. "Now it's just gaps in his memory, he says."

Wait a minute. What was he saying? "You think El—I might be a…gap…in his memory?" she asked incredulously. Wasn't that a bit too convenient?

"Fortunately, his memory seems to be coming back.

What do you do in Bozeman?" Jabe asked, changing the subject.

Without thinking, she said, "I own a boutique. With my sister."

"Really? Is it profitable?"

Oh, so he thought she'd gotten herself pregnant to get the Calloway money. "Very," she said, then reminded herself she was supposed to be Elise, and added, "My sister runs the shop. I'm a theater stage designer."

"Very enterprising," Jabe said, eyeing her even more closely. "You build sets locally?"

"I just returned from a theater tour in London," she said smugly, proud of her sister's talents and her success, completely forgetting she was suppose to be El. "I'm not after your money, Mr. Calloway. I am more than capable financially of raising this child alone if that becomes necessary. I came here to give your son one last chance to decide whether or not he wants to be part of this baby's life. It would appear, he's already made his decision."

Jabe Calloway seemed to flinch at her candor. His blue eyes took on a remote look. His face contracted in pain. For a moment, she thought he might be ill.

"Are you all right?" Marni asked in concern.

He blinked at her as if he'd forgotten she was there, took a bottle of prescription pills from his pocket, popped two in his mouth and washed them down with a glass of water on the table next to him.

"I'm fine. Just allergies. What did Chase tell you about my relationship with him?"

Another test? Marni met his gaze, wishing he hadn't asked. "I know the two of you have never gotten along."

"Did he tell you why?"

Marni looked at the older man, sensing something far more complex than what Elise had told her about Chase and his father. "He said you were a hard, uncompromising man who cared more about money than people and that you use your money to extract a high price from your sons.'' She could see that the words hurt him, but also that they must have rung true. ''I'm sorry.''

Jabe Calloway looked away for a moment and when he turned his gaze back to Marni's, his blue eyes glistened. ''Do you love my son, Ms. McCumber?''

''Very much,'' she said, remembering the look on El's face when she'd talked about Chase. ''And I believed he loved me.''

Jabe nodded slowly, and with a visible effort pushed himself to his feet. ''You will join us for dinner.''

''Thank you, but I have to get back—''

''I insist,'' he said, cutting her off. He must have seen the look in her eye. He quickly softened his tone. ''If you would be my guest for dinner, I'll arrange for you to have a chance to speak with my son again without any interruptions.''

''I can't see that it would do any good,'' Marni said, sounding as discouraged as she felt.

''You might be surprised,'' Jabe said. ''My son is a reasonable man. Right now he's extremely frustrated by his immobility and his inability to remember everything. He hates being cooped up. Especially here.''

''All right.'' What could one dinner hurt? She owed it to El to at least give Chase a chance.

Marni worked her body out of the couch's soft cushion and let Jabe usher her to the family dining room.

''Set another place,'' Jabe ordered as he swept Marni into the room. ''Next to me. Elise McCumber will be our dinner guest.''

Marni figured the latter part was addressed to the family now seated around the huge slab of an oak table. While they might not have a choice, they didn't pretend to be happy about it. Especially Chase. He met her gaze with an irate scowl. Marni got the impression he would have gotten up and left, but someone had moved his crutches out of his reach, which no doubt added to his irritation.

At the foot of the table, Vanessa's expression was one

of shocked disbelief. For a moment, Marni thought the woman would raise an objection.

Instead, she brushed back her perfect pageboy and said, "Cook says the roast is going to be overdone."

"I *like* my roast overdone," Jabe said, pulling out the chair the housekeeper procured for Marni before taking his place at the head of the table.

Vanessa snapped, "Hilda, you may serve dinner now."

The moment Jabe sat down he began the introductions. Starting on Marni's right, he went around the long rectangular table. "Lilly is my youngest son's wife."

Marni recognized the heart-shaped face and large dark eyes from earlier when she'd seen the woman peeking out the window under the third-story eave. A petite, pretty woman, Lilly wore a pale pink dress that hung from her frail frame. Her white-blond hair was pulled severely back into a knot at her slim neck and the only color in her face was her eyes.

She murmured, "Nice to meet you," and drained her wineglass with a trembling hand.

"Lilly, you're hitting the wine a little hard tonight, aren't you, dear?" Vanessa asked too sweetly.

"I'm worried about Hayes," Lilly said as she motioned the housekeeper to refill her glass.

Jabe frowned at the empty chair next to Lilly, then at Vanessa. "Where *is* Hayes?"

"He had to go to Bozeman," Vanessa said.

"What is he doing in Bozeman?" Jabe demanded.

"I certainly wouldn't know. He only told me he planned to be back before dinner. I can't imagine what could have detained him." She looked over at Lilly as if Lilly knew but just wasn't telling out of meanness.

Jabe sighed and continued his introductions. "My wife, Vanessa." He skipped over her quickly. "And this is my middle son, Dayton."

Dayton Calloway had his father's blue eyes and a head of dark hair that he'd had meticulously styled, unlike

Chase's more unruly soft locks. A dark mustache curled across Dayton's upper lip like a thin mean caterpillar. While no way near as handsome as Chase, he was good-looking in a petulant, dark sort of way. Marni got the immediate impression that he didn't like her for some reason.

He didn't get to his feet as Marni was introduced. Instead, he just nodded. Out of the corner of her eye, Marni saw Jabe scowl and mutter something directed at his wife about bad manners. Vanessa frowned and glared at Marni as if it were Marni's fault.

"Felicia is Dayton's wife," Jabe continued. A sharp-featured brunette with green eyes, a more than ample chest and a bad disposition sat between Dayton and Chase. Marni knew about Felicia's bad disposition the same way she knew the price of the expensive ethnic-print maternity dress and matching jewelry the woman wore. Marni had sold it to her at her Bozeman boutique—last week.

"You look familiar," Felicia said, eyeing her suspiciously.

The truth seemed the best approach. "I believe you trade at the boutique I'm part owner of in Bozeman." She looked at Chase to see if he registered any shock to hear she owned a boutique. Chase didn't look up; he sat turning the thin stem of his wineglass in his strong fingers, showing no sign that he was paying the least bit of attention to any of this.

Felicia's gaze narrowed. "Yes, I remember now. But when I saw you last week you weren't pregnant."

Marni laughed. It sounded hollow even to her ears. "You probably have me confused with my sister. We look a lot alike." Boy, was that putting it mildly.

Felicia didn't appear convinced, but lost interest as Hilda served dinner: a beef roast the size of Montana, followed by huge bowls of mashed potatoes, brown gravy, fresh green beans, another of hot homemade dinner rolls and butter.

Marni felt famished, having not taken time all day to eat. She ladled gravy over her beef and potatoes, buttered a hot roll and slathered butter on her green beans. Her love of food was one of the reasons she'd never had Elise's slim model-like figure.

Hilda brought Vanessa broiled chicken, cottage cheese and crudités, and Felicia a plate of what looked like Chinese food. Lilly seemed to be the only Calloway woman who didn't ask for a special-order meal. She took a spoonful of everything that was passed to her then hardly touched the food she'd put on her plate. But she polished off the remaining wine at her end of the table, ignoring Vanessa's reprimanding looks. Marni declined wine when Hilda came around to fill her glass, needing all her wits about her. It wasn't until later that she realized pregnant women weren't supposed to drink alcohol and she was a pregnant woman, by all appearances.

Everyone ate in silence, not that Marni minded. She concentrated on the food, rather than the strange family dynamics. The roast was excellent, not in the least overcooked. Halfway through her meal, she glanced up to see Chase staring at her, his expression unreadable. But she noticed he hadn't touched his food any more than Lilly had.

"I enjoy a woman who likes to eat," Jabe said, smiling at Marni.

"This is delicious," she said, a little embarrassed by her appetite.

"You're eating for two," he said. "It's healthy to eat even if you're not expecting."

Vanessa mumbled something under her breath and pushed away her diet plate in what could only be described as disgust. The room grew painfully quiet.

Marni finished her roast beef, thinking about El and the baby. At least she knew her sister wasn't going hungry or not following doctor's orders. By now, Mary Margaret McCumber would have Elise at the family farm. If anyone could get El to do as she was told, it was Mother, Marni thought with a smile.

The door to the dining room swung open and a man in

western attire rushed in, apologizing for being late as he took the chair next to Lilly.

"Hayes," Lilly said, lifting her wineglass to him in a less than sober salute. "We were so worried about you." She didn't sound as if she meant it in the least.

Clean-shaven, Hayes Calloway also had his father's blue eyes, a little lighter version of Chase's hair color and a softer, gentler, more handsome face than his brother Dayton.

Hayes seemed to eye his wife warily before brushing a kiss across her pallid cheek. Then he spotted Marni and looked startled to see that they had a guest. Marni got the impression the Calloways didn't have many dinner guests.

"Hayes, this is Elise McCumber," Jabe said. "She's a...friend of Chase's."

Hayes stumbled to his feet, his eyes widening in surprise. "Hello."

"Why are you so late?" Jabe demanded.

He looked past Marni to his father. "The roads are covered in ice and the visibility was so bad I hit a deer on the way home."

"Are you all right?" Vanessa cried, although he obviously was fine.

"What about the damage to the truck?" Jabe asked.

"The truck?" Hayes asked, anger flickering in his gaze as he sat down and began to dish up his plate. "The truck is repairable."

"The truck is the least of our worries," Vanessa cut in, sending a look at Jabe.

He grumbled but returned his attention to his meal.

Marni watched Chase pick at the food he'd put on his plate. He looked as uncomfortable as she felt. She caught both Hayes and Dayton stealing curious glances at her. But then, why wouldn't they be? They had to wonder who she was, what she was doing at their dinner table, seven months pregnant, and why she was sitting next to Jabe as if part of the family.

What *was* she doing here? More and more she felt she was on a fool's errand. What possible good would it do to talk to Chase after he'd already denied even knowing her. And now it sounded as if the roads were probably getting worse by the minute. But she had to give it one last try with Chase. For El's sake.

"I hate to eat and run," Marni said pointedly to Jabe.

He nodded, letting her know he remembered his promise, but then said, "We couldn't possibly let you leave with the storm as bad as Hayes says it is. Not in your fragile state."

Fragile state indeed. "You don't understand, I have to work tomorrow."

Jabe shook his head. "By now the road out of here will be impassable."

"He's right," Hayes said. "It's much too dangerous. Especially in your...condition."

Marni started to argue that she'd driven icy roads all her life, having been born and raised a Montanan, but to her astonishment it was Chase instead of Jabe who cut her off.

"It's settled," Chase said, slamming down his wineglass. "You'll stay the night and leave first thing in the morning after the roads are plowed and sanded."

Marni groaned inwardly, but knew there was no point in arguing. She'd leave in the morning. After she'd finished her business with Chase. What was one night in a haunted house with people who hated her, anyway?

In the deathly silence that followed, Vanessa signaled for Hilda, who hurriedly cleared the dinner dishes and brought in a bottle of champagne on ice and a huge cake with one large pink candle and Congratulations! scripted across the white icing in bright pink.

Marni stared at the cake. She had a strong feeling it wasn't for her and Chase. In fact, she suspected she'd put a damper on a family celebration by showing up when she did.

Vanessa irritably motioned Hilda away the moment the housekeeper had poured the champagne and lit the candle.

"We have something to celebrate tonight," Vanessa announced. Her smile looked strained as she glanced almost warily at Jabe.

Jabe appeared surprised. And maybe a little worried.

"Felicia and Dayton have an announcement," she said and took her seat again.

Dayton got to his feet. "Felicia saw her doctor today and it's a girl," he announced without preamble.

If Marni thought the news would be met with cheers, applause or even halfhearted congratulations from the rest of the family, she was mistaken.

Lilly let out a startled cry, spilling her wine, then rushed from the room. Hayes looked to Marni as if he felt he should say something on behalf of his wife, then hurried out after her. Following their departure, a hush fell over the room. It was Chase who broke it.

"Let me be the first to congratulate you." He raised his glass in a toast. "Dayton. Felicia. To the firstborn grandchild of Jabe T. Calloway. A girl." His gaze shifted to his father. "Jabe finally has what he wanted, a grandchild." A tension Marni couldn't comprehend danced in the air like Saint Elmo's fire.

Jabe got slowly to his feet. He picked up his glass and raised it. Marni started to raise hers, then realized the rest of the family hadn't touched their champagne.

"To my first grandchild," Jabe said, his voice cracking with emotion. Or anger. Marni couldn't tell which.

He looked over at Marni. Her glass seemed filled with lead as she lifted it and he touched the rim of his glass to hers with a tinkling sound that echoed through the room. "To my first grandchild," he repeated.

Marni lifted the glass to her lips. No one else in the room had moved. She took a sip of the champagne, realizing that everyone was staring at her. She quickly put the glass down.

"What's going on here?" Dayton demanded sourly.

Jabe looked at Chase.

Marni thought she could have heard a snowflake drop in the room.

"We may have double reason to celebrate," Jabe said to Dayton. "I may have been blessed with not one grandchild, but two. It seems Elise is also carrying my grandchild. It appears it will be my *first* grandchild." He shifted his gaze to Chase. "Chase's child."

Felicia gasped. Dayton let out an oath. Vanessa looked across the great expanse of table at Marni, hatred in her eyes.

But it was Chase's reaction that worried Marni the most. He got up, hopped over to his crutches and left the room without a word.

Chapter Three

Jabe excused himself and went after his son, leaving Marni alone in the dining room with what was left of the family and their dagger-throwing glares. The silence in the room was stifling. But it didn't last long. An argument between Chase and his father ensued outside the dining-room door.

"How dare you make such an announcement without even discussing it with me first," Chase bellowed.

"Keep your voice down," Jabe warned him. "You can't just pretend you don't know her."

"I *don't* know her!"

"That's ridiculous," Jabe said. "She told me in no uncertain terms how you feel about me. You must have made her...acquaintance. No one outside the family could paint such an unattractive—or accurate—picture."

"This is all your fault, you and your damned ego," Chase said. "I told you not to change your will. I warned you not to do this. Now look what you've done."

"I offered you a chance to run my business, you turned it down."

"You aren't going to lay this on me! I wouldn't be surprised if you were behind this."

"What are you talking about?" Jabe demanded.

"That woman. I wouldn't be surprised if you put her up to this. You just don't give up, do you?"

"That's ridiculous," Jabe snapped. "You owe it to yourself to find out if she really is carrying your child."

"And I'm telling you I've never seen her before in my life."

"If you talk to her, you'll find she's very convincing," Jabe said.

"Well, she's going to have a damned hard time convincing me. I happen to *remember* the women I sleep with."

"How can you be so sure?" Jabe asked, sounding almost reasonable. "Think of all the other things you haven't been able to remember since the accident."

"Believe me, I'd remember *her*," Chase shot back. It sounded as if he'd started to leave, his crutches clopping across the floor.

"She doesn't seem the type to lie about something like this."

Chase's hobbling stopped. "What type is that, Jabe? A woman like my mother?"

Marni shot a look at Vanessa. She'd paled visibly.

"I won't have my first grandchild be a bastard," Jabe boomed, his voice an iron glove of authority.

"It was good enough for your first *son*," Chase retorted just before a door slammed and silence filled the dining room again.

Marni felt her head swim. Chase was Jabe's firstborn son, wasn't he?

"I'm sorry, dear," Vanessa said to Dayton as he got to his feet again.

"Leave it to Chase to throw cold water on any family celebration, and Father to be…Father." He gave Marni a mocking bow, and snagging a bottle of wine Lilly had missed, headed out through the kitchen with Felicia trailing along behind him.

Chase certainly knew how to empty a room, Marni thought, then noticed with regret that she'd been left alone with Vanessa. And Vanessa looked as if she might start a food fight if given any provocation. What kind of family had El gotten herself involved with? What had Marni gotten herself into?

Jabe returned to the room, looking tired. "I apologize for..." He couldn't seem to find a word for what had happened. Neither could Marni. "But I assure you, I am a man of my word, Elise. You will have a chance to speak with my son before you leave. In the meantime—" He turned to Vanessa. "See that Elise gets a room and anything else she needs for the night." With that he turned and left.

After a long sigh, Vanessa rang for the housekeeper and instructed her to prepare a room for their guest. The way she said "guest" made it sound like "ax murderer."

Marni noticed that the candle had burned down on the untouched cake. It flickered, barely alive, in a pool of wax. Vanessa snuffed it out with the serving knife in one swift swat and stabbed the knife into the heart of the cake with a good deal of what appeared to be pent-up aggression.

Her hostess sat for a moment surveying the empty room before she looked again at Marni. She opened her mouth seemingly to speak and closed it, as though she'd thought better of it. Instead, she cut herself a thick slice of roast beef, stuck it and a half inch of butter into one of the rolls and took a healthy bite. As she chewed, she scrutinized her houseguest as if deciding how best to dispose of her. It seemed Jabe dictated she be nice to Marni. But if looks could kill...

Marni stared down into her empty plate, considered having another slice of roast beef herself, vetoed the idea and sat thinking about the conversation she'd just overheard. She didn't care about any of the particulars except one. Chase was sticking to his story that he didn't know her. He didn't even want to believe it was because of his temporary memory loss. The problem was: No man forgot Elise McCumber.

"You must be tired," Vanessa said after she'd polished off the last bite. "I'll show you to your room." As they got up, she instructed Hilda to save her a piece of cake. A very large one. Marni got the impression Vanessa had just fallen off her diet.

"I'll leave it in your sitting room," Hilda said conspiratorially.

Vanessa shot Marni a look, daring her to say a word.

Not likely. As they entered the foyer, Vanessa glanced toward the library. "If you'll excuse me for just a moment," she said. Not waiting for a reply, she strode down the hall through the open doorway, closing the door firmly behind her.

Marni grimaced as she imagined the choice words Vanessa must be sharing with her beloved husband at his moment, then turned her thoughts to her own precarious situation.

Snowed in. Miles from everything. Seven months pregnant. Or so it seemed. Forced to spend the night in this huge, old—quite possibly haunted—house. With people who definitely hated her. Pretending to be her beguiling sister. All because of a man who swore he'd never seen her before—nor it seemed—her identical twin. How had she talked herself into this?

She hadn't even had a chance to really speak to Chase. And she couldn't for the life of her understand the strange reactions of these people. Why had Vanessa been so happy about Dayton's child but so upset by Chase's? Was it just because this baby was conceived out of wedlock? Or did it have something to do with the argument she'd heard outside the dining-room door about Jabe's firstborn being a bastard?

And why hadn't Elise told her any of this? Maybe Elise hadn't known, Marni realized. She groaned. It seemed clearer and clearer that Elise didn't know much about Chase Calloway. But how much could you learn in only four days?

Marni turned at the soft sound of footsteps directly behind her. Lilly stumbled around the corner, the wine in her glass sloshing onto the floor as she came to a lurching stop at the sight of Marni.

She smiled as she tried to rub the wine into the hardwood floor with her shoe, then staggered over to Marni, leaning toward her confidentially. "It isn't going to work, you know." Her words slurred. "You think I'm a fool? You think I don't know what you're really after? Pretending you're carrying Chase's baby. You don't fool me."

"Lilly, do you want to sit down?" Before you fall down? Marni looked around for a chair. There were none.

Lilly didn't answer. She glanced down the hallway toward the library and dropped her voice. "You don't really want him. It's the money. You're after the baby money."

Baby money? "Lilly, I don't know what you're talking about," Marni said softly, not sure why they were almost whispering, but feeling a little seasick just watching Lilly sway back and forth. She motioned toward the stairs. "Perhaps if we sit down—"

"The first grandchild," Lilly said, following Marni to the stairs. She plopped down hard on the first step, spilling more of her wine onto her dress. It looked like blood against the pale pink of the fabric.

Marni sat down beside her. "What difference does it make if I'm having Jabe's first grandchild or the fifth?" she asked.

"Like you don't know," Lilly said with a smirk. "He told you about the change in Jabe's will. He probably told you everything."

Right, like Chase had told Elise anything. "What does the change in Jabe's will have to do with the first grandchild?" she asked again.

Lilly straightened. "Jabe wants someone he can leave his...empire to. Chase turned it down. So Jabe changed his will to leave a fortune to his first grandchild," she said, bitterness buoying her in a way not even strong, black coffee could have. "The other two sons end up with almost nothing."

"Why would he do that?" Marni exclaimed, realizing now exactly what she'd witnessed at dinner. Jabe Calloway had pitted his sons against one another, a baby race, and Elise had unwittingly become a part of it and was now it appeared, the leading contender. No wonder Dayton and Felicia had been so upset.

"It should be my money," Lilly said. She drained her glass and set it on the step beside her. Her gaze bobbed up to sear Marni with a hateful look. "Not yours."

Marni heard the library door open and the sound of Vanessa's voice drift toward them.

"I assure you I knew nothing about this will," Marni said quietly, but she could tell Lilly wasn't listening, her attention drawn to the library instead.

"I had the first grandchild," Lilly whispered as she stumbled to her feet. "But Vanessa killed it."

"What?" Marni cried, jumping to her feet. Surely Lilly was too drunk to know what she was saying.

But Marni felt a chill as she witnessed the fear she saw in the woman's eyes as Lilly lurched around the side of the staircase at the sound of Vanessa's high heels thumping across the hardwood floor toward them. Marni started to follow Lilly, afraid the woman would hurt herself in the state she was in, but Lilly motioned for her not to. The pleading in her wide-eyed gaze stopped Marni. What was she so afraid of? Vanessa? Or Vanessa catching her this inebriated?

Marni watched in surprise as Lilly touched the wall behind her and a narrow door silently slid open. Lilly slipped into what appeared to be a passageway and disappeared, the door sliding shut behind her with only a whisper.

"Are you ready?" Vanessa demanded.

Marni jumped as she swung around to find Vanessa glaring at her. The conversation in the library must not have gone well.

"Is something wrong?" Vanessa asked, her gaze narrowing as it settled on the empty glass resting on the bottom stair where Lilly had left it.

"You just startled me," Marni said quickly.

Vanessa nodded suspiciously. Then she picked up the empty wineglass with obvious annoyance, and placed it on the marble-topped table to the left of the stairs. "Hilda should have your room ready." Without giving Marni a backward glance, Vanessa started up the stairs.

Marni followed her up the wide circular staircase, realizing that the longer she was in this house, the more questions she had about Chase and his family. She shook her head, confused but too smart to ask Vanessa anything.

As she climbed the stairs, Marni found herself looking over her shoulder. *You're getting a little paranoid. Yeah? Well, who wouldn't be in this house?* She tried to laugh off the feeling that she was being watched. Spied on. That someone definitely didn't want her here. She almost laughed at the thought. *No one* wanted her here and it wasn't as though they'd made a secret of it.

As Vanessa led her toward the third floor, Marni glanced back again, thinking about Chase Calloway. She had so many questions, but only one that really mattered. Could it be possible he was the man Elise thought he was and this was just a misunderstanding because of his memory loss? Then why, her skeptical side questioned, is he so adamant that El couldn't be carrying his child?

Marni had almost reached the top of the stairs when suddenly her right foot slipped. She grasped for the railing but wasn't close enough to reach it. She felt herself teeter and start to fall backward. Two strong hands grabbed her.

"Are you all right?" Hayes cried as he steadied her.

It took Marni a moment to assure herself she wasn't at that moment cartwheeling to the bottom of the long, curved staircase. She looked up, wondering where Hayes had come from so suddenly, and realized he'd been waiting in a small alcove on the stairs. As odd as that seemed, Marni was thankful he'd been there. It also explained that paranoid feeling that someone was watching her. She almost laughed in relief.

"Thank you. I must have slipped." Marni spotted the cause of her near accident—a colorful silk scarf on the stairs—about the same time as Hayes and his mother did.

Vanessa's hand went to her throat, her look one of shock. "Did *I* drop that? I didn't even realize I was wearing it." She stepped back down the stairs to pluck up the scarf. "How careless of me."

"Mother," Hayes said, the reprimand clear in his voice. "She could have been killed and the baby—" He stopped, distress in his expression.

"It mustn't happen again," Hayes said to his mother.

Vanessa looked as if he'd slapped her. "It was an accident." Her voice sounded close to tears.

A chill wrapped its icy fingers around Marni's throat as she watched Vanessa retie the scarf around her neck. *It mustn't happen again?*

"Go find your wife," Vanessa said to Hayes. "She needs you."

Hayes glared for a moment at his mother, a silent accusation in his eyes that even Marni couldn't miss before he turned and left.

Vanessa led the way to what Marni guessed was the guest bedroom. What had Hayes meant by "It mustn't happen again"? Had there been other falls down the stairs? Marni wondered as she stepped through the doorway Vanessa now held open for her. Is that how Lilly had lost her baby? Or had he meant another baby mustn't die in this house? Whatever, it gave Marni a chill not even the fire in the small rock fireplace in the corner could throw off.

The bedroom was spacious and not quite as masculine as the library was, even with the king-size log bed, matching log furniture and antler-based lamps.

The covers had been turned down on the bed and the flannel sheets looked inviting. So did the huge claw-foot tub she glimpsed in the bathroom.

Marni glanced a little apprehensively at the adjoining bedroom door, however.

Vanessa must have noticed. "The room next door is Chase's."

Whose idea was that? Marni asked herself.

"It locks from either side," Vanessa said.

"Thank you," Marni said, still curious about the woman's antagonism toward her. That *had* been an accident on the stairs, hadn't it?

Marni noticed a light blue striped shirt and a black velour robe had been left for her on the bed. Both garments were obviously male. Vanessa frowned when she saw them and Marni wondered whose they were.

"There are candles beside the bed. When it storms, the power often goes out. If there is anything else you need..." Her voice trailed off, then, "Breakfast is at eight."

Marni could see that being forced to be nice was taking its toll on the woman. "I'll be gone first thing in the morning," she said. "Right after I talk to Chase."

If she thought that news would please Vanessa, she was sadly mistaken. The woman gave her an icy stare. "Good night," she said and left, closing the door firmly behind her.

Marni stood in the middle of the room suddenly too tired to move. What a day! She felt worn-out by everything that had happened and even more tired by trying to understand Chase Calloway and his decidedly weird family. That wasn't fair, she told herself. She'd thrown his family into turmoil by showing up in an advanced stage of pregnancy claiming to be carrying Chase's child.

She considered knocking on the adjoining door and trying to talk to him, but it was late and she didn't feel up to it. Morning would be soon enough to have her final say before she left.

Marni walked to the window and looked out into the storm. Outside, a Montana blizzard raged. Snow fell, dense and deep, smothering the mountain landscape with cold white. It was as beautiful as it was confining. A white Christmas. Marni had to remind herself Christmas was just days away. Little in the Calloway house reflected the season. And something told her there wouldn't be much Christmas spirit at the Calloways' this year.

She started to move away from the window, but stopped as she heard a faint sound. It seemed to be coming up through the heat vent. She leaned closer, surprised to hear a baby crying softly. Marni frowned. All that talk about the first grandchild at dinner... Whose baby was this? she wondered.

The sound stopped as abruptly as it had begun. With a shiver, Marni stepped away from the window to lock the hallway door. A hot bath. That's what she needed. Something to get her mind off El, Chase, his family, this house—

As she entered the bathroom, Marni stopped, shocked by what she was doing. Waddling. She was taking this whole pregnancy thing way too seriously.

She started filling the tub, splashed in a generous amount of the vanilla-scented bubble bath she found on a shelf at the foot of the tub and hurriedly undressed, anxious to get the maternity form off and end this ridiculous charade at least for a few hours.

But as she slipped into the tub sans Sam and let the bubbles caress her nakedness, she felt a stab of regret that took her a moment even to recognize. She missed Sam.

With a groan she sank under the water. What was wrong with her? She'd never even thought about children of her own and now she was getting attached to a maternity form? No, not a maternity form, she thought as she surfaced. A pretend child named Sam. Chase Calloway's son. Geez.

She heard a soft knock at her hallway door and started to call that she was in the tub but stopped herself. The last thing she wanted was another confrontation with someone else in this family—especially right now, naked in the tub, with her bubbles dissolving and her body unpregnant.

Whoever it was knocked again. Softly. As if they didn't

want the rest of the house to know they'd come to see her? Chase? Surprised, she listened as the person tried the knob. *Please let it be locked.* The knob started to turn. And stopped. Locked. Footfalls retreated down the hall. Marni let out the breath she'd been holding.

Relieved, she leaned back in the tub and closed her eyes, doing her best not even to think about Chase Calloway. But her thoughts went to him as swiftly as an arrow shot from a bow. What was his story? And more to the point, how could Elise have fallen for such a disagreeable man?

The water began to cool and Marni climbed out and quickly dried herself, curious to know who her earlier visitor had been. Would her caller have come in if the door hadn't been locked? It appeared so. She doubted it was Chase. It seemed odd that he'd use the hallway door instead of their adjoining one. It seemed even odder anyone would try the door when she didn't answer the knock.

Whoever it was might return, she thought, realizing she'd have to put the maternity form back on. She didn't relish the idea, but it was better than getting caught unpregnant by Chase Calloway. No amount of explaining would get that man to believe her.

But at least she could get comfortable. After putting the form back on, she wandered into the bedroom, picked up the loaned shirt from the bed and pulled it on over the maternity form. It was large enough that the soft fabric covered her to her knees.

Her earlier tiredness came back suddenly and she couldn't wait to climb between the flannel sheets of the massive bed. That's when she remembered she hadn't locked the door between her room and Chase's. Buttoning the shirt on her way, she waddled to the door and reached for the knob. The door must not have been closed soundly. The moment she touched the knob, the door creaked open and a deep, angry voice bellowed, "What the hell do you want?"

Marni jumped at the sound of Chase's voice. "I—" She

grimaced as she heard him limping across the floor toward her, the crutches beating a path to her.

The door banged open and Chase filled the space between their rooms. "Look, woman—" His gaze dropped from her face to her chest. She caught the smell of brandy on his warm breath as he leaned toward her. "Is that one of *my* shirts? What the hell are you doing in my shirt?"

"Someone left it for me," Marni said defensively. "The way your mother acted, I just assumed it was Jabe's." Her chin went up to show him she wasn't afraid, but her traitorous feet stumbled back a step from the fury in his eyes.

"My mother?" His gaze narrowed. "That proves how little you know about me. Vanessa's not my mother."

Marni stared at him. Well, *that* explained a lot. Did Elise know *anything* about this man? "Dayton and Hayes are your..."

"Half brothers." Chase hobbled toward her, forcing her into a corner. "How can you pretend we were lovers and this is my baby, when you know nothing about me?" he demanded.

Marni felt the hellfire of his gaze and wanted to proclaim her honesty but it was hard to do, all things considered. She lifted her chin again and met his blue eyes, frantically trying to imagine what Elise would say in answer to his very reasonable question. She had no idea, having never met a man like Chase Calloway. All she knew was that he made her nervous. Self-conscious. Unsure of herself.

"I thought I heard a baby crying," Marni said, motioning toward the heat vent, belatedly realizing he'd see right through her clumsy attempt to change the subject.

"A baby? There is no baby in this house." His gaze dropped to her swollen form. "Yet."

No baby? But she'd heard a baby crying. Or had she? Her eyes widened. No, it couldn't be. This pretend pregnancy made her waddle, even vulnerable to emotions she couldn't remember ever having before. But surely it didn't make her imagine crying babies?

She realized Chase was waiting for an answer to his original question. She felt at a loss as to how to reply.

He gave her an impatient look and she knew she'd have to say something. She took a deep breath and, closing her eyes, concentrated. She imagined she was Elise and that this man standing in front of her was her lover. Her eyes flew open; she felt the flushed heat of embarrassment rush to her cheeks as the sudden, crystal-clear image of the two of them unclothed branded itself on her brain.

"Admittedly," Marni said shakily as she sidestepped away from him, "there is a lot I don't know about you and your family." Practically nothing. "All I can tell you is the...truth." She almost choked on the word.

"The truth?" Chase asked, sounding skeptical.

She nodded as she turned to face him, suddenly reminded of the disastrous results the other times she'd pretended to be her twin. "The truth is..." She tried for that slight catch in her throat El had when she talked about Chase. It came out more like a croak. "I'm in...in love with you."

For a moment, she thought he'd laugh in her face. Instead, he let out an animal growl and thumped over to her, slamming any and everything in his path out of the way with his crutches. He stopped, towering over her, his eyes hard as ice chips.

"Don't you see how dangerous this game is you're playing?" he demanded, his voice reverberating through her.

She commanded her feet to stand their ground. He couldn't scare her, she assured herself with only a slight tremble.

"Cut your losses and give up this charade," he said, dropping his voice to a menacing softness as he leaned closer. "You are no more pregnant with my child than you are in love with me."

She couldn't argue that. Not that he gave her a chance.

Before she could move, he took her face in his hands. She felt his calloused hands, warm and strong, on her cheeks. The hands of a man who did an honest day's work.

That picture didn't quite fit with the one she'd already painted of him. But she didn't have time to worry about that now. In the depths of his gaze, she saw what he planned to do. Unfortunately, there wasn't time to react before he took her mouth as he'd probably no doubt taken her sister's body, with an intensity that stunned her. And for those few moments, she *was* El. And she knew the power this man had over her twin.

Abruptly he broke off the kiss and shoved himself away from her. "You and I have never kissed before," he said, his voice as rough as his hands. "Believe me, if we had, I would have remembered." He limped a few feet away on his crutches and turned to glare at her.

Marni fought the urge to cry out. In frustration. Her body ached, reminding her how long it had been since a man had kissed her. Had one ever kissed her like that?

Worse yet, he'd been testing her and she'd failed miserably. Failed to pull off her fraud. And failed El. She already felt like a traitor to her sister for just letting the man kiss her.

"Let me give you some advice, Miss McCumber," he said, his voice sending a shiver through her. "You picked the wrong man to fool with. I don't know who you are or what you want, but if you're smart, you'll get away from here as fast as you can. You and your baby aren't safe in this house."

He left, the threat hanging in the air as he slammed the door between their rooms.

Chapter Four

Long after Chase left, Marni lay on the big log bed, her arm protectively around Sam as she stared up at the ceiling and mentally kicked herself. What had she hoped to accomplish by coming here? When was she going to learn that she couldn't solve everyone's problems?

As for the kiss...

She tried to excuse it. It was only a test and a test kiss didn't amount to anything. She shouldn't feel guilty. Really, if she was going to pretend to be Elise, these things were bound to happen. Men kissed El unexpectedly, passionately, soundly.

Not that Marni would let it happen again. One test kiss per sister's boyfriend, thank you. But if it should—

Marni groaned. Why was she agonizing over one silly little kiss? Instead she should be worrying about how El was going to take the bad news. She'd tried to call her sister before climbing into bed but the phone line was dead. Probably the storm.

She stopped a moment to listen, almost sure she'd heard footsteps out in the hallway again. As she drew the covers up around her shoulders, she assured herself the house didn't feel exceptionally imposing or hostile and that all those grunts and groans, creaks and crackings were just from the storm outside. This was Chase's doing. Him and his "you and your baby aren't safe here."

Only silence came from the adjoining room. Chase had no doubt gone to bed and was sound asleep by now. So much for his guilty conscience keeping him awake.

She'd really believed that once she had him alone, she could get him to admit his part in Elise's pregnancy. At least she would have accomplished that much. Not that he planned to do anything about it. But instead, he wouldn't even consider she might be part of his lost memory. If indeed he suffered from such a convenient affliction.

Marni squeezed her eyes closed and searched for sleep, wishing she'd grabbed a book from the library. Nothing could distract her mind faster than a book.

Her stomach growled. How could she be hungry when she'd devoured such a large meal just hours ago?

She tried to ignore the hunger pangs and the mental picture that kept flashing in her brain. Cake. A moist white cake, rich with buttery frosting.

Her stomach rumbled loudly. She opened her eyes. It would be incredibly rude to raid the refrigerator. Not for a woman who was eating for two, she argued, as she slid her legs over the side of the bed.

The embers had burned down in the fireplace and the storm's icy chill settled in along with Chase's warning. He didn't know her very well if he thought he could scare her that easily.

She reminded herself that he didn't know her at *all*. He knew Elise. And the truth was, Elise probably wouldn't have budged from her bed until morning.

Marni opened her bedroom door cautiously and peered out. The hallway was empty. And dark except for a light at the far end beyond the stairs. The house seemed to hunker in silence as if waiting for something. For her, the voice of reason warned. But a piece of cake, rich with frosting, was calling. The cake won. She stepped out and, quietly closing the door behind her, tiptoed down the hall.

A cold draft crawled over her bare feet. She pulled Chase's robe around her. The robe was thick and warm and like the shirt, smelled faintly of its owner, a scent that was both disarming and comforting.

When Marni reached the stairs, she trod down them carefully, her near accident still too fresh in her memory for comfort.

Someone had left a light on and Marni wondered if she was the only one up raiding the fridge. The thought of running into Vanessa almost changed her mind. Marni tiptoed across the foyer, peeked into the dining room, then headed for what she figured would be the kitchen.

The kitchen was spacious like the house. But unlike the house, it had a warm, almost homey feel to it. Marni guessed it was probably because Vanessa never set foot in it. It was the first room that Marni could say she actually liked. And it was blessedly empty.

She found the cake without having to raid the fridge, cut herself a large slice and sat down at the table. The cake was delicious. She licked the frosting from her lips as she eyed another piece. Oh, what would it hurt?

As she was scraping her plate to get the last of the crumbs, she marveled at her increased appetite. Was it just nerves? Or was her body somehow kidding itself into believing she really was eating for two?

Whatever it was, she had to quit or she'd gain a ton.

A short while later, she made her way toward the library. The house groaned and moaned around her. Snow piled up at the windows and cold crept along the bare wooden floors like snow snakes.

Marni had started down the hall when she heard something that made her freeze in midstep.

Crying. At first she thought it was the baby again. Then realized it wasn't the same sound she'd heard earlier coming up through the heat vent. The heart-wrenching sobs pulled at her and she found herself trailing the sound past the library toward the back of the house.

A faint light shone from a far corner of what appeared to be the living room. The thick, dark curtains along the bank of windows were open to the night. The darkness outside blurred in a thick lattice of falling snow.

Lilly Calloway sat slumped in a large log rocker, in a golden circle of light from a floor lamp beside the chair. She clutched something in her arms and rocked, Marni noticed with a start. Beside the rocker on the floor sat a half-empty wine bottle. The room smelled faintly of gardenias.

Marni reminded herself again that this was none of her business. She should backtrack and go up to bed. But the woman's wail tore at her heart.

"Lilly?" she asked softly, half expecting the woman to rebuff any attempts to console her. After all, Marni was a stranger. And no one in this house had been what she would call friendly.

Neither the crying nor the rocking stopped.

Marni stepped around in front of the woman. "Lilly?"

Lilly slowly raised her head, her rocking motion slowed. The storm outside lit her pale heart-shaped face and Marni saw what the woman clutched in her arms. A rag doll, its face worn and grayed, its yarn hair matted with age. Lilly glanced down at the doll crushed in her arms. For a moment, she made no sound. Then her eyes swam with tears and great, huge sobs racked her body.

Marni knelt and opened her arms to the woman. The rag doll tumbled to the floor as Lilly fell into Marni's embrace. "There, there," Marni whispered, sympathizing with the woman's pain. She couldn't imagine what it would be like losing a child. "It's all right."

As the crying subsided, Marni heard the scrape of a boot sole on the wooden floor. She looked up with a start, not sure who she expected to see.

Even in shadow and even if he hadn't had the crutches, she would have known Chase Calloway. He filled a doorway. Not only with his body but with his anger.

He stood, watching her, suspicion in every line of his body. She could feel the heat of his gaze on her as surely as she could feel the reproach in that gaze. She glanced down at Lilly, wondering what made Chase so angry with her, that he thought she was pregnant or that he thought she was trying to trap him? When she glanced up again, he was gone.

Marni didn't know how long she held Lilly. The crying had stopped, but the slim arms still held her tightly, as if Marni were Lilly's only anchor in some blizzard far worse than the one outside this room.

After a while, Marni looked down to find Lilly had dropped off to sleep on her shoulder. Carefully, Marni laid her back into the rocker and covered her with a knitted afghan from the couch. Lilly whimpered softly but continued to sleep the sleep of the dead. Or the inebriated.

Marni switched off the lamp and left her in front of the bank of windows and the storm, hoping Lilly slept off the wine before she attempted the stairs.

On the way to her room, Marni stopped at the library and quickly found *Pride and Prejudice.* As she turned out the light and headed for the stairs, she told herself she was ready at last for some sleep of her own.

But back in bed, Marni lay, listening, waiting for Chase to come storming in to admonish her for interfering in family business. After a while, when she heard no sound, she opened the soft, worn volume to chapter one, realizing it had been years since she'd read this book.

The first line jumped off the page at her. Marni groaned as she thought of Chase Calloway. Who was this impossible single man in possession of a good fortune her twin had fallen in love with? Certainly not a man in want of a wife—or a baby, as Elise had been led to believe. That was one truth at least Marni acknowledged.

A few pages into the book, she heard Chase return to his room, heard the clomp of the crutches as he approached the door adjoining their rooms. She held her breath. Then she heard him lock his side of the door. Instead of relief, Marni felt a wave of anger. Did Chase think he had to lock his door to protect himself from her? Did he really think she'd come to his room tonight and throw herself at him? The man couldn't be that big a fool, could he?

Tossing the book on the night table, she threw back the covers and swung her legs over the side of the bed, set on sharing a few choice words with Mr. Chase Calloway, even if it meant through a three-inch-thick door.

The lights flickered, and before her feet could touch the floor, went out. Marni held her breath, waiting for them to come back on. They didn't. And she had a feeling they wouldn't. As Vanessa had reminded her earlier, the electricity often went out during snowstorms in Montana. This far from civilization, it could be out for hours. Even days. Great. And just when she thought things couldn't get any worse.

A thud came from the adjoining room and Chase swore loudly after stumbling into what sounded like a piece of good-size furniture. She smiled, ashamed but no less amused. Served him right for being such a jerk.

Content, she slipped back under the covers. The embers in the fireplace cast a pale patina over the room. If she had been anywhere else, she might have thought it cozy. Outside, the snow fell in a dense suffocating silence. Marni watched it for a few moments, trying not to think about the other people in this house. The night seemed colder, Marni thought, or maybe it was just knowing the electricity had gone off. She felt alone and far from home. At least Elise and the baby were fine, she assured herself. Then she closed her eyes, hoping for the oblivion of sleep.

Chapter Five

December 21

Morning came like a blessing. But unfortunately, Marni's nightmares followed her into the daylight. One dream in particular haunted her: Chase standing over her, his blue eyes dark with evil as he told her she would never have the baby. Then something in his hands. An ax? Marni shivered and looked toward the window.

If the remnants of her bad dreams weren't enough, she found herself still trapped by the snowstorm raging outside. Wind plastered snow to the windowpanes and sent icy gusts hammering at the glass.

With a curse, Marni threw off the covers and lumbered from the bed, keenly aware of Sam. She hurriedly dressed, hoping to speak to Chase before he went down to breakfast. But when she tapped softly at their adjoining door, she received no response. She tried the door. It wasn't locked. When had he unlocked it? She thought about him standing over her in the dream. The dying firelight in his eyes. The ax in his large calloused hands.

"Chase?" She stepped into his room. What surprised her was the open suitcase lying in the bottom of the empty closet. Marni frowned as she surveyed her surroundings. The room was exactly like the one she'd spent the night in. A guest room. Chase didn't live here. She shook her head, continuously amazed at how little her twin knew about the man she'd fallen so desperately in love with. The man who'd fathered her child.

The bed didn't look as if it had been slept in and Marni guessed it probably hadn't, judging from the appearance of the chair pulled up in front of the fire. The cushions were crushed as if he'd battled them in the night searching for comfort and sleep. Marni smiled, taking some pleasure in the thought that Chase might not have slept as soundly as she'd suspected.

As she headed downstairs, she found herself keeping a firm grip on the railing. Her near accident the night before had proved to her just how uncoordinated she'd become thanks to Sam. She couldn't even see her toes.

None of the family appeared to be up yet, although it was nearing time for breakfast. She could hear someone in the kitchen banging pots and pans, and smell the rich scent of coffee. Coffee sounded wonderful, although she wasn't sure a pregnant woman should be drinking caffeine. Marni peeked into the dining room, hoping to sneak a cup anyway.

"Mr. Calloway and his son are in the library," a voice announced behind Marni, making her jump.

She swung around to find Hilda looking harried and flushed. "There's coffee and juice in the library. Mr. Calloway said you'd be joining him."

He did, did he? She wondered which son was with him and hoped it was Chase.

Without a word, Hilda hurried away and Marni headed down the hall toward the library. The sound of angry voices drifted out, making her hesitate long before she reached the library door. She recognized the two male voices at once, confirming what she'd hoped, that Chase was in there with his father. In the cold light of morning, Marni was more determined than ever to get things settled between them—one way or another.

She stepped through the open library door and stopped abruptly at the sound of Chase's angry words.

"You're going to get Elise and her baby killed if you don't do something about this mess."

Chase stood, hunched over his crutches, in front of the blazing fire. His father stood next to him, a hand on the thick-timbered fireplace mantel as if he needed the support. Both had their backs to her.

"Why do you have to be so damned stubborn about this?" Chase demanded. "Isn't it enough that someone tried to kill *you?*"

Marni slipped behind the end of the bookcase, aware she planned to spy on the pair shamelessly. But if Elise and the baby really were in danger— She told herself not even to try to justify her actions. Silent as a mouse, Marni peeked around the edge of the bookcase.

"Ridiculous," Jabe snapped, pushing himself away from the fireplace. "It was just some fool in a pickup going too fast. Didn't see us until it was too late, if he saw us at all." Jabe dropped into a chair in front of the fireplace and reached to pour himself more coffee from the pot on the end table. "Probably some drunk driver."

"Like hell," Chase said, turning on his father. "A drunk driver tried to run you down only minutes before you were threatening to change your will? Not even you can believe that. You just don't want to admit you made a mistake in the first place with this first grandchild foolishness. Or is it that you can't face that it has to be someone in this family or someone closely connected to this family that's trying to kill you now?"

Jabe raised his head to look at his son. "Is that the reason you've been staying here? You think my life is in danger?" He sounded touched that Chase would try to protect him.

Marni was touched as well by this side of Chase Calloway, and surprised.

"You saved my life that night," Jabe said. "I owe you, son, but—"

"You don't owe me anything," Chase snapped. "It was a reflex action, one if I'd given some thought to, I would probably have done differently."

Jabe clearly didn't buy that any more than Marni did. No matter what Chase said, he cared about his father. And it seemed he'd saved Jabe's life in some heroic feat that had left him with a broken leg and memory loss. Marni almost felt guilty for still doubting Chase's memory loss. Almost.

"I just don't want you to concern yourself with my welfare," Jabe said.

"It's not only your fool neck on the line anymore," Chase retorted. "What about this woman and her baby? What about Felicia's baby? Are you willing to jeopardize all their lives, as well?"

"Why would anyone want to harm my grandchildren?" He sounded shocked that Chase should even think such a thing.

Chase dragged a hand through his dark locks in obvious frustration. "Because of that damned will of yours."

"Have either Elise or Felicia been threatened in any way?" Jabe asked reasonably.

Chase let out a curse. "By the time that happens it could be too late."

Jabe shook his head. "I'm not going back on my decision when I don't believe for a moment that my grandchildren or their mothers are in any danger."

Chase sliced a hand through the air between them. "I've never been able to reason with you. I thought you'd finally come to your senses that night in November right before the hit-and-run, I thought you realized how foolish this first grandchild thing was. Why don't you be honest with yourself for once. The only person you care about is yourself and what you want. That's the way it's always been." He turned and hobbled toward the door.

Marni ducked back behind the corner of the bookcase and tried to flatten herself to the wall, suddenly aware how ludicrous that notion was. Sam stuck out like the prow of a ship. Marni groaned silently. The last thing she wanted was to get caught in this compromising position by Chase Calloway.

"By the way," Chase said, the sound of his crutches halting, "I saw the face of the person driving that truck right before it hit me."

A tense silence filled the room.

"I'm going to remember and then I'll know who in this family hates you more than I do."

Marni held her breath as Chase stormed out, slamming the door behind him. It took her a moment to digest everything she'd overheard and to realize Chase Calloway had trapped her in the library by closing the door and sealing off any surreptitious escape. She was cursing her inquisitive nature when she heard Jabe get up from his chair.

"You can come out now," he said wearily.

Marni grimaced as she stepped from behind the bookcase. How long had Jabe known she was there? Shamefaced, she brushed imaginary lint from the front of her maternity top, trying to think of something appropriate to say. Jabe saved her the effort.

"Chase is confused," he said as he reached into his pocket and pulled out a bottle of prescription pills. She watched him shake two into his hand and toss them down with the last of his coffee.

"When Chase's memory comes back he'll realize that he was mistaken about a lot of things," Jabe said with conviction. His gaze settled on Marni and seemed to soften at the sight of her pregnant form. "My son is very stubborn. Go after him. Try to make him see."

Marni stood for a moment, wondering what she could make Chase Calloway see. "Where—"

"He'll go to the horse barn," Jabe said as he turned back to the fire.

Dismissed, Marni slipped out of the library, took her coat from the front closet where Jabe had put it the night before and trailed Chase out into the snowstorm. Through the swirling snow, she saw him hobbling toward the largest of two barns set back in the pines.

Marni came in through the barn door to find herself on an upper level overlooking an empty arena. The air smelled of horses and leather. She took the stairs and wound her way toward the back of the barn, passing tack rooms and what looked like an office. Both were empty.

She found Chase leaning on his crutches next to a stall containing the most beautiful horse she'd ever seen. The name on the stall door read Wind Chaser. Marni remembered Elise telling her that the Calloways had investments in a little of everything, real estate, all kinds of businesses and horses. *Not just horses, El.* Wind Chaser had to be one of the top quarter horses in the country.

Marni shuddered to think what a horse like that would be worth. She was starting to realize how high the stakes were in this family intrigue. She wondered how much money Jabe Calloway had saddled his first grandchild with. Enough that Chase thought it was dangerous for El and the baby.

Marni stood for a moment, just inside the doorway, watching Chase. He crooned to Wind Chaser, his voice low and soft, his manner both gentle and strong as he stroked the horse's sleek neck. The animal responded with soft nickers, obviously enjoying Chase's touch. And Marni could see how a woman might respond to this side of Chase, as well. She imagined that soft gentleness in his touch, the feel of his fingertips on her cheek, brushing across her lips, trailing down her neck…

He must have sensed her behind him. He turned, the kind look on his face disappearing instantly. "You," he said in disgust.

She stepped closer. The horse in the stall stomped, throwing its head and snorting as if it felt the same way about her.

"I'd keep your distance if I were you," Chase said

softly, calming the horse both with his tone and the stroking motion of his hand along its neck. "Wind Chaser can be dangerous when he's upset."

Marni wondered if it was the horse he was worried about or himself. But she didn't go any closer. Nor did she turn and leave. Was it only her imagination or was Chase Calloway still trying to scare her?

When he turned around again, Chase almost seemed surprised to see her still standing there. "What?" he asked with obvious irritation.

She bristled, especially after the argument he'd just made on her behalf with his father. How could he keep contending that he didn't know her, didn't care anything about her or the baby?

"You certainly have a lot of hostility toward a woman you've never laid eyes on before," Marni noted. "Are you angry with me because you think I'm lying or because I'm not?"

"Understand something." He sounded almost patient. "I've never wanted children of my own, never planned to have any and when Jabe—"

"But I thought—" So it had been a line when he told Elise he wanted children. Just as Marni had suspected. She glared at him angrily.

"What?" he demanded, looking defensive.

"You told me that finding a woman to love and having children were all that was missing from your life."

He looked horrified, then burst out laughing. "You couldn't force those words out of me at gunpoint."

The gunpoint part appealed to her. "I guess your usual seduction lines must be one of those holes in your memory."

He growled and moved away from the horse, which snorted and stomped as if their conversation agitated him. Marni knew that feeling as Chase advanced on her and she found herself backstepping away not only from his anger but also the memory of what had happened last night.

"I might have lost some of my memory, but I haven't lost my mind," Chase snapped. "I've never wanted children and I've never made that a secret to *anyone*."

Marni bumped into the solid wall of the stable and realized he'd backed her into a corner. Again. He was so close his warm breath caressed her cheek, she could feel the heat of him, a powerful male energy that hummed in the air between them. A smile played at his lips; he thought he'd trapped her. The only way out would be to go over the top of Chase Calloway. It was an option she was keeping open.

"Last summer when Jabe told me he planned to change his will if I didn't agree to come into the business, I tried to talk him out of it," Chase said quietly as if he was glad to have her undivided attention at last. "When that failed, I distanced myself from the whole mess. Then you come along claiming to be carrying my child. Very suspicious, if you ask me."

She looked down at Sam. "Is that why you can't admit this is your baby, because it will make it look like you're after the money?"

Chase let out a curse. "If you really knew me, you'd know I don't want the money. I don't want anything from my father. I never have." He fixed a look on her that made her squirm. "Doesn't it amaze you how little you know about me? It sure amazes me."

"I couldn't help but overhear you and your father in the library," Marni said, quickly changing the subject.

"I'll bet," Chase said. "You always make a habit of eavesdropping?"

She started to inform him that if he didn't want his arguments overheard he should tone them down, but saved her breath. The truth was, she was guilty of far worse than simple eavesdropping.

"You really believe—" She had to catch herself. "My baby is in danger?"

Chase shot her a look. "I told you that last night. Did you think I was joking?"

"I thought you were only trying to scare me."

"You should be scared." He shook his head at her in irritation. "I saw you last night with Lilly. Look, do yourself a favor. Don't get involved with this family. Especially Lilly."

"Lilly needed someone last night. I was just being kind."

He let out a curse. "Kind could get you killed." He raked a hand through his hair. "I'm trying to protect you."

"And why is that? You say you don't know an Elise McCumber and you couldn't be the father of her baby. So what do you care?"

He gritted his teeth. "I don't want to see you get hurt. Or your baby. And if you care about this baby, the best thing you can do is admit that you and I were never lovers and that the baby isn't mine."

"And if I don't?" she asked. Earlier, Marni had almost found something she could like about Chase. A man who would save his father at personal risk to himself. A man who would argue for the safety of pregnant women and their unborn children. That was a man she could like. There was nothing likable about the man standing in front of her now, however.

"How much money do you want?" He tugged his checkbook from the hip pocket of his jeans. "Name your price. I'll pay you double what my father is paying you."

"I don't want your money," she told him. "Nor did your father pay me to say I'm having your baby."

His look said he didn't believe her. "You think you can pass this kid off as the first grandchild and get more?" Chase shook his head. "I'll fight you," he said, anger making his voice crackle. "As soon as that baby is born, I'll prove it isn't mine and you won't get a dime. I can't imagine what my father hopes to gain by this."

She fought to contain her temper. "I don't want your

money or your father's. I didn't even know about your father's stupid will until Lilly told me last night.''

He glared suspiciously at her. "You probably hadn't heard about my accident either or my memory loss, right?"

"As a matter of fact—"

"How convenient," he said.

"My thought exactly."

He raked a hand through his dark curls. "You don't get it, do you?" he said as he leaned closer.

Reminded of last night and the disastrous test kiss, Marni flattened herself against the wall.

He looked at her, amusement dancing in all that blue, then moved back just enough to give her breathing room. She got the impression that he wasn't going to let her go until he was through with her.

"If someone tried to kill my father to keep him from changing his will," Chase said, biting off each word, "then imagine what that person would do to keep your baby from inheriting all that Calloway money."

Marni thought about Vanessa dropping her scarf on the stairs and wondered if there was any truth in what he said or if this was like everything else, an attempt to frighten her away?

"Let's get back to this memory loss of yours...."

He glared at her a moment, her distrustful tone obviously not lost on him. "I have what they call selective memory loss."

She raised an eyebrow. "*Selective* memory loss?" *Give me a break!*

"My memory's coming back," he assured her quickly. "I remember most everything. There's just a few...holes."

Right. Marni studied him, unable to get past the *selective* part of his memory loss and the *hole* Elise and the baby had supposedly fallen in. "How do you know that...I'm not one of those holes?"

"I know. I don't have to prove it to you or anyone else."

Why did he sound so defensive if he was so positive?

Because he isn't sure, Marni thought. Maybe his memory loss was more severe than he wanted to admit. But that still didn't explain why he wouldn't even consider Elise might be part of those lost memories, did it?

"This—" she had trouble even saying the word "—*selective* memory loss of yours, did the doctors say all of your memory will come back?" Marni thought about what she'd heard in the library. If Chase had really gotten a glimpse of the driver of that truck right before the accident, he might have seen the attempted murderer. Even knowing Chase for as short a time as she did, she knew trying to remember that must be driving him crazy. Possibly it explained why he was so angry at her; she'd added to his frustration by being another one of those holes in his memory.

"It's only a matter of time before I remember everything," he said, the threat clear in his voice.

She wanted to say something smart to wipe the smugness from his face. Wouldn't he feel foolish when he remembered Elise? "What about the accident itself?" she asked instead. "Will you be able to remember it?"

"The doctors say I won't but they don't know me."

Jabe was right about Chase's stubbornness, she decided. But while Jabe saw the quality as a flaw in his son's character, Marni saw it as a strength.

But what if he never remembered the face of the truck driver? "If you're right about the driver deliberately trying to run your father down, your life might be in danger, as well. The driver is probably worried you'll remember."

Chase actually smiled. "Are you starting to believe me?"

Was she? "It doesn't matter what I believe," Marni told him. "But I have to wonder, if you're so positive we were never lovers, why are you so worried about me and the safety of my baby? Could you be afraid to remember?"

He narrowed his gaze. "Afraid?"

"Afraid of the feelings you might have for me or this baby." She expected anger. Denial. Recriminations.

She didn't expect him to laugh.

The sound filled the barn as he leaned toward her on his crutches and placed a large palm on either side of the wall beside her head.

Chase was a little too close for comfort. Nor did she like the glint in his eyes. But he had her trapped, and he knew it. He pinned her to the wall with the intensity of his look. She held her breath as he let his gaze travel leisurely over her face, pausing at her lips, as predatory as a wanton kiss.

"Were we passionate lovers?"

"I don't see how that has anything to do with this," she replied primly, feeling her cheeks burn.

"You don't?" He seemed to be fighting back a smile. "As intimate as you say we've been, why look so shocked by my question?"

"Because this has nothing to do with sex."

He lifted one dark eyebrow. "It looks to me like it has a great deal to do with sex." He dropped his gaze to Sam.

She assured herself she could hold her own with him. Even with the memory of last night's kiss still fresh in her mind and on her lips. Even with her limited experience with men. And her total lack of experience with a man like Chase Calloway.

"How long have we known each other?" he asked innocently enough.

"Since June," she said, surprised at how nervous he was making her.

"How did we meet?" he inquired, not moving closer but making her intensely aware of the space he dominated.

"In a fender bender. I ran into you."

"Then there should be a police report, insurance forms, some sort of record."

So proof was what he was looking for. She put a protective hand over Sam; how much more proof did the man need? "We didn't call the police or our insurance companies because there wasn't any real damage."

"If you'd run into a truck I was driving, I would have insisted we call the police, even if there wasn't any visible damage."

"But for some reason you didn't that day," she said.

He seemed to ignore that. "Nor can I remember the last time I drove one of the ranch trucks."

"You can't remember a lot of things," she said. "But you do drive the trucks as part of your job, right?"

He stared at her. "You think I work for my father?" he asked incredulously.

"I just assumed—"

"How could we have been lovers and you not know what I do for a living?" Chase interrupted.

Good question. "You led me to believe you worked for Calloway Ranches."

"You're saying I lied to you?" he demanded, obviously not happy with the prospect of being called a liar.

"Misled me, possibly?" she suggested carefully. How could Elise have gotten things so messed up? "So there isn't any way you could have been driving the ranch's white truck last June?"

He frowned. "I didn't say my father doesn't try to involve me in the family business every chance he gets."

"So that proves nothing," she said, discouraged.

He rummaged a hand through his hair. "How long did we date?"

She was at a loss for words to describe Elise's four-day love affair. Marni couldn't imagine falling that hard in four months, let alone four days. "It was love at first sight."

Chase laughed. "You have to be kidding."

"It was magical," Marni said defensively.

He arched an eyebrow. "Really?"

"Something that only happens once in a lifetime," she added and stopped, having run out of clichés.

"How long?" he demanded.

She swallowed. "Four days."

"Four days!" Disbelief. Shock. Incredulity. He shook his head and laughed. "Four days?"

"It happened very fast."

"I'd say." He reached out and traced his thumb across her lower lip. His thumb pad felt disarmingly rough. "That must have been some four days. I must have kissed these lips often during those magical, fun-filled four days."

It was clear in his eyes what kind of woman he thought her to be. She turned her head and he pulled back his hand, the smile dissolving into a piqued frown. He thought her a liar and a fraud. Among other things. She wanted to knee him, but taking down a man on crutches seemed lower than even the way he was behaving.

"I see that you don't believe two people can fall in love…quickly," she said.

"You're wrong." He speared her with those pale blue eyes. "I believe two people can fall in love instantly. Just not me."

"You're immune to love?" she asked, adopting his disbelieving tone.

"I don't have time for it, and since I never plan to marry—"

"No children *or* marriage?" she interrupted in surprise.

"That's what I've been trying to tell you. I don't get involved."

"But what if you did this time? What if you…" She swallowed. "Couldn't help yourself?" Her cheeks flamed red hot. She wanted desperately to explain to him that she wasn't referring to herself but Elise. Elise had a way with men that caused them to do things they would never do with any other woman.

He leaned back and lazily let his gaze explore the curves beneath her open coat. "I can see where I'd definitely be tempted, I'll give you that." He seemed to be enjoying this a lot more than she was.

"Maybe," he said softly, "it's just a matter of... jogging...my memory."

Marni didn't like the sound of this or the predatory look in his eyes. "I came here to discuss what we were going to do about the baby," she said quickly, realizing Sam was the only thing keeping them apart right now. "Not to—"

"To what?" he asked with wide-eyed innocence.

CHASE MADE a dozen excuses for what he was about to do. All of them were honorable and made perfect sense. Especially in his current state of mind. Was this woman part of some memory loss? Or was she simply taking advantage of the situation? He had a right to prove that she wasn't his lover, that the baby she carried wasn't his and that she was the conniver he suspected she was. She wasn't the first woman who'd tried to wrangle the Calloway name with a baby that wasn't his.

Except this woman was different. That he wanted to kiss her again was the least of it. He needed to kiss her to prove to himself that he was right. He couldn't have forgotten her, memory loss or not. Last night he'd been so sure that once he kissed her he'd know the truth. But kissing her had only left him more confused. The attraction had been explosive. More than he wanted to admit. Maybe he *did* have a four-day affair with her, his traitorous mind tempted. Or maybe he just wanted to kiss her again for purely prurient reasons.

"I think we should talk about this," she said, her voice cracking.

"About what?"

She opened her mouth to speak but no words came out. There was something about her mouth... The provocative way her lips parted. The soft moan that escaped her throat last night when he'd pulled her into his kiss. The powerful seductive feel of her. It had been so...magical?

He wasn't sure what decided him or if it had been an actual decision at all. Suddenly he had a need to feel her skin as strongly as the need to remember her. He needed to explore the dark recesses of his mind to find if she was lodged there, the same way he needed to explore her body. Purely to get at the truth, of course. If he felt her skin against his, he would remember, his mind assured him. And oh how he wanted to feel her naked against him. He couldn't remember ever wanting a woman the way he wanted this one right now. What was it about her?

His fingers slid down the soft, silken column of her neck. At the hollow of her throat, he could feel the thunder of her heart beneath his fingertips. What he saw in her golden brown eyes startled him, but not half as much as the intensity of his body's reaction to her. Desire fired her gaze the way it blazed in his loins. My God, was it possible? Had they really been lovers?

"Elise." His voice came out a hoarse whisper. His hand dropped to the round curve of her breast.

She jumped as if she'd been scalded with boiling water.

Chase frowned at her reaction, all his suspicions coming back in an instant. Why did she seem as startled as he was by the strength of the chemistry between them? And as unsure about him as he was about her? "Do I make you nervous?"

"No," she croaked.

"I would think you'd be used to my touch," he said quietly, watching her face. Who was this woman? Certainly not one he'd ever spent four amorous days and nights with, he thought with no small regret. He told himself he'd known it hadn't been true all along. What was it about her that had made him doubt that?

Whoever she was, he was now more determined than ever to find out what she was up to.

MARNI FELT HER BODY begin to vibrate, a fine high vibration that raced along in her blood. She leaned against the wall, trying to get her feet back under her. This wasn't going the way she'd planned. She had to get out of here

before she betrayed her twin. Out of this barn. Away from
Chase Calloway. She just didn't know how to do it grace-
fully. She'd already stirred up his suspicions again. She
could see it in those pale blue eyes of his.

If she were really his lover— She couldn't keep deluding
herself that another kiss might unlock his lost memories. If
that were true, it would take Elise's kiss—not her own. And
this time, Chase had a lot more than a kiss in mind. It was
put-up or shut-up time and Marni was in over her head.

He looked at her, his gaze challenging her. "What's
wrong?"

"We can't do this."

His smile was merciless. "We've already done this. As
they say, it's too late to close the barn door after the cow
has gotten away."

Her hands went to his chest to push him away. She felt
the heat of his skin through his shirt, felt his heart race
beneath her palms, and her own instantly match that treach-
erous beat as his lips descended on hers.

A door banged open. "Chase?" Dayton sounded peeved.

Chase swore softly as his gaze met Marni's, his lips lingered for a moment, hovering over hers, then he smiled,
his message clear: This was only a temporary reprieve.
"We'll finish this later."

"Chase?" Dayton snapped. Over Chase's shoulder,
Marni could see Dayton squinting into the darkness of the
stable area, trying to find them. "You're holding up breakfast and you know how Mother hates—" He faltered as his
gaze fell on them. Annoyance turned to curiosity. "Everything all right?"

"Everything's just fine," Chase said without turning
around. "Isn't it?" he asked Marni softly and then faced
his half brother.

Marni leaned against the wall, her heart hammering, her
very breath trapped in her throat, her body quaking like an
aspen in the wind. She wasn't sure what shocked her more.

Chase's behavior. Or her own. She'd wanted to kiss him again!

Worse than that. She actually felt regret that Dayton had rescued her when he did. What was happening to her? This wasn't like her at all.

Inwardly she groaned as a thought struck her. If Chase had this effect on every woman, no wonder Elise had fallen so madly in love with him. But Marni couldn't help wondering how many other women were lost in the man's selective memory loss.

"Vanessa's going to be fit to be tied," Dayton said, sounding as if he looked forward to it since it would be Chase's fault and not his own.

The two brothers exchanged a look. Marni could feel the tension stretch dangerously between them.

Dayton looked away first. "Hey, don't kill the messenger. She just sent me out to get you both into breakfast. Also you have a phone call, Chase."

"Took you long enough to tell me." He shot Marni a look over his shoulder that held both promise and threat, then he turned and hobbled out the side entrance Dayton had come in, the door closing behind him in a gush of cold air and snow.

The spell broken, Marni took a breath to steady herself. Always sensible. Always confident. Always in control. What had happened to *that* Marni McCumber? Chase Calloway. That's what had happened. Chase and this stupid pretense. She wasn't just pretending to be pregnant. She was trying to be another woman, a woman Marni McCumber couldn't even pretend to be.

What was it about Chase Calloway that could be so irritating and at the same time so...tempting? She took a ragged breath and realized Dayton hadn't moved. He leaned against the barn wall, studying her in a way that instantly made her uncomfortable at being alone with him.

She started past him but he stepped in front of her to block her exit.

"So you're having Chase's baby?" he asked, something dark and intimidating in his blue eyes.

"It's really none of your concern," she said, realizing he wasn't going to let her past until he had his say.

"Do you know anything about breeding...horses?"

Marni wanted to wipe that smug, self-satisfied look off his face. The last thing she'd do was let him see that he frightened her. "No, do you know anything about interior design?"

He looked confused, some of the smugness gone.

"I was just curious who decorated the house," Marni said. "Your mother?"

Dayton looked wary. "Yes, she wanted it to reflect my father and his position."

Marni wondered what position of Jabe's the house reflected. Overbearing, domineering and pompous came to mind. "Then Vanessa was an interior decorator before she married Jabe?"

Dayton's horrified expression confirmed that she'd scored a bull's-eye. "My mother has never...*worked*. She was a Landers of Boston before she became a Calloway."

A Landers of Boston? He made it sound like royalty, the same way he made "work" sound like a dirty word.

She had to bite her tongue not to share her thoughts on the work ethic with him. A job might be just what Vanessa Calloway needed.

"Where are the McCumbers from?" Dayton asked, his nose lifting into the air.

"Montana," she said proudly. "I'm fifth-generation."

"How nice," he said, not even pretending to mean it. "That would make this child you're carrying...?"

"A sixth-generation Montanan," she said.

He gave her a weak smile. "If you knew anything about breeding...horses, you'd know the value of the foal is based on its lineage. That's why you'd never breed a Thoroughbred with a nag."

Marni felt as if she'd been slapped. "I don't know much

about breeding horses," she said, surprised at how calm and restrained she sounded, "but I do know a jackass when I see one." She shoved past him but not before she'd seen the look on his face. Pure hate.

She felt a shiver as she hurried toward the house.

Chapter Six

Marni rushed through the back door and nearly collided
with Vanessa.

"Breakfast is going to be late," Vanessa announced angrily, then turned on her high heels and stalked back down
the hall to the dining room.

Marni mugged a face at her back, wishing the storm
would stop and she could get out of this place.

"I wouldn't keep my mother waiting," Dayton warned
as he came in the back door and swept past her.

"I'm sure you wouldn't," Marni mumbled as she removed her coat. She wanted to tell Vanessa what she could
do with her breakfast and Dayton what he could do with
his so-called breeding and Chase what he could do with
his—

Come on, Marni, who are you really angry with? She
took a deep breath and reluctantly admitted none of those
people were really to blame for the way she was feeling.

Dayton, the blizzard, the cold, snowy hike from the barn
and even Vanessa couldn't distract her thoughts from her
recent encounter with Chase. She made several attempts to
downplay her reaction to his touch and finally gave up. The
bottom line: She wasn't equipped for this. Pretending to be
Elise was too much for her.

"I hope you're hungry," Jabe said, coming out of the
dining room to take her coat.

"Not really." Just the thought of another meal with the family—and Chase—

"Wait until you taste Hilda's pancakes," Jabe said as he hung her coat in the closet and closed the door. "You'll change your mind."

"I need to get out of here," she said, sounding as panicky as she felt.

He raised an eyebrow, but didn't ask how things had gone in the barn. "I'm afraid we're snowed in. Until the storm lets up, you have no choice but to stay," he said, patting her hand as he led her toward the dining room. "This is all going to work out. You'll see."

Right, Marni thought. She couldn't imagine things getting any worse.

Most of the family were already seated, overdressed and just as silent and unfriendly as they'd been at dinner last night around the table now laden with plates of pancakes, bacon, ham, eggs, fried potatoes and biscuits and gravy.

As she sat down, Marni noticed two chairs remained empty. Lilly's. And Chase's.

She wondered how they got out of breakfast when she couldn't. Not that anyone really seemed to want her there. Except Jabe. Vanessa didn't even bother to look up from the soft-boiled eggs and dry toast Hilda slid in front of her. Dayton and Felicia gave Marni a brief contemptuous look. She felt Hayes studying her, but when she met his gaze she saw more curiosity than vindictiveness.

"Lilly's not feeling well this morning," Hayes said as if someone had asked. When no one responded, he returned his attention to the large plate of food in front of him, his appetite noticeably improved over last night's.

Marni got the impression that this wasn't the first morning Lilly hadn't shown for breakfast. She was no doubt sleeping off a major hangover.

Just about the time Marni began to wonder what had happened to Chase, he came in, frowning as he took his chair. She wondered if the frown was due to her or his phone call. It dawned on her that the phone must be working again. She'd call Elise right after breakfast. Elise would be sympathetic to Chase's memory loss; she'd find hope in it. And they'd get through Christmas.

Maybe there'd be a Christmas miracle. And Chase would get his memory back on Christmas Eve and remember his love for Elise and their baby. Marni was so lost in her safe fairy tale that she forgot she wasn't hungry. As Jabe passed her plate after plate of food, he quickly proved he was right about her appetite. She lathered butter and thick homemade peach preserves on a pancake and took a bite, unconsciously closing her eyes to savor it.

At the sound of a soft chuckle, her eyes flew open and instantly she felt the heat of embarrassment wash over her as she saw it was Jabe. She sneaked a glance at Chase, only to find him watching her, looking amused.

"What do you think of Hilda's pancakes?" Jabe asked, still chuckling.

Marni smiled and licked the sweet preserves from her upper lip. "Amazing. I'd love her recipe." She'd make them Christmas morning for the whole family to celebrate Elise and Chase's engagement—

"*You* cook?" Felicia asked.

"My mother insisted we all learn to cook and sew, even my brothers," Marni said, warmed by the pancakes and a subject dear to her heart, her family.

"How many brothers do you have?" Jabe asked.

"Four. They're all older than—" she felt the near slip on her lips "—me and my sister."

Both Hayes and Dayton glanced up. "There's more at home like *you?*" Dayton asked, making what could have been a compliment sound just the opposite.

"My sister is nothing like me," Marni said quickly in Elise's defense.

"Your mother sounds like a smart woman," Jabe commented.

"I think I'm going to throw up," Felicia announced,

sliding her chair back from the table. She tossed down her napkin and rushed from the room.

Dayton watched her leave with only mild concern.

"Morning sickness," Vanessa said.

"Did you suffer morning sickness?" Jabe asked Marni as he passed her more pancakes.

"I was fortunate," she said, busying herself with the pancakes, eyes averted. "I missed that part."

"Where were you raised?" Jabe asked.

Yesterday his questions had been pointed and part of a test. Today they seemed kindled out of a sincere desire to know more about the woman who was about to give birth to his grandchild. Elise's baby. His first grandchild, Marni reminded herself with growing apprehension.

She told him about growing up in rural Montana, climbing trees, swimming in the creek, playing baseball, camping in the back pasture under the cottonwoods.

She realized with a start that she'd been describing her own childhood—not Elise's. Elise had been more prissy, playing with dolls, holding elaborate tea parties on the front porch and refusing to bait her own hook when she did go along fishing. While Elise didn't have the patience to sit and wait for a fish to bite, she could spend hours planning elaborate skits, which she directed after charming her siblings into participating.

Marni shot a look at Chase, surprised that she seemed to have his full attention, although from the look on his face, he wasn't enjoying her stories. He looked angry and upset. Had something she said made him remember one of El's childhood stories? Was it possible he would remember everything before Christmas? Remember Elise and give her that happy ending El and the baby so deserved? And let Marni forget all that foolishness she'd felt in the barn?

"Your childhood sounds idyllic," Jabe said.

"It was," Marni said, her hand going to Sam without her realizing what she was doing. "I always thought if I ever had children, that's what I'd want for them."

"You haven't always planned to have children?" Chase asked.

She met his gaze. "No," she answered truthfully. "I always saw myself as a doting aunt." She looked down at Sam again. "Sometimes I still have trouble seeing myself as a mother."

"I'm sure Chase is having the same problem seeing himself as a father," Dayton commented wryly.

"Fatherhood is something a man shouldn't take lightly," Chase said.

Marni couldn't tell whether that was meant for Jabe or Dayton. Both busied themselves with breakfast.

"How was your phone call?" Dayton asked Chase.

"Odd, but it seems the phone lines are still down," Chase answered, not looking up from his plate.

"Huh," Dayton said. "Must have gone down about the time I came out to the barn to look for the two of you."

"Yeah, that's what I thought you'd say." Chase glanced up at Marni, concern in his gaze.

Marni swallowed. Dayton had purposely gotten rid of Chase? What for? Just so he could insult her? Or had he had something else planned for her and changed his mind? She concentrated on her food, telling herself she'd never let Dayton get her alone again.

"Dayton didn't get to tell you last night at dinner," Vanessa said, smiling at her husband. "But Felicia's further along than we all thought. Almost seven months."

That brought everyone's attention up from their breakfasts.

"Seven months?" Jabe demanded, spearing the last piece of ham. "She doesn't look that pregnant."

"She's always watched her figure," Vanessa said, and added pointedly, "Not all women blow up like a balloon when they're pregnant."

Feeling her face burn red hot, Marni chewed her last bite of pancake in the thick, tense-filled silence that followed. When she dared sneak a look at Chase, she found him smiling in obvious amusement, not in the least sympathetic to her predicament.

AFTER BREAKFAST, Jabe announced that he'd picked up the weather report on the mobile radio. Bozeman Pass was closed and some parts of Interstate 90 were open only to emergency traffic because of blowing and drifting snow.

"In other words, we're snowed in," Dayton said, not looking any more pleased by the news than Marni. The road down to Maudlow was impassable and would stay that way until the county plowed it. Or until the Calloways plowed themselves out.

"No reason to start plowing until it quits snowing and blowing," Jabe said. "It would just drift back in behind the plow."

Marni had the unpleasant thought that Jabe might be just trying to keep her here. But as powerful as Jabe Calloway was, he couldn't control the weather, she told herself.

She listened as he barked orders to his two youngest sons and realized that Dayton and Hayes were both involved in the family business with jobs that often took them away from the ranch. Not menial chores such as mucking out the barn since hired hands normally took care of the horses.

But not today. The crew wouldn't be able to get into the ranch to work because of the storm. That meant Dayton and Hayes would have to do all the chores, something that didn't go over well with either of them, judging from the looks on their faces.

But they didn't argue and it became obvious who ran Calloway Ranches, and who took orders. Jabe could be a hard man, she decided. He was used to getting his way. And his sons seemed to dance to his tune. All except one.

"Why don't you stay off that leg and see that Elise doesn't get bored," Jabe ordered Chase irritably after everyone else had left the table.

Chase gave his father a patient smile. "With her active

imagination, boredom is the last thing she has to worry about.''

Active imagination, huh? If he only knew.

Chase got to his feet and, leaning on his crutches, smiled down at her. "But don't worry, I'll take care of her."

The threat in his voice sent a shiver through her. Just the thought of the two of them alone again together— Everything be damned, she couldn't go on pretending to be Elise. She couldn't let what almost happened in the barn happen again.

"Chase, there's something we need to talk about."

He smiled. "Whatever the lady wants."

Marni didn't like the look in Chase's eyes as Jabe got up from the table. "I'll see that no one interrupts the two of you," he said and closed the door behind him.

Marni didn't like the sound of that. "Look, I'm not the woman you think I am," she said.

"Why don't you let me be the judge of that," Chase said, coming around to her side of the table. "We're completely alone again. That *is* what you wanted, right?"

She got to her feet, backing away from him. "I didn't want to get you alone to—"

"But you did want to get me alone again," he interrupted. "Or did you finally want to tell me that we've never been lovers, never spent four days together, let alone four 'magical' nights and that there is no way you're carrying my child?"

Damn him. That's exactly what she wanted to tell him. And a confession is exactly what he wanted. If she told him the truth now, he wouldn't even listen. All he'd hear was that he'd been right all along: She wasn't pregnant, wasn't his lover and had never been. He'd laugh at the whole twin-sister routine and throw her out into the storm.

"You're going to feel pretty foolish when you remember everything," she said, realizing immediately it wasn't the catchy comeback she'd hoped for.

"When I remember, I fear you're going to regret it."

She didn't doubt that for a moment.

CHASE FOUND HIMSELF backing her into a corner again and looking forward to it. He stopped himself, remembering only too well what had almost happened earlier in the barn. He had to get a grip. After all, he was trying to prove to her that they'd never been lovers. He'd start by trying to reason with the woman. Then if that didn't work...well, there was always making love to her on the dining room table.

He sat down and tried to see past her cute sweet face to the gold digger he knew her to be. Whoever this woman was, she had come here on false pretenses to pass off another man's child as his own, hoping to capitalize on his misfortune and his father's wealth and ego. Well, Chase wasn't about to let that happen.

After sitting through breakfast, listening to tales of her childhood, he was all the more convinced that nothing she could say or do could convince him he'd been her lover. She was the kind of woman he'd avoided since puberty. There was no way he'd have ever let himself get close to her. Miss McCumber and her perfect childhood were much too dangerous.

"There are a lot of reasons you and I never had a four-day affair," he said, trying to replace the emotions she stirred in him with something safe like good old familiar anger. He'd show up this charlatan for the liar she was. "Number one, you're not my type."

She raised an eyebrow but took a chair a safe distance from him. "And what type is *your* type?"

He didn't want to admit what that had always been. Simple and safe. "Tall, leggy, busty..."

"Shallow?" she offered.

"Noncombative," he said, not liking the way this was going. "Do you have a problem with that?"

She shot him a wide-eyed innocent look. "What man

would want a woman who might intellectually challenge him?''

He growled. ''Why do women think men want to be challenged? Maybe we just want peace and quiet.''

She rolled her eyes.

''Number two,'' he said through gritted teeth. It amazed him how she could make him doubt himself, make him think against all his arguments that maybe somehow she *had* been part of his memory loss. He'd never thought of pregnant women as beautiful or intriguing or...sensual. But this one— If she had her way, she'd have him thinking he was falling for her. ''Why would I ask you to lunch after you'd just run into my truck?''

''I think we both know the answer to that one,'' she said, giving him a dirty look. ''You obviously thought I *was* your type.''

He cursed himself for starting this. ''Where did I take you for lunch?''

''Guadalupe's.''

''That tiny, out-of-the-way Mexican-food place?'' he asked in surprise.

''I take it that isn't where you usually wine and dine your...bustier dates?'' Her innocent look had a sharp edge to it. ''Maybe you didn't want us to be seen.''

He frowned, wondering if that was exactly what he'd been thinking, if he had indeed taken her there. Which, of course, he hadn't. ''What did I order?''

She gave him a blank look.

''You don't remember,'' he accused. He always ordered the same thing at Mexican-food restaurants. If she'd said anything but chile rellenos, he would have known she was lying. For just a moment, he thought he had her.

''I don't remember, I was...nervous.''

He definitely made her nervous, he knew that. ''What did you have?'' he asked, studying her.

''Chile rellenos. My favorite.''

He groaned inwardly. Her favorite was his favorite. Oh,

brother. And on top of that, he liked her appetite as much as his father did. "You're not exactly a light eater, are you?"

She lifted her chin. "Do you have a problem with that?" she asked defiantly.

He had to laugh. It seemed to surprise her. "No. I find it...refreshing." *Just like you find her refreshing?* "Did I kiss you during dinner?"

Marni shook her head and avoided his gaze. He couldn't imagine how any man had impregnated this woman. She seemed so...chaste. He remembered the way she'd reacted to his kiss last night. The way she'd reacted to his touch in the barn. Just the memory stirred something inside him he didn't want stirred.

"We didn't kiss until...later at the...motel," she said.

What? He stared at her. "You're kidding?"

She looked away. "You were...shy."

Right. "I would have kissed you at dinner. Just looking at that face of yours—" He raked a hand through his hair and glared at the ceiling. "If I'd taken you to Guadalupe's, I would have requested a private booth in the back, candlelight even though it was lunch and chile rellenos for both of us. I would have kissed you the moment the waiter walked away."

"How can you be so sure?" she asked, seeming to fight for breath under his gaze.

"Because that's what I'd like to do with you now," he said honestly.

She swallowed. "Take me to Guadalupe's?"

He found himself on his feet, balancing on his good leg. "Kiss you."

She shot up out of her chair. "We already tried that. It didn't jog your memory."

"I don't give a damn about my memory or what happened months ago," he snapped, realizing how true that was. "All I care about is what's happening right now." He was on her before he knew what he was doing.

She looked scared. "You've forgotten about the baby."

"Not likely," he said, looking down at her protruding stomach, the only thing that was keeping them apart—other than the enormous lie she was telling. "That's all I've thought about since yesterday when you walked through the door. You. And the baby." He'd driven himself crazy, knowing she wasn't locked somewhere in his faulty memory, torturing himself with the impossible thought that she was.

"There's only one way to prove that I've never made love to you." He shoved aside the food and plates on the table in one swift noisy movement and lifted Marni up on the table, wondering how far he'd go, how far he'd have to go. He knew how far he wanted to go. "Trust me, I'll be gentle."

Chapter Seven

Oh, no, he plans to take me right here. Right on the dining-room table! "You wouldn't!" Marni cried.

"After those four days we spent together, surely you realize I would do more than make love to you on a dining-room table," Chase said.

No, she told herself. He wouldn't dare.

But she couldn't forget the way he'd made her feel in the barn. She'd wanted to kiss him, wanted him to touch her, wanted him to— *Oh yes, she'd wanted him to make love to her.* Not that she would have let him. Not that she would ever betray her sister. But she wanted him.

And what if the desire she'd thought she'd seen in his eyes had been real? What if he'd wanted her as badly as she'd wanted him? What if he wanted her now—at all costs?

He swung her legs up and spun her around and back, until she lay lengthwise on the table in front of him. Panicked that he might not be bluffing after all, she struggled to get up, but he bent over her face, his breath tickling her cheek as his lips skimmed across her skin in search of her mouth.

She turned her head away from his kiss, and realized that if he was just trying to scare her, he was doing a good job of it. "Chase, let me up. I don't find this in the least bit humorous."

"Humorous?" He laughed softly as he trailed kisses down her throat to the V of her maternity blouse. "Honey, I'm not trying to be humorous."

With a shock, she felt him unbutton the top button on her maternity blouse and realized where his mouth was headed next. *Oh no.* "Chase, pleas—"

His kiss cut her off before she got any further. Last night his lips had taken, demanding nothing in return. This kiss staked claim to her, demanding every ounce of her, warning her of his intentions in a way his words never could have done. This kiss brooked no argument and her traitorous body acquiesced without even a whimper.

She closed her eyes. Tasting him. Savoring him. Letting his lips transmit alien, wonderful, tantalizing sensations to the rest of her body. Amazed to feel her breasts tingle, nipples harden to taut peaks, her aching center long for his touch, for his mouth, for his— Her eyes flew open and she let out a cry of pure agony.

Chase jerked back, his heart a thunder in his ears. He stared at her as he tried to catch his breath. She lay, breathing hard, her eyes wide, her body trembling slightly. He saw that he'd freed the first two buttons on her blouse, laying bare the fair freckled skin above her full breasts.

He stepped back, realizing how close he'd come to taking her right there on the table. The realization frightened him more than he wanted to admit. She filled him with a need so powerful—

She sat up, swinging her legs over the side of the table as she pulled down her skirt and then quickly buttoned her shirt, smoothing it over her swollen belly, tears in her eyes.

He felt like a teenager, as embarrassed by what he'd done as she looked. The words *I'm sorry* came to his lips but he wouldn't let himself say them. The effect this woman had on him scared the hell out of him. He called on the anger, reminding himself that the child she carried was some other man's. He let the wave of jealousy that followed that thought fuel his anger.

"I wondered just how far you would go with this charade of yours," he said, grabbing his crutches as he backed toward the door. "Now I know."

It wasn't until he'd gone out the back door, felt the snow against his face and taken a deep breath of the cold winter air that he let his defenses down. His chest hurt with an ache so foreign to him— He tried not to remember the look of hurt on her face or the way her gaze clutched at his heart. *My God, he was falling for this woman.* It wasn't possible. Not in just twenty-four hours. Then he felt a jolt so strong it made him stumble. *What if she's telling the truth, what if this happened last summer and that baby she's carrying really is yours?*

HE MADE HIS ESCAPE to the barn amazingly fast considering his disability, Marni thought. She stood, leaning against the dining-room table, too shaky to leave the room, too embarrassed. Her pounding heart filled with guilt. Tears of shame stung her eyes.

Chase's first kiss had been unavoidable. The almost kiss in the barn was foolhardy at best. This... She glanced back at the table, the dishes and food pushed aside, and closed her eyes, trying to block out the sensation of his lips, his hands on her skin.

She opened her eyes at the sound of someone entering the room and lifted her head high, ready to put on a strong front for the family members she knew must have been waiting outside the door, listening to each sordid sound.

"What has my son done now?" Jabe demanded.

Obviously seeing how distraught she was, Jabe ordered her hot chocolate with marshmallows and led her into the library, even giving her his chair in front of the fire.

"I wish I could explain Chase to you," he said after adding more logs to the fire. He took the chair beside her and handed her a large mug of hot chocolate from the tray Hilda had brought in.

She took a sip, still fighting tears. She rarely cried. She'd always seen it as a weakness, one she didn't have the time or energy for. But right now—

"He seems so cold, so distant and unfeeling," she said. "And other times— Has he always been like that?"

"I wouldn't know." Jabe seemed to hesitate. "I never knew my son until he was fourteen. I didn't even know he existed before then."

Marni stared at him in shock.

"I don't know how much my son has told you about his childhood."

As far as Marni knew, Chase hadn't told Elise much of anything, especially about his childhood. "Not a lot."

He sighed as if he dreaded what he was about to say. "Chase's mother was the most beautiful woman I've ever known. Her name was Lottie, short for Charlotte. Lottie was my first, my last, my only true love."

Marni frowned to herself. Poor Vanessa. She'd be a fool not to know how Jabe felt and Vanessa was no fool. No wonder she came off as mean-spirited toward Chase.

"Lottie was…to put it bluntly…from the wrong background. Her father worked for mine. So when she came to me and told me she was pregnant with my child—"

"You sent her away."

"My father discharged hers and gave her money to have an abortion, at least that's what he told me." Jabe had the decency to look ashamed. "I was engaged to Vanessa by this time. We'd met at college and her family and mine were…compatible. I thought I would forget Lottie."

"What happened to her and Chase?"

"They had some hard times." He looked away, his face drawn. "Lottie wasn't well. Chase took care of her the best he could until almost the end."

Chase took care of himself *and* his mother? He was only a child!

Jabe looked into the fire. "Chase finally came to me for help. I realize now how hard that was for him. He was-fourteen, proud even then and just as stubborn. He hated me for what he felt I'd done to his mother.''

Marni felt sick to her stomach. She thought of Chase and that easy, loving gentleness he had with the horses.

"I might as well tell you the rest, Chase probably will." His words filled her with dread.

"I wanted something of Lottie so badly that when Chase came to me, I made him a bargain. If he would acknowledge that he was my son, I would help his mother."

"How could you do such a thing?" Marni cried without thinking. Trying to buy his son. How hateful of him. How incredibly selfish. She could see why Chase had told Elise the things he had about Jabe. Chase had to hate his father. And yet he didn't. He was here at the ranch now because he thought Jabe's life was in danger.

"I only wanted what was mine," Jabe said defensively.

And at any price. Just as he had now, changing his will in an attempt to get the grandchild he so desperately wanted.

"Poor Chase," she said, not wanting to think of the childhood he must have had. No wonder he didn't want children of his own or marriage. "He must have needed your help desperately to agree to your terms."

"He's never forgiven me no matter how hard I've tried to make it up to him."

Marni almost felt sorry for Jabe, for the anguish and regret she heard in his voice. Almost. "What happened to his mother?"

"Chase thought my money and influence could save her. All I could do was to make her last months as painless as possible."

Marni felt tears rush to her eyes. She turned away. Oh, Chase. She tried to imagine him as a boy, caring for his mother, and finally at fourteen, coming for help to the father who'd abandoned them. How hard it must have been. And then to have his mother die anyway. He must have felt betrayed in so many ways.

"You see why it's important that Chase not make the same mistake I did," Jabe said.

Marni saw that Jabe Calloway's motives were anything but selfless. He wanted a grandchild and he didn't seem to care how he accomplished that, even if it meant buying one. Or helping her convince Chase that he was the father of Elise's child.

If only the storm would let up and she could take off this silly maternity form and go back to being Marni McCumber, the sensible, the confident, the woman in control of her life, and more important, the woman in control of her feelings.

"Is there a chance that my baby's in danger because of your will?"

"There is nothing to worry about, I assure you."

Marni wished she shared his confidence. "Why is Chase so worried then?"

"Chase is a worrier by nature."

"I can see that he might not be too trusting," Marni said.

"Especially with me?" Jabe said. "I'll admit I've made some mistakes in my life. That's why I want to try to right them with a grandchild. Is that so wrong?"

"Yes," Chase said from behind them. Neither of them had heard him come in. He stood leaning on his crutches, his face twisted in anger. "Because you try to buy what you want. You've tried to buy me from the first day I met you. You tried again when you changed your will. If I'd come into the family business, you wouldn't have put a price tag on your first grandchild."

"So I wanted you to be a part of the family business more than I even wanted a grandchild," Jabe bellowed. "Is that so heinous?"

"Could you leave Jabe and me alone?" he said to Marni without looking at her.

Glad to escape the tension she felt in the room, she left without a word, closing the door behind her. She wanted to be as far away from Jabe Calloway as she could get and wished Elise wasn't carrying Chase's child for more reasons than she wanted to think about.

As she started for the stairs, she realized that she'd lost one of her earrings. The thought of having Hilda find it in the middle of the dining-room table sent her scurrying in to look for it. She found the small silver loop on the floor where it must have fallen and quickly replaced it in her ear. As she was coming out of the dining room, she saw Lilly emerge from under the stairs and heard the soft whisper of the secret passage door closing. Lilly saw her and touched her lips in a mock plea for secrecy and silence, then lifted the glass in her hand in a salute before she headed up the stairs. Marni watched her in concern but she seemed steady enough.

After a few moments, Marni walked over to the spot where the door had opened in the paneling and felt along the wall for a few minutes but no secret doorway opened at her fingertips. If she hadn't seen Lilly appear, she wouldn't have believed the passage existed. Nothing about the wall gave any indication there was a paneled doorway hidden in it.

And where did the passageway go? She remembered Lilly's face peering out of the tiny window below the third-story eave. Is that where she'd come from? Why all the secrecy? Surely Lilly didn't think she was successfully hiding her drinking problem from anyone.

As Marni turned, she collided with Felicia.

"Did you lose something?" Felicia asked, one dark eyebrow shooting up with interest.

She had that same know-it-all look on her face as her husband. Smug. Self-satisfied. What she didn't look was pregnant. The irony of it made Marni smile.

"I was just admiring the beautiful wood," Marni said.

"You like it?" Felicia asked in surprise. She wrinkled her perfect little nose. "It's a little too dark for my tastes."

"It's like the house, it reflects Jabe and his position," Marni said.

"Really?" Felicia's interest in the pretentious house seemed to wane. "When exactly is your baby due?" she asked, her gaze dropping to Marni's protruding stomach.

"Valentine's Day," Marni said.

Felicia looked as if she might want to throw up again. "I heard that you've befriended my sister-in-law."

The change of subject was so abrupt it took Marni a moment to realize Felicia was referring to Lilly. News definitely traveled fast in this house. But Marni did wonder how Felicia had found out. She doubted Chase had mentioned it to Felicia, a woman Marni figured he wished was still in one of those deep, dark holes of forgotten memory.

"Lilly was upset," Marni said. "I just tried to comfort her."

"Lilly is always upset," Felicia said disagreeably. "Upset, drunk and—" She looked up, her eyes darkening. "Dangerous."

"Dangerous?" Marni repeated.

Felicia nodded conspiratorially. "I hate to be the one to tell you this, but Lilly has never been well, and since the baby...died."

"How did it die?" she asked, reminded of Lilly's claim that Vanessa had killed it.

Felicia did a poor job of pretending discomfort. "It says crib death on the poor little thing's death certificate," she whispered. "The baby had somehow suffocated."

When Marni didn't question her about the "somehow," Felicia added, "The truth is, Vanessa found Lilly leaning over the crib with a pillow in her hands and the baby dead. She murdered her own daughter and now she wanders this place crazier than a loon, clinging to that damned stuffed doll and crying."

Marni shuddered at the picture Felicia painted of Lilly.

"That's why I wanted to warn you," she said earnestly. "If you're smart, you'll stay away from her. She could be a threat to you." Felicia let her gaze drop and Marni's hand went protectively to Sam.

Having obviously accomplished what she'd set out to, Felicia turned and strolled away. Marni watched her go, unable to throw off the image of Lilly standing over her daughter's crib, a pillow in her hands. Nor could she forget the sound of the baby crying coming up through the heat vent, when there was no baby in the house.

Chapter Eight

Marni hurried up the stairs to her room, wanting to avoid further contact with Chase's family for a few hours. She tried not to think about what Felicia had told her. It was obvious Lilly needed help, if for nothing more than her drinking problem. So why wasn't someone in this family seeing that she got it?

Marni felt uneasy and almost...afraid as she closed her bedroom door behind her and locked it. Afraid not of Dayton, Felicia or even Lilly, but something less tangible, a feeling of misfortune that seemed to permeate this dark, joyless house.

She checked to make sure the adjoining-room door was locked, as well, feeling silly and strangely paranoid. She couldn't remember ever being afraid before. Not even of the dark.

Part of it is the storm, she told herself as she went to the window to stare out. From the gray of the sky, huge snowflakes continued to fall, spiraling down to form a suffocating blanket of white.

She felt trapped. In this house. In her own dark thoughts. She couldn't stop thinking about Lilly and her infant daughter. Nor about Chase and his mother.

She knew so little about Chase. Elise knew even less. Why hadn't Elise known he had a different mother from Hayes's and Dayton's? That he'd been a bastard. That he hadn't even known his father until he was fourteen. That he didn't work for Calloway Ranches. What *did* he do for a living? And why hadn't he mentioned any of this to El?

Had he purposely kept things from her or had the two never talked about anything...important? But according to El, they had talked about marriage and children. And El thought he worked for Calloway Ranches. Was it just because he'd been driving one of the ranch trucks? Or had he led her to believe he worked for his father?

Marni couldn't shake the sense that something was desperately wrong here. Or maybe she was just feeling how wrong it was to pretend to be Elise, especially considering her own reaction to Chase.

Unable to call her twin until the phone lines were restored, Marni busied herself building a fire in the fireplace, hoping the physical activity would stop her thoughts of Chase and his family. But when she had the fire going, she couldn't stand still long enough to enjoy its warmth. Instead, she paced the room, worrying about Elise and the baby and what she was going to tell her twin when she could finally call. Marni stopped pacing at a sound in the hallway.

She listened. There it was again. A fumbling, stumbling sound outside her bedroom door. Lilly?

As Marni went to unlock the door, she expected to find Lilly weaving outside.

But when Marni opened the door, the hallway was empty. She stood for a moment, listening, then looked toward the stairs. The thought of Lilly trying to maneuver the steps in an inebriated state sent Marni hurrying to the top of the stairway. She glanced down over the railing.

Silence filled the house. "Not a creature was stirring," Marni whispered.

Wrong. She caught a movement at the base of the stairs, then saw a flash of pale pink.

Marni groaned, remembering Lilly's earlier drinking. She could be much worse by now. Someone needed to see

that she was all right. With another groan, Marni hurried
after the woman, ignoring that little voice in her head that
told her to mind her own business.

As Marni reached the first floor and turned the corner
toward the dining room, she saw to her surprise that the
secret panel beneath the stairs stood open. She halted for a
moment, looking into the narrow darkness. Lilly wasn't her
responsibility. Maybe she should heed Felicia's warning
about Lilly and go back upstairs.

With a sigh, Marni stepped closer. *When are you going
to stop being such a sucker for anyone in trouble?* "Lilly?"
she whispered as she stuck her head into the opening. There
was just enough room inside for the narrow stairway. She
could heard the soft pad of footfalls on the steps disappearing up into the darkness.

Why had Lilly left the door open? Was she so inebriated
she forgot to close it? Or had she known Marni would
follow her?

Marni felt a chill as she took one tentative step into the
passageway. *Don't do this. This is stupid. This is scary.
This is crazy.* But she couldn't shake off the feeling that
Lilly Calloway was in trouble. That's why Lilly had come
to her bedroom door. That's why she'd left the hidden panel
open. For some reason, Lilly wanted her to follow.

At least Marni hoped that was the case as she started up
the stairs, the steps curling up and up in a tight spiral that
seemed unending in the semidarkness. Natural light seemed
to filter down from somewhere at the top.

A few steps and Marni heard the secret panel close below
her. Her heart thumped wildly. Who'd closed the door?
Someone downstairs? Or did it close on its own? What did
it matter? That avenue of escape was gone and instantly
the stairwell seemed more claustrophobic than before. She
felt as if she'd been sealed up in the walls of the old house
never to be seen again.

She brushed away such ridiculous thoughts, hoping they
were indeed ridiculous, as she climbed more quickly.

That's when she heard it. At first she thought it was her imagination. Her hand dropped to Sam as she stopped to listen and catch her breath.

It was faint, but definitely a baby laughing and cooing softly. The sound brought goose bumps to her skin. She shivered, telling herself there was no baby in this house. Someone just wanted her to think there was. But that frightened her all the more. *Why* would anyone want her to think there was a baby here? What possible purpose could they have?

Marni heard a door open overhead. And close again softly. She hurried up the steps only to have them end in a wall. A skylight above her let in what little light there was in the passageway.

Beyond the wall, she could still hear the baby, no longer laughing and cooing, but fussing. She could hear another voice now. A woman's voice, trying to soothe the infant.

Marni examined the wall. She could only assume it also had a secret panel she would have to press. She ran her hand along the dark wood, the memory fresh in her mind how she'd been unable to open the lower door the time she'd tried. Her heart rate skyrocketed as her fingers felt frantically along the wood. A scream rose in her throat.

She felt a narrow vertical notch in the wall and realized with body weakening relief that Lilly hadn't closed the door all the way. Slipping her fingers in the groove, she pushed and the door began to slide open, reinforcing Marni's hope that Lilly had wanted her to come up here.

Marni slid the door aside and stepped into what appeared to be an attic. The air smelled of dust and age, but definitely felt warmer than in the stairwell. Furniture stood like sentinels in front of the doorway. Marni started around a huge antique bureau, remembering Lilly's pale face peering out from the small window on the third floor. Unless she missed her guess, this was the room.

"Lilly?" Marni called, her voice little more than a whisper as she stepped around the bureau. Deeper in the attic, the baby started to cry as a woman's voice tried to hush it.

The rich wood of armoires and chiffoniers, credenzas and tallboys gleamed, the feeling of another, gentler lifetime in the valuable antique pieces. Why didn't Jabe and Vanessa use these wonderful antiques instead of the massive log furniture that looked so out of place in the old Victorian house?

Marni had started to take a tentative step deeper into the room when she heard a rustling sound like taffeta and the scrape of a shoe as someone moved across the floor. She froze behind a massive armoire.

Until that moment, she'd believed it was Lilly who'd maneuvered her up here.

Now she wasn't so sure. The step had sounded sure. Not like that of a woman who'd had too much wine to drink. What if it wasn't Lilly who'd lured her up here? All she'd seen was a glimpse of Lilly's pale pink dress in the shadowed darkness and just the hint of a staggered gait.

The baby quit cooing. The room filled with silence, thick and heavy. Cold fear raced across Marni's skin as quick and frightening as a spider.

"Elise?"

Just that one word, whispered hoarsely in the darkness. Marni's pulse thrummed in her ears. Goose bumps skittered across her flesh. She held her breath, no longer pretending her fear wasn't warranted.

"Poor Elise," came the whisper again.

Marni recoiled at the hatred in the voice, bumping into the bureau behind her. Instantly she realized her mistake. She'd given away her location. The armoire beside her came toppling over.

CHASE CLOSED the barn door, pleased he'd accomplished what he'd set out to. His arms ached from the hours he'd spent stacking hay and pulling feed sacks down from the storage loft. His good leg ached from standing on it for so

long, his casted leg ached from trying not to stand on it.
He felt exhausted after all the weeks of inactivity. But he'd
been too busy even to think about Miss McCumber. Most
of the time.

On top of that he'd had the joy of listening to Dayton
and Hayes grumbling and complaining as they shoveled out
the horse stalls.

All except for Wind Chaser's stall. The stallion wouldn't
allow either of the brothers to get near it. Chase had found
no small satisfaction that he was the only Calloway the new
horse at the ranch would tolerate. Although he did wonder
what had upset the horse to such an extent. Probably the
storm, he told himself. Or maybe the horse liked it at Calloway Ranch as much as Chase did and realized they had
that in common.

Chase felt good as he came through the back door of the
house, assured that his physical exhaustion would keep his
mind from wandering to that one particular pregnant
woman.

But the moment he closed the door behind him, he felt
her presence. And something even worse. A concern for
her that he'd promised himself he wasn't going to allow.
The house felt too quiet. He started to worry that he
shouldn't have left her alone, even with Jabe and others
around—maybe especially with them around. He'd been
keeping a close eye on Dayton and Hayes, up until about
thirty minutes ago when he'd lost track of time and them.

Chase picked up the hall phone and dialed her room. No
answer. He pushed open the kitchen door and stuck his
head in. "Have you seen Elise?" he asked Cook.

She looked up from the open door of the woodstove
oven. The smell of a large piece of prime rib wafted toward
him as she closed the oven door.

She shook her head and went back to her cooking as if
she had better things to do than keep track of his women.

Chase swore under his breath as he headed for the service elevator. The stairs were just too dangerous on

crutches, although he'd tried them out of stubbornness his first day only because Jabe had insisted he not.

He wondered where everybody was. Probably in their rooms, avoiding each other. If he knew Vanessa, she'd be working out in the exercise room off the master bedroom. Felicia would be doing her nails or something productive like that. Lilly, well, who knew where Lilly might be. He'd seen her sneaking around the house like a drunken ghost in the days he'd been here. No wonder Hayes spent so much time on the road.

And the same could be said of Dayton. He and Felicia seemed to lead separate lives as far as Chase could tell. He doubted a baby would change that. It made him glad he had no intentions of ever getting married, let alone having children.

By the time the elevator groaned to a stop on the third floor, Chase had pretty well convinced himself that Miss McCumber was none of his concern. It wasn't as if he really believed she was carrying his baby. But still he stopped at her door and knocked softly. When she didn't answer, he went to his own room and built a fire, then slumped in the chair in front of it, watching the flames dance along the logs, determined to relax and not think about her. Especially the part where he'd almost taken her on the dining-room table. Whatever had possessed him?

He tried to steer his thoughts to business, all the work he'd have when he finally got out of here. He'd already made up his mind. He was leaving the moment the roads opened. And as for Jabe—well, he was on his own. If Miss McCumber wanted to stay here and continue her charade, that was her problem.

Chase swore again. Wishing she fit his image of a gold digger. If she'd been more like Felicia it would have made things a whole lot easier. But instead, she was so damned wholesome-looking and so...chaste. If he didn't know better, he'd think her a virgin.

Nor could he forget the sight of her kneeling beside

Lilly's chair in the garden room, holding the crying, obviously sloshed woman and trying to comfort her. It was that compassion, along with everything else, that threw him. And the feeling that she wasn't the kind of woman who fell in love with just any man, had a four-day tryst and didn't take the proper precautions. She seemed so...nice.

He had to find her. Not to make sure she was all right. No, he had to find her just so he'd know what she was up to.

He knocked at their adjoining door. When she didn't answer, he tried the knob. Locked. He knocked again and listened for even the slightest sound. When none came, he used the key he was sure his father had left for him in the lock and opened the door without even a twinge of guilt.

He'd expected to find her napping or sitting in the chair before the fire, ignoring his knock. He found neither.

Damn. Where had she gone? What was she up to? Trouble. Because trouble dogged women like her who got too involved in other people's lives. As he went to the window, he assured himself she deserved every moment of whatever disaster befell her. He'd half expected her car to be gone.

Of course, it wasn't. She couldn't get out even with four-wheel drive: The snow was too deep. But, to his surprise, he saw that the storm had stopped. Someone was out plowing the ranch yard. It wouldn't be long until the county snowplow would be coming up the road. And Miss McCumber would be going down the road.

She wouldn't be happy about that, he told himself. She had probably planned to stay here until she got what she wanted. And she seemed to want Chase Calloway. The fool woman.

Turning from the window, Chase decided he'd check downstairs for her again. The best thing he could do for both of them was to get her out of this house. He'd started for the door when he heard what sounded like thunder rumble over his head. He looked up to see dust sifting down from the rafters and realized that a large object had just hit the floor over his head. He stared at the ceiling and frowned. What was someone doing in the attic?

MARNI HAD ONLY an instant before the towering antique closet came crashing down. She fell back into a chest of drawers as the armoire toppled, smashing the credenza behind it as it fell in a loud thunderclap of splintered wood and destruction.

Marni felt the massive wardrobe graze her arm, breeze past her face and hit the maternity form with a force that knocked her breath out. Then it crashed into the credenza, flattening it as if it were built of toothpicks. Marni stood staring down at the pile of splintered wood as she fought to corral her racing heart. She wasn't hurt. No harm was done.

She heard a door open and close on the far side of the room and the sound of footsteps retreat down creaky stairs.

Relief. She leaned back against the chest of drawers, reassuring herself again that it had been a close call but she was all right. She looked down, surprised to see that her borrowed maternity shirt was torn from where the armoire had hit her protruding stomach. She stared at Sam. The form would survive. But would a real baby have? Her blood turned to ice.

All she wanted was out of the attic. She hurriedly stepped over the shattered armoire and around another large wardrobe and stopped. To her left, a child-size door creaked open. From inside, Marni could hear the sound of the baby cooing softly. Her heart thundered in her chest as she slowly knelt to gaze through the crack between the door and the jamb.

Light from a small round window under the eave at the back of the room illuminated the eerie scene. A window much like the one Marni had seen Lilly peering out of yesterday afternoon. Next to the window sat a rocker with a ball of pink yarn on the seat, a pair of knitting needles and two tiny baby booties, the second nearly completed.

The air suddenly filled with the startling cry of a baby. Marni jumped, her heart a sledgehammer inside her chest. An antique crib had been pushed back into a shadowed corner of the room. A mobile of hideous-faced clowns spun slowly above it in an invisible draft. From inside the crib the baby started to cry softly.

Marni had to bend down to see in through the doorway and as she did, she noticed the scrape on the floor where someone had recently moved a large object away from the door.

She stuck her head in tentatively, but the room was empty except for the rocker and the crib. Carefully she slipped in, surprised to find she had room to stand once inside.

As the baby whimpered, Marni moved toward the crib and, calling on all her courage, looked over the side.

Something the size of a baby lay wrapped in a pink baby blanket. With trembling fingers, Marni pulled back the blanket.

A face leaped out at her. She fought back a scream as she realized what was lying in the crib. The blank eyes stared up out of a grayed worn face. Not a baby. But a doll. Lilly's rag doll.

Marni tried to still her thundering heart as she pushed the doll and the blanket aside to reveal a small tape recorder.

"Hush now," a woman said as the baby began to cry again on the tape. With a start, Marni recognized the voice. "Stop that fretting," Vanessa said impatiently.

Marni hit the stop button on the recorder. The baby quit crying. Vanessa fell silent.

Marni felt sick as she stared down at the crib and the doll baby inside it. Who had done this? What was Vanessa's voice doing on the tape? Was this Lilly's way of coping with the loss of her baby? Or someone else's sick way of tormenting Lilly?

Behind her, Marni heard a sound. She spun around. The child-size door shut.

Blindly, Marni flung herself at the closing door.

Chapter Nine

"What the hell?" Chase cried as the door hit him. He dropped the flashlight in his hand. The light spun in an arc, illuminating the source of his pain, then the flashlight hit the floor with a thud at Miss McCumber's feet. "I should have known it would be you."

She looked up at him. "It amazes me that any woman could have ever fallen in love with you." She handed him the flashlight.

"Yeah, well, that makes two of us." He pointed the beam at her.

"Do you mind?" she said, shielding her eyes.

He shifted the circle of light to a spot on the floor between them, but not before he'd noticed two things that surprised him. Her disheveled appearance. And the fear in her eyes. "Want to tell me what's going on?"

Marni glared at him as she drew her shirt together over her swollen stomach. "I was almost killed!"

Leave it to a woman to magnify things.

"I'm the one who got hit with the door," he told her, then recalled the fear in her eyes. Surely just catching her snooping around the house hadn't put that scared look on her face. And it wasn't as though he could frighten her even when he'd tried.

"Why should I expect you to believe me?" she said.

"You're a mess," he said softer than he'd meant to. He

reached out to wipe a smudge from her cheek with his thumb. "There's probably a good reason why you're up here."

She looked as if she might cry. But she also looked damned and determined not to. He watched her face, amused and intrigued by her. She wasn't like anyone he'd ever known. And yet, sometimes she reminded him a little of himself.

"So why don't you tell me about this hair-raising experience you had," he said, brushing hers back from her face.

She pulled away and didn't seem all that willing to tell him anything. But he realized something had happened up here that had upset her. Not only was she a dusty mess, it looked as if she'd torn her maternity top. Both filled him with concern, a concern that made him angry. He fought the urge to tell her she had no business in the attic, no business here at all.

"I was worried about Lilly," she began hesitantly.

He bit his tongue to keep his mouth shut. Hadn't he warned her not to get involved with this family? Especially Lilly?

She seemed surprised he hadn't said anything and, obviously encouraged by his silence, charged ahead with her story.

He amazed himself. He kept his mouth shut through the climb up through some secret staircase, as ridiculously stupid as that was, right to where the armoire crashed and she was almost killed, even though he could tell she was purposely leaving out details for whatever reason he could not imagine, probably just exaggerating how close a call it was.

"Didn't I tell you that you were in danger?" he demanded when he couldn't stand it anymore.

"I thought Lilly was in trouble," she cried in high indignation.

"*Lilly* was in trouble?" Chase asked, trying to control his anger, which was matched only by his fear for this woman. It surprised him how relieved he felt that she hadn't been hurt. "It sounds to me like you're the one who's always in trouble." He hobbled toward her. "Do you have any sense at all? Going up hidden stairways to old attics following a woman who at best is an alcoholic and at worst is...unstable?"

"I thought it was a cry for help."

"You're the one who needs help," he retorted. "You just can't seem to stay out of other people's lives, can you?"

"Like yours?"

"Show me this fallen armoire." He handed her the flashlight. "Unless you're afraid to go back there."

Her chin came up, her eyes darkened like clouds before a hailstorm. "Maybe you *should* see it for yourself."

He didn't like the sound of that.

She led him around several large pieces of furniture and he realized he'd had no idea any of this was up here. It surprised him and made him wonder about Jabe Calloway and what else he kept hidden.

She stopped, waiting for him to maneuver the last few steps on his crutches.

He rounded the corner of a huge buffet and came to an abrupt stop. "What the hell?" He took the flashlight from her and flicked the light over the fallen armoire, his gaze widening in horror as he saw the armoire and the splintered credenza beneath it.

"My God, you could have been killed."

"I know, that's what I told you," she said with no small amount of satisfaction.

"Are you sure you're all right? And the baby—"

She gave him a *now*-he-cares look. "I'm fine. The baby's fine. But there's something else you'd better see."

He let her lead him back to the small door she'd nailed him with earlier. Taking the flashlight from his hand, she shone it inside the room.

Chase bent down to peer in. "A nursery?"

"For a dead baby," she said, giving him a chill. "I *told* you I heard a baby crying." He watched her duck through the doorway. It took him a little more effort to get through the door, even when he left his crutches outside the room.

She went to an antique crib set back against the wall and reached inside.

Instantly, he heard a baby fussing, then start to cry. Something about the sound freeze-dried his blood. Then Vanessa's voice came on the tape.

He limped over and hit the stop button on the tape recorder, a feeling of abhorrence in the pit of his stomach when he saw the worn rag doll lying in the crib.

"See why I'm worried about Lilly?" he demanded.

"She wasn't the only one on that tape. You heard Vanessa's voice."

"That makes Lilly even more perverse," Chase shot back.

"Maybe Lilly wasn't the one who did this. Or pushed over the armoire."

He looked at her. "I thought you said you followed Lilly up here?"

"I thought it was Lilly. At the time."

He raked a hand through his hair. "Based on what?"

"Based on..." She took a deep breath and avoided his gaze. "I saw a flash of pale pink like Lilly wears, and the person seemed to kind of stagger."

He couldn't believe it. "You're not even sure it was a woman?"

She didn't even have to open her mouth. He saw the answer on her face.

"So you have no idea who pushed over the wardrobe. Or if it was even meant for you."

She stepped away from him to finger a hand-knit baby blanket thrown over the back of the rocker, the only other piece of furniture in the small room. "It was meant for me. The person said my name and..."

"And what?" he asked, knowing she and her baby were

the targets, but wishing she could give him another explanation.

"It was just a hoarse whisper from the other side of the armoire. The person said, 'Elise? Poor Elise.' Then I bumped against the chest of drawers, and I guess there was no doubt where I was. The armoire toppled over."

He swore under his breath and almost launched into another one of his tirades—not that they seemed to have any effect on this woman. He could tell her that her life and her baby's was in danger until he was blue in the face and she'd still do whatever she damn well pleased, especially if she thought someone else was in trouble.

Why couldn't she be like Felicia, self-centered, mercenary, coldhearted? Just to make his life simpler. He saw her freeze in motion, her fingers on the baby quilt, her gaze directed at the seat of the rocker.

"What is it?" he demanded.

"There were knitting needles and a pair of almost finished pink baby booties on this rocker just minutes ago—" Her gaze leaped up to his; she looked as if she'd seen an apparition. "Do you smell that?"

He caught the scent on a slight breeze that seemed to whisper through the attic. He recognized it immediately. Gardenia. Lilly's cloying perfume.

"Come on, you're getting out of this house." He crawled from the small room, anxious to breathe fresh air, anxious to get out of the attic. He picked up his crutches and took a few steps before he realized she wasn't beside him. He turned to find her standing outside the nursery door, glaring at him.

"We're just going to pretend we didn't find this room?" she demanded. "That the armoire toppled over on its own? That Lilly doesn't have a drinking problem or worse?"

He hobbled back to her. "Don't you get it?" he said through gritted teeth. "Someone tried to kill you and your baby up here today. Forget Lilly. Forget her problems." He gazed into her eyes. She looked frightened and he wondered if he'd gotten through to her. He doubted it. If she was scared, it was for someone else—not herself. The woman was incredible. "Just worry about yourself right now—and this kid of yours."

"What is that, your philosophy of life?" she demanded. "Every man for himself?"

"It works for me."

He could tell she was gearing up for an argument, but he didn't give her a chance. "The storm has stopped. Get packed. You're getting out of here, whether you like it or not." He steered her through a labyrinth of boxes, more furniture and old trunks to a doorway that opened onto the attic stairs. "Give me the keys to your car and I'll get it warmed up," he said when they reached her bedroom door. "Stay here until I get back. Lock your door. And don't argue."

MARNI MCCUMBER had never taken orders well. Especially from men who thought it was their birthright to give them. But most especially from a man like Chase Calloway. The all-out arrogance of the man!

She stood in the middle of her bedroom, indignant and defiant. Pack? She had nothing to pack. She took off the ruined maternity top and threw it in the trash. She'd have to wear Chase's shirt since she had nothing else. Once she'd retrieved her coat from the closet downstairs, she'd be as packed as she could get. So what was she supposed to do until then?

She felt herself begin to tremble. All the anger ran out of her and she stood in the middle of the floor, shaking. Chase was right. She had to think about Elise and the baby. That falling armoire had been for her sister—not Marni McCumber. But no one knew about Elise, Marni thought, hugging herself to keep out the cold fear. Elise and the baby were safe. For the time being.

She went to the window. It had indeed finally stopped snowing. Bits of blue broke through the grayness, bringing shafts of sunshine that made the snow sparkle like prisms. She could see Dayton behind the wheel of a Calloway Ranch pickup, plowing snow from the ranch yard. She was going home. Home for Christmas. Isn't that what she wanted?

She caught a glimpse of Chase hobbling on his crutches from her car toward the barn. If she could have gotten the window open, she would have thrown something at him. "Whether she wanted to leave or not"? Was he kidding? She'd never even wanted to come here, let alone have to stay two days and pretend to be seven months pregnant and put up with Chase Calloway all that time.

So why was he going to the barn now? Probably to do something with the horses. Chase had a way with horses. And some women, she reminded herself. Maybe all women.

She watched him reach the barn and was surprised to see that Jabe had been waiting for him. Even from this distance, she could tell they were arguing. She figured that's all they did. She wondered what about now. The will? Elise's safety? Or would Chase tell Jabe about Lilly? Would he try to convince Jabe that his daughter-in-law needed help?

Marni couldn't see Jabe Calloway being very sympathetic to Lilly's plight. Actually, there wasn't anyone in this house who seemed to care about Lilly. Except Hayes. Maybe. She promised herself she'd call Hayes once she got to Bozeman and tell him about the nursery in the attic. Surely he'd see that his wife got help. That was the least she could do, no matter what Chase said about not getting involved.

She hugged Sam, remembering the hoarse whisper, "Poor Elise," just before the armoire fell. She was involved as long as there was any chance Elise and the baby were in danger.

Marni glanced toward the barn again. Chase and his father were no longer standing in the doorway. In the distance, she could hear a snowplow coming up the county road. She told herself she was as anxious to get out of here as Chase was to have her go. She already felt she'd betrayed her sister just letting the man kiss her, let alone—

Marni swung around at a sound behind her, remembering belatedly Chase's instructions to lock her door.

The remorseful expression on Lilly's face scared Marni as much as the realization that the woman had just sneaked quietly into Marni's room, closed and locked the door and now stood with her hands behind her back.

"Lilly," Marni said, all her surprise and fear echoed in that one word. "I didn't hear you come in."

She smiled, her lips turning up, her eyes turning hard as stones. "You've been listening to them, haven't you?" She stepped closer, her hands still hidden behind her back.

Marni watched Lilly approach with uneasiness, desperately trying to assure herself that she had nothing to fear.

"The storm's over," Marni said, her nerves taut. What was the woman hiding behind her? "Chase has gone out to start my car for me. He should be back any minute and then I'll be leaving." She hoped.

Lilly didn't seem to hear. Her gaze skittered around the room. "What did they tell you?" she asked, drawing nearer. "Did they tell you I'm crazy? That I've never been well? Did Hayes tell you that I never loved him? That I married him for his money?" She stopped within a few feet of Marni, their gazes locked. Marni smelled alcohol and gardenia, the same scent as in the attic. "Did they tell you I killed my own baby?"

"It wasn't your fault that the baby died," Marni said. "Sudden infant death syndrome is—"

"Is that what Vanessa told you?" She smiled. "They lie to protect the family name. They play tricks on me. They do things to make me think I'm crazy. To even make me think I killed my own baby."

Marni looked into Lilly's eyes, her heart urging her to reach out to this obviously hurting woman. Her brain screaming for her to run.

"I should hate you," Lilly said, her gaze falling to Sam.

"But I know it's not your fault." Suddenly Lilly brought her hands out in front of her. Marni stumbled back against the windowsill before she saw what Lilly held.

"I'm sorry they're pink," Lilly said.

Oh my God. Marni stared down at the pair of hand-knit pink baby booties nestled in Lilly's palms. The same ones she'd seen earlier on the rocker in the attic.

"Pink was the only color yarn I had," Lilly said as she closed the distance between them. "I started knitting them for—" She looked up, tears flooded her eyes.

"They're beautiful," Marni said, taking the tiny booties Lilly held out to her. "Thank you." She cradled them in the palm of one hand, her heart a drum pounding in her ears. Lilly had been in the attic. The booties proved it.

But as she looked at the woman, Marni thought of how Lilly had finished the last few stitches of the booties to give them to the baby she thought Marni carried. A baby she thought was stealing everything from her dead one.

Marni felt a surge of emotion at Lilly's generous gift. Her eyes filled with tears as she pulled Lilly into her arms and hugged her, expecting the thin body to be frail. Instead, Lilly felt incredibly strong.

Lilly pulled away first, seemingly embarrassed, then looked toward the door as if she'd heard someone out in the hallway. Chase? "I have to go."

Marni's heart broke at the fear she saw in the woman's face. "I'm worried about you. What is it you're so frightened of?"

Lilly looked up at her and seemed surprised by Marni's concern. "They wouldn't hurt me. A woman who's too drunk, too crazy, to know what they're planning." Her eyes darkened. "It's you they want—"

She stepped to the door, hesitated for a moment to listen, then was gone in a flash of pale pink, leaving only the hint of her perfume and her imbibed wine wafting through the room like a ghost.

Marni looked down at the tiny pink booties still nestled in her hand.

"You're not going to keep those?" Chase said from the open doorway, making her jump. "For all you know, she tried to kill you in the attic earlier."

Why then did her heart tell her differently?

"You'd be a fool to trust her," he said. "But you're also a fool if you think you and your baby will be safe as long as you continue to claim you're carrying my kid."

He shook his head in disgust as she placed the booties in her purse. "I've started your car to let it warm up. I'm sure you'll want to get going as soon as possible."

"You're so thoughtful," Marni said, not even bothering to hide her sarcasm. Chase turned and thumped down the hallway.

As Marni followed, she couldn't help feeling that she was abandoning Lilly. And that Lilly Calloway was in more serious trouble than Marni McCumber ever imagined.

Chapter Ten

By the time Marni retrieved her coat, Chase was already leaning on his crutches beside her car with a scowl on his handsome face. Exhaust rose thick and white, a spirit curling up into the sunny December day. Everywhere, the snow sparkled, diamond bright.

Marni followed the freshly shoveled path to the car, the knowledge that she'd failed her twin making her steps heavier than when she'd arrived. She'd failed Elise in more ways than she wanted to think about. At least she could put it all behind her once she left here. But Elise—

"I wish I could promise you that once you drive away, you'll be fine," Chase said as he opened the door for her. "It's not too late to straighten things out before you leave."

She climbed in and buckled her seat belt without looking at him. "Jabe has assured me—"

"Have it your way. But don't say I didn't warn you." Chase slammed the door before she could finish. She watched his broad back retreat toward the house and told herself the best thing she could do would be to drive off. Nothing would be accomplished by rolling down her window and yelling something rude at him.

But the thought of letting Chase Calloway have the last word was too unbearable. She rolled down her window. "If you select to remember you have a child—" She was going to say, "Call me." But Elise didn't have a place yet. And

Marni McCumber wasn't Marni McCumber. "Call my sister. It's the only McCumber in the Bozeman phone book."

Chase turned, his narrowed gaze a pale blue that perfectly matched the wide-open Montana sky. She thought he'd say something nasty. She wanted him to. She told herself she'd been much too kind to Chase Calloway. He'd tried to frighten her, to intimidate her, to confuse her. She wanted to tell him just what she thought of him. All he had to do was say one word, any word and—

His gaze widened and she blinked in shock as he threw down his crutches and half hopped, half ran back to the car, jerked open the door, unsnapped her seat belt and, to her amazement, pulled her out and carried her toward the house.

For a moment, Marni was too stunned to speak. The moment passed. "Put me down, you—"

He did. But not until he'd kicked open the front door of the house and placed her inside as if putting down a very rare piece of glass. "Stay here," he commanded. Then he turned and hobbled/ran back to the car.

Marni rushed to the window to stare after him, shocked to see that her car appeared to be on fire. Smoke rolled out from under the hood and she could hear flames licking at the metal. She watched in horror as Chase reached in, turned off the engine and popped the hood latch. The flames licked up and out, bright orange; the smoke billowed higher and for a moment, Marni lost sight of Chase. Faster than most men can move without one leg in a cast, he had the hood thrown up and was dousing the engine's fire with shovelsful of fresh snow.

Marni let Chase ease her into a chair in front of the fireplace in the library. The room grew quiet after Jabe had sent the rest of the family away. They hadn't gone easily, still asking questions about the fire and what was going on.

Marni was glad when they were gone. Unable to stop shaking, she watched as Chase rang Hilda for hot chocolate.

Neither she nor Chase said anything to the man standing in front of the fire. Jabe looked pale and shrunken. He stood, holding on to the mantel, watching them with a look of total disbelief.

For a long moment, he didn't speak, then, ''It was definitely not an accident.'' It was more a clarification than a question.

''The car was rigged so the engine would catch fire, very amateurish,'' Chase said and Marni wondered how he knew anything about such things. ''This one worked off the heat of the engine. Whoever rigged it planned for the car to catch fire somewhere down the road after the engine got hot. They didn't plan on me starting the car and letting it warm up for such a long time.''

Marni listened to Chase's voice but heard only one thing: Someone had tried to kill her because they thought she was Elise McCumber. Again. Because they thought she was carrying Jabe Calloway's first grandchild. This was no possible cry for help from a woman in pain. This was attempted murder. She met Jabe's blue-eyed gaze. ''You said I was safe.''

Jabe let out a low curse and headed for the liquor cabinet. ''You need a little brandy to steady you.'' His hands shook as he splashed some into a snifter.

''She doesn't need brandy,'' Chase snapped. ''She's pregnant.''

Just then Hilda came in carrying Chase's crutches in one hand and a cup of something steaming in the other. Chase tossed the crutches aside and pressed the cup of hot chocolate into Marni's hands. She curled her fingers around it, hoping the warmth would help melt the core of icy fear inside her.

Chase laid a hand on her shoulder. Warm. Reassuring. She hadn't wanted to believe that he might be right. She thought he was just trying to scare her. Her perception of him kept changing. A kaleidoscope of characteristics. She wondered how many people got to see the real Chase Calloway. Obviously Elise had.

He removed his hand and Marni felt a sense of loss. She took a sip of the hot liquid, forcing the cold to retreat. But nothing could scare off the fear. Someone had really tried to kill her. As crazy as that sounded. This was no toppling armoire. This was so much more deliberate. So much more frightening. If they'd succeeded, they would have only killed Marni McCumber and a maternity form. Of course, after that they'd have realized their mistake. Marni felt a shudder and took another sip of hot chocolate.

"What are you doing?" Jabe demanded.

She looked up to see Chase dialing the phone, knowing he was bluffing because the phones weren't working. Marni had tried again earlier to reach her sister.

"I'm calling the sheriff," Chase said.

"Hang up the phone," Jabe ordered. "This is a family matter."

"Like hell." Chase finished dialing. "Someone in this *family* is an attempted murderer, and has to be stopped."

"I know how to stop this," Jabe said. "And I will, if you hang up that phone. Now."

Chase slowly replaced the receiver. "You'll change your will?" he asked, his voice rough with anger or fear, probably a little of both, Marni suspected. No matter what Chase said, he felt responsible for her and the baby. He'd just risked his life for them.

Jabe looked down at the brandy he'd poured into the glass and drained it in one swallow. "Yes," he said, carefully putting down the glass.

"Get Hilda and Cook to witness it," Chase ordered. "Make sure everyone in this household knows."

Jabe winced, obviously still having trouble accepting that someone in the house had tried to kill Marni. His gaze met hers. He looked as if he wanted to apologize but must have realized the futility of a mere "sorry." With weary steps, he walked to his desk and pulled out a sheet of Calloway

Ranch letterhead and a pen. Slowly he lowered himself into the chair.

The door to the library slammed open and Dayton came back into the room. "Now that Mother isn't here, would one of you like to tell me what the hell is going on?"

"Someone in this house tried to kill Elise," Chase said.

"By setting her car on fire?" Dayton said. "That's ridiculous."

"Chase says the car was rigged to catch fire," Jabe said wearily.

Dayton laughed. "What does Chase know about rigging cars to catch fire?"

"You forget the neighborhood where I grew up," Chase said.

Dayton closed his mouth and glanced over at his father sitting at the desk, pen in hand.

"He's changing his will," Chase said in answer to his brother's unanswered question.

A vein popped out on Dayton's forehead. "You mean to tell me you're going to change your will because this...woman's car caught on fire?"

"What do you care?" Chase asked. "I'd think you'd want the will changed back because right now it appears my child would benefit."

Dayton threw a mean look at Marni. "If she's even carrying your child."

"Stay out of this, Dayton," Jabe warned. "I'm changing my will. It's my decision. Now all of you get out of here so I can finish and put an end to this."

Dayton stomped out.

"Come on," Chase said to Marni as he took her half-empty cup and placed it on the coffee table, then helped her up from the chair.

"Shouldn't you be using your crutches?" she asked after watching him take a few painful steps beside her.

He swept them up and settled his weight on them. He looked exhausted, his face drained and sooty, and yet he was more handsome than she'd ever seen him, she thought with a stab of guilt.

"Are you leaving the ranch?" Jabe asked his son.

"Not until that codicil is written and witnessed." Chase turned and led Marni out of the room.

They took a service elevator that Marni hadn't known existed up to the third floor. In the cramped confines, the air between them seemed to vibrate with an intimacy that took away the last of the cold she'd felt. Marni stared at the floor, unable to meet Chase's gaze. She felt the need to say something, thank him, tell him she was sorry she hadn't believed him when he'd told her she was in real danger, but she didn't trust her voice. Not standing this close to him.

The elevator door opened and she stepped off, not sure where they were going or why.

"We need to talk," he said and led the way to his room. She took a deep breath and followed.

Chase headed directly to the bathroom but left the door open as he washed up. Marni felt too nervous and upset to sit. She wandered over to the window and looked down at her car, its hood blackened from the fire. It still seemed incomprehensible.

"Once he signs the will, you should be safe," Chase said from the bathroom doorway.

She turned to find him drying his hands gingerly with a towel.

"Your hands," Marni cried, hurrying across the room to him to take them in her own. Both of his large callused hands were red. "They're burned."

"They're fine," Chase said, pulling them back. "My gloves took most of the heat."

She wanted to argue that he needed to put something on them but bit her tongue. He was right; his hands were fine. She looked up at him, and suddenly she was doing something she never did.

Chase saw what was coming. Her lower lip began to

quiver. Her eyes filled, making the golden brown shimmer like rare silk. He watched as one large tear broke free and rolled down her cheek. Damn. He hated it when a woman cried. He hated it because he felt helpless. Downright clumsy. He dropped his crutches and pulled her to him, careful not to smash the baby between them as he took her in his arms. She came reluctantly, but finally surrendered to his awkward hug, bending slightly to press her face into his chest and yet keeping her baby safely away from him.

They stood that way, him balancing precariously on his one good leg while she clung to his shirt and cried. After a moment, she dried her eyes and stepped back, her composure and confidence quickly returning. She was no wimp; he'd give her that.

"Thank you," she said with one last sniffle.

He waved her thanks away. A hero he wasn't. And if anyone should know that, it was her. In fact, just being around her made him more aware of what an ass he could be.

He looked at her flushed face and wished— Hell, he wished she *was* part of his memory loss. He wished they *had* been lovers. He wished— He looked at her swollen abdomen. For a moment there, he even almost wished that she really was carrying his baby.

He shook his head at his own foolishness. One moment he was absolute in his knowledge that they could never have been lovers and the next... He limped over to a chair, his casted leg aching, and dropped into it. He hoped to hell he hadn't done so much damage to it that it would have to be reset. He couldn't stand more weeks of immobility, not after being trapped in this cast since the accident back in November.

"I'm sorry things didn't work out for you," he said.

He saw the effect of his words in her expression and mentally kicked himself for being such a jerk. But only moments before, there'd been a soft gentleness to her that made him feel protective. A vulnerability that pulled at some masculine need in him to shelter and care for her.

She raised her chin, all pride and determination again. She reminded him of a porcupine. Prickly enough to make him keep his distance. He and every other man. Last night he'd lain in his bed thinking about the man who'd made love to her. Chase could forgive her for trying to pass off the kid as his to assure her child of a healthy financial future. What he couldn't forgive was her letting some other man past that reserve of hers.

He shook his head, a surge of jealousy that defied comprehension going through him, knowing it made no sense.

"You think your father changing his will is going to make me less pregnant?" she asked. She sounded weary but there was still fight in her.

"No, just not pregnant with my child," he said, feeling like the heel he was. "Once there isn't a price on this baby's head, I'm hoping you'll recant your story. There won't be any reason for you not to." He had no idea for what motive, other than greed, someone had wanted her dead. But who knew what hateful forces were housed in this old mansion. It worried him.

As soon as Jabe finished the will and had it witnessed, Chase intended to contact the police, no matter what his father said, family or no family.

She looked away. "You're that sure I'm not carrying your child?"

He wanted to laugh. He was positive. Because she wasn't his type. Because he was a workaholic who didn't have time to date, let alone take four days off for a wild affair. Because he wasn't a wild affair kind of guy. Because he would never have let a woman like her close enough.

Right. How did he explain what had almost happened on the dining-room table? Or the way she made him feel—in spite of every reason he'd given her for why he couldn't, wouldn't and hadn't felt that way about her last summer.

Chase got to his feet slowly and went to her, forcing

himself to meet her gaze, battling feelings so alien to him he wanted to blame them on his injury.

"The only thing I'm sure of is that you and I have never made love," he said softly. "Not yet, anyway."

SHE SHOOK HER HEAD, unable to speak. No, they'd never made love. She felt numb. From her near accidents. From something inside her. A regret she didn't dare put a name to.

For twenty-four hours she'd tried to tell herself that Chase Calloway was the father of Elise's baby. And for twenty-four hours he'd been telling her he wasn't.

All Marni knew was that she wasn't carrying Chase's child. Or any child for that matter. Sometimes she forgot that. Sam seemed so real. Even now, it was hard to let go. He'd been her connection to Chase. Pretend though it was.

Marni felt the warmth of Chase's gaze wash over her.

He reached out to thumb away tears that spilled down her cheeks.

Was she crying again? She never cried.

"My father should be finished with the codicil by now," Chase said softly. "I'll give you a ride to Bozeman."

She met his gaze, surprised that even with him believing he wasn't the father of her baby, he still felt compassion for her. Now that Jabe had changed his will, there was no reason not to—and every reason to—tell him the truth. "There's something I have to tell you first."

CHASE STOOD looking at her, his heart suddenly heavy. For twenty-four hours he'd been trying to convince her—and himself—that he couldn't have fallen in love with her.

And yet isn't that what had happened? He'd known her less than a day. And somehow she'd gotten to him in a way no other woman ever had. No other woman ever could.

"There's something I have to tell you," she repeated. "Maybe you'd better sit down."

It was almost funny. What could be worse than telling him he'd had a four-day affair with her and she was carrying his child and he couldn't remember even one sensual, sexual moment of it? What could be worse than making him want to be that man?

He looked at her and felt something clamp down on his guts. Stumbling, he limped to the chair and took her advice. He dropped into the rocker and tightened his fingers around the arms.

"You're not pregnant with my baby, are you?" he said, his voice barely audible.

Tears welled in her eyes. She shook her head.

Hadn't he known that all along? So why did it hurt to hear her say it? Because he'd been playing a game with himself, pretending he was the man she described, some fool who'd fallen head over heels and spent four days making love, four days in some magical, once-in-a-lifetime world, throwing caution to the wind. A man Chase Calloway had never been, could never be.

He looked into her guileless face. "You and I have never made love."

She shook her head again.

He tightened his grip on the chair arms. "Let me guess, we never even met before yesterday."

A tear rolled down her cheek and he cursed his stupid, gullible heart. He'd fallen for it. No, he thought, he'd fallen for her.

"I'm not Elise McCumber," she said, taking a swipe at the tears. "I'm Marni McCumber."

"Marni?" Same last name? The only McCumber listed in the Bozeman phone book. The sister, the one he was supposed to call when he remembered his affair with Elise.

"I'm Elise's sister. Her identical twin. I'm not even pregnant." She patted her protruding stomach. "It's a maternity form."

He stared at her. "Why?" It was the only word he could get out.

"Elise is the one who's seven months pregnant with your baby. Not me."

He found his feet somehow. He didn't even feel the pain in his cast. "What?"

"Elise is having complications and has to stay in bed until the baby is born. She talked me into pretending to be her and coming here because you wouldn't take her calls."

"That was Jabe's doing, not mine." Not that any of that mattered. "You're trying to tell me…" What *was* she trying to tell him? He waved a hand through the air, lost his balance without his crutches and sat back down in the chair hard. He didn't even feel it. He felt nothing.

"My twin sister, Elise, is pregnant. With your baby." Marni fished through her purse and pulled out her wallet. She handed him a photograph of two women. Both looked like the woman in front of him.

He stared at the photo, then at her. Identical twins. My God.

She looked up at him. "I never cry." With that she burst into tears again.

Chase stared at her. "You're trying to tell me that you came here pretending to be pregnant on behalf of your twin sister?" He should have been stunned she'd go to such lengths. But knowing her the way he'd come to in such a short time, it made a strange kind of sense. It was the kind of thing this woman, Marni McCumber, would do for someone she cared about. He cursed softly under his breath but found himself wanting to laugh out loud.

"I had to. Elise was so upset I was afraid if I didn't come here she would. And she can't because she has to stay in bed. I did it for the baby."

The baby. "Do you really believe I'm the father of her baby?" he asked, trying to come to terms with the fact that there were two women out there who looked like this one as he got to his feet again.

"Yes, even though you don't remember what my sister is like."

"If she's anything like you—"

"She's nothing like me," Marni cried. "She has a way with men. Don't feel bad. You're not the first to fall for her."

He laughed as he closed the distance between them. Didn't she realize how ridiculous that was? If he'd fallen, he'd fallen for her, Marni McCumber, not her twin. "You're trying to tell me that your sister is irresistible and because of that, it proves I'm the father of her baby?"

"Yes," she repeated.

"Marni." He liked the sound of her name on his lips. He tilted her chin up so he could see her face.

"I look awful when I cry," she said bashfully.

"You look wonderful all the time." Even…pregnant, he thought. "You're the one who's irresistible."

She pulled free. "Please don't say that," she said, looking down at the floor again.

"You felt bad about kissing me because of your loyalty to your sister?" Chase said.

"Of course."

He smiled. He respected loyalty above all else. But his smile faded quickly when he realized things were worse than he could possibly have imagined. Wasn't it bad enough, the way he felt about this woman? And now she was telling him that he'd impregnated her sister? That he was in love with her twin? Impossible.

"Don't you see?" he asked softly. "I couldn't be the man your sister fell in love with." He took her shoulders, refusing to let her go without a fight. "The things you told me that I was supposed to have said, they aren't me. Don't you see? Something isn't right about all this." He looked into her eyes. "You sense it, too, don't you?"

"I want to," she said, wiping her tears.

He smiled at her, cursing his memory loss. If only he could remember enough to prove to her that there was some kind of mistake. Then what? he asked himself.

He looked into her tearful face. Hell if he knew. He was still trying to sort it out.

And right now he had the craziest urge to kiss her. To pull her into his arms, to hold her against him, to kiss away her tears.

He pulled Marni to him, telling himself the last thing he was going to do was kiss her.

But he would have kissed her. He would have held her, maternity form and all, if not for the gunshot that thundered through the house.

Chapter Eleven

Chase rushed out of the room as fast as Marni had seen anyone move on crutches. She stared after him, desperately trying to make sense of the sound she'd just heard. It wasn't until the service-elevator door clanged shut that she found her feet.

She raced down the hall to the top of the stairs. Below she could hear the hammer of hurried feet. The sound of voices raised in panic.

"Was that a gunshot?"

"Where did it come from?"

"Is everyone all right?"

"Oh, my God, no!"

"Where's Lilly?" The last voice was Hayes's; he sounded more afraid than the others.

Then a woman screamed and all hell broke loose.

Hysterical cries and someone trying to calm her. When she reached the main floor, Marni saw that everyone had congregated outside the library door.

No, not everyone, she realized as she headed toward them. The one person conspicuously missing was Lilly. Marni's heart dropped to her feet as she looked into their faces. Whatever had happened, it was bad.

Hilda sobbed into her apron while Felicia yelled at her to shut up. Hayes had his arm around his mother; both looked shocked and all Marni could think of was Lilly. Where *was* Lilly?

"What is it?" Marni asked, apprehension making her nauseated. She heard the elevator door clang open. "What's happened?" she repeated as Chase hobbled toward them, his face strained with worry.

"It's Jabe," Felicia said to Chase as if he'd asked the question. "He's killed himself."

Marni saw her own shock and disbelief mirrored in Chase's face as he pushed his way through to the open library doorway.

"He's dead," she heard Dayton say from inside the room. Marni looked past Chase to see Dayton standing beside his father's desk. Jabe sat where they'd left him. He appeared to be slumped in the chair, his head to one side. Blood ran from his temple down the smooth, soft leather of the chair to pool on the hardwood floor at his feet.

Marni closed her eyes, feeling ill, but the image stayed with her. Jabe sprawled in the chair at his desk. His right arm dangling at his side. His fingertips almost touching the pistol that had fallen from his hand to rest in the blood on the floor.

"Don't do that!" Chase barked.

Marni opened her eyes to see Dayton jerk his hand back. He'd been about to pick up the gun from the floor.

"Don't touch that!" Chase repeated, limping over to his father. Forcing Dayton to step out of the way, he felt for a pulse. After a few moments, he cursed under his breath and looked up at Marni.

She felt a shudder at the anguish she witnessed in his eyes.

"Shouldn't we get him covered up or something?" Dayton said.

"Don't touch anything," Chase ordered.

Dayton's face reddened. "What the hell is wrong with you, Chase? It was suicide not—"

"Who found him?" Chase demanded, cutting off his half

brother as he opened the desk drawers with the tip of a pencil and searched inside.

"I did," Dayton said.

"Was the will on the desk?" Chase asked.

"No," Dayton said with a frown. "There wasn't anything on the desk, I don't think. I don't know. I didn't notice. I saw him and I called for Mother."

Chase sighed and raked a hand through his hair. "And you didn't see anyone else in this room or see anyone leave?"

"I was just down the hall when I heard the gunshot. I opened the door and Father was the only one in the room," Dayton said. "No one went in or out." He seemed to realize where that left him. "You don't think I killed him?"

Marni watched Chase finish his search of Jabe's desk, knowing he was looking for the will Jabe had been writing when they left the room. So where was it now?

Lilly suddenly appeared beside Marni, her eyes large and haunted.

"Lilly," Hayes whispered. "Where have you been?" He stepped toward her as if he meant to comfort her.

She sidestepped him and took Marni's hand in her cold clammy one. Marni could smell the booze on the woman's breath and felt Lilly's body tremble as she asked, "It's Jabe, isn't it?"

"Shouldn't we call a doctor?" Vanessa cried, her voice high and brittle.

Chase shook his head. "Call the sheriff."

"The sheriff?" Dayton echoed. "It's obvious Father killed himself. What do you need the sheriff for?"

"Someone call the damned sheriff!" Chase yelled as if he hadn't even heard Dayton. "And close off this room."

No one moved. Hilda cried harder.

Chase looked up, his gaze meeting Marni's again. She stared at him, trying to understand the fury she saw in his eyes.

"Just call the sheriff, dammit. From the barn," Chase

snapped when Dayton started to pick up his father's phone. "The phone's still dead. Use the two-way radio in the barn."

Dayton threw his half brother a lethal look, then stormed out of the room, sending the family scattering down the hallway.

All except Marni. She stood alone at the edge of the room, hugging Sam, watching Chase with concern. He had gone deathly still after everyone left. For a long moment, he'd just stood looking down at his father. Then he'd taken one of his crutches and swung it wildly. It came down on the edge of the hearth and broke in a loud crack, but not as loud as the curse that Chase cried out. The sound tore at Marni's heart. She wanted desperately to reach out to him, and even stepped toward him, then stopped, afraid he wouldn't accept comfort from her.

He threw the other crutch across the room and turned to see her still there.

"I wish I'd killed the bastard myself," he said, the cold rage in his voice sending a chill through her.

He picked up his one good crutch and limped toward her. "Let's wait somewhere else until the sheriff comes."

They went into the room where Marni had found Lilly crying last night. Chase sat on the arm of the couch.

"I'm sorry about your father," Marni said quietly.

He closed his eyes for a moment. "You know what this means? Elise McCumber and her baby are in danger until that will turns up." He opened his eyes, his gaze fell on her and softened. "You're in danger."

She hugged Sam. "Why would someone first try to kill your father to keep him from changing his will and now kill him to keep him from changing it back?"

Chase shook his head. "Especially when it's my baby who will benefit." He eyed her. "Or so it would seem. The thing is, Elise McCumber isn't carrying my baby any more than you are." He gave her a look that said he'd prove it to her.

Marni wished with all her heart that he could.

"Why would a man so hell-bent on having a grandchild kill himself? There is no way my father killed himself. No way."

Marni had to admit she couldn't see Jabe Calloway committing suicide. Especially now.

"And where is the will he was writing when we left him? Dayton said there was nothing on the desk when he came into the room. There's nothing in the wastebasket or the drawers. I checked. Whoever killed him either took it or destroyed it."

"But why? The way it stands right now, the money goes to the first grandchild."

He moved to the window. "As long—"

"Don't say it, Chase, you're scaring me."

"You are still in danger," he repeated, turning to look at her.

"You mean Elise."

"Everyone in this house believes you're Elise McCumber. That's why you have to take off that damned maternity form. Now."

CHASE WATCHED in frustration as the sheriff and coroner did their thing, knowing each had come to the same conclusion: Jabe Calloway had committed suicide.

"He didn't kill himself," Chase said, making Sheriff Tom Danner look up from his notes. Jabe's body had been removed from the library.

"What makes you say that?" Danner asked.

"He was too selfish to kill himself," Chase said, unable to control the anger he heard in his voice. "It would have made too many people happy."

The sheriff shook his head. "I knew your father—"

"Then you knew what an overbearing bastard he was," Chase said. "Do you really think he killed himself?"

Danner rubbed his jaw and eyed Chase warily. "All the evidence certainly makes it appear to be a suicide. He was shot in the side of the head at contact range from the right side with a .38 registered to him." He glanced at Chase. "He was right-handed and the gun is on the right side of his body. There's no evidence of a struggle. The angle of the shot, the fact that only one shot was fired and the location of the gun all would support suicide, and I'd bet we'll find powder burns on his hand. The only thing missing is a suicide note."

"No, the only thing missing is the codicil to the will my father wrote just before he was killed," Chase said.

"He was changing his will?"

"His original will left an equal share to each of his sons," Chase explained. "He changed it recently so the first grandchild would get the lion's share of his estate. When I left him in this room, he was changing it back."

"Who stands to benefit at this point?"

"It would appear I do." He could feel the sheriff's gaze on him, warmer than the fire.

Danner studied him. "Well, unless you killed him, what would be the point?"

"I wish I knew. All I can tell you is that someone in this family didn't want Jabe to change his will back."

"Maybe the autopsy will come up with something," the sheriff said, closing his notebook and putting it into his shirt pocket. "Your father was a complicated man. Who knows what his last thoughts were."

His last thoughts? "If we knew them, we'd know who killed him," Chase said.

"Or we'd know that he left a financial mess for you kids," Danner said. "Knowing your father, that's a possibility."

"Yes," Chase said, not even trying to hide his bitterness. "His first thought was always his children."

THE BIG OLD HOUSE grew unusually quiet after the sheriff and coroner drove away, the lights from the ambulance flashing brightly against the fresh snow. Marni watched from the bedroom window, her hand on the maternity form she still wore. She couldn't take if off. Not yet. Not until she knew that Elise would be safe.

Still in shock Marni watched until the lights died in the distance. The sheriff said he had been planning to head out this way as soon as the roads opened anyway. Someone by the name of Mary Margaret McCumber had called, worried about her daughter.

He promised to call Mrs. McCumber and let her know her daughter Elise was fine and would be calling from Bozeman. Sheriff Danner had offered to give Marni a ride but Chase had insisted he would take her. Where was Chase? He'd promised to come to her as soon as he'd finished with the sheriff. In the meantime, he'd made her promise to stay in the bedroom with both doors locked.

Marni caught a glimpse out of the window of someone hurrying to the barn and recognized Chase's tall, lean figure limping across the snowy yard. What was he doing going to the barn again now?

Marni heard a sound and turned to see that someone had just slipped a note under her door. She rushed over to pick up the piece of paper and, against her better judgement, opened the door to look out. The hallway was empty.

She closed the door quickly and unfolded the piece of paper. "Elise, meet me at the barn. It's urgent, Chase."

Marni looked down at the note, unsure. Who had delivered this? She'd just seen Chase hobbling out to the barn. And she'd never seen Chase's writing. Not only that, she'd promised she'd stay in her room. She remembered how Dayton had tricked Chase into leaving her alone in the barn with him. She didn't want that to happen again.

But the note said it was urgent.

Suddenly more worried about Chase than herself, Marni hurried to the barn. The last of the day's sun made the snow-covered earth glow white. The pines hung heavy and the air smelled fresh and crisp.

Marni pushed open the barn door and stepped in, expecting to find Chase inside. She stood for a moment, waiting for her eyes to adjust to the dim light. The tack room was empty, so was the office. She moved to the edge of the arena and looked down at the soft trampled ground. Empty.

A horse whinnied from the stable area, drawing her in that direction. As she opened the stable door, she could hear one horse in particular. She caught a glimpse of Wind Chaser about the same time she saw Hayes.

Hayes stood back from the stall, a look of concern on his face as he stared at the stallion. Wind Chaser thrashed around, his hooves pounding the ground beneath him, his eyes wild.

"Something's wrong with this horse," Hayes said to himself, frowning. He seemed to sense Marni and turned to smile tentatively.

"I was looking for Chase," Marni said and started to turn.

"I was the one who sent the note," Hayes said. "Not Chase."

"But I just saw him—"

Hayes nodded. "I sent him over to the other barn so I could talk to you alone."

Marni felt a chill wrap its icy fingers around her neck. "What about?"

He moved toward her. "You've been great with Lilly."

"Lilly?" Is that all this was about?

"The thing is, there is so much you don't know. I'm just afraid that Lilly might do something—" He glanced behind him, back at Wind Chaser, and when he turned, stumbled into her, bumping the maternity form. "I'm sorry, I—" He looked from her belly to her face and back again. "My God." He stepped back as if burned. His eyes widened as he stared at her.

Marni felt her heart sink. Hayes knew she wasn't carrying Chase's child! Wasn't carrying *any* child. "I can explain."

But she didn't get the chance. Behind them, Wind Chaser let out a high-pitched whinny followed by the sound of splintering wood. She and Hayes swung around.

Everything happened so fast. The scent of gardenia. The stall door banging open. Wind Chaser, hooves flying as the horse reared, eyes wild.

Marni stumbled back and fell hard, knocking the air out of her. She heard Hayes let out a cry. And the sound of the horse, above them.

She rolled over to find Hayes lying crumpled beside her, silent and bleeding. She crawled over to him.

"Elise," he said, his voice barely a whisper. He reached out to her; she took his hand and held it.

"Don't try to talk, Hayes."

"The baby. You have to protect the baby."

"Hayes, it's all right—"

He squeezed her hand and shook his head. "No." His grip loosened. His eyes closed.

"Hayes!" Marni cried. Then she saw the rise and fall of his chest. Thank God, he wasn't dead.

Behind her, she heard Wind Chaser snorting and stomping the dirt. Slowly she turned to look over her shoulder, hoping he'd gone back into his stall, knowing there wasn't much chance of that. The horse stood only a few feet away. He snorted and stomped the dirt, then reared again. She screamed and curled herself protectively around Hayes as the hooves came down.

"EASY, BABY," Chase said, his words soft. Marni opened her eyes, expecting to see Chase leaning over her. Instead, he stood between her and the stallion and his soft words were not for her, she realized, but the horse.

It took a moment to realize exactly what he was doing. Putting distance between her and the horse. "Be careful," she cried as she watched Chase advance on the stallion.

"Hush, and don't move," Chase ordered softly, the softness obviously still for the horse.

He moved slowly toward the stallion, murmuring soothingly as he backed Wind Chaser toward an open stall. "Easy, boy."

The stallion stomped and swung his head. Marni watched in amazement as Chase cajoled the horse into the empty stall and closed and latched the door.

He turned and limped over to her. "Are you hurt?"

She shook her head as she tried to sit up, her muscles like jelly. "Hayes—"

Chase turned to his half brother, checked for a pulse then rushed to the office and the two-way radio. She listened to him call for a medical helicopter. Then call the house on an intercom.

"There's been an injury in the barn."

He reappeared and pulled off his coat to lay it over Hayes. Then he pressed his leather glove to the wound on Hayes's head to stop the bleeding.

"What were you doing out here?" he demanded, not looking at her.

She could hear the controlled anger in his voice. After all, he'd ordered her to stay in her room. She wondered if Chase did anything but order people around. "I got a note from you saying to meet you in the barn. That it was urgent."

"I didn't send the note."

"I know that now," she said in exasperation. "Hayes did. He said he'd sent you to the other barn so he could talk to me alone."

"What about?"

"He seemed to want to talk about Lilly." She remembered the smell of Lilly's perfume just after she'd turned to see the stall door standing open. Had she imagined it? Or had Lilly been in the barn?

Chase made a disgusted sound. "You came out here, knowing how dangerous it was?"

"I saw you come out here, then I got the note. I was worried about you."

"About me?" He swore under his breath. "How did the stallion get out?" he asked, obviously changing his tack.

Marni wished she knew. "I found Hayes near Wind Chaser's stall. The horse was agitated." How did she explain what had happened next?

Chase turned to blink at her. "Are you telling me Hayes is the one who left the stall door open?"

Marni looked over at Wind Chaser in confusion. "No, the door was closed. We had turned our backs when I heard the sound of splintering wood. The stall door banged open. Just before that, I think Hayes realized I wasn't really pregnant. And I think Lilly was here," she added.

Chase turned on her, a look of shock on his handsome features. "What?" was all he got out before Vanessa came bursting into the barn, followed by Dayton and Felicia, then finally Lilly.

Vanessa threw herself to the dirt beside Hayes and wept openly, showing much more emotion for her son's injury than she had for the death of her husband.

Lilly stood staring down at her husband, her face the color of snow, her eyes dark and wide. "It's God's will," she whispered, making Marni look up at her in surprise. It was then that Marni noticed that unlike Vanessa, Dayton and Felicia, who had rushed straight from the house, Lilly wore her coat and boots.

Vanessa shooed Chase away, taking over the care of her son. Chase helped Marni to her feet. She still felt woozy as he led her over to Wind Chaser's empty stall. The boards on one side had been splintered by the horse's hooves. The door hung open. Marni watched Chase inspect it. He pulled a piece of broken wood from inside the latch and motioned for Marni not to say anything until they were outside.

"Is that what I think it is?" Marni asked.

"It looks like someone jammed the stick into the latch so it wouldn't lock all the way," Chase said when they were a good distance from the barn.

"That's crazy. Anyone who came into the barn could have been Wind Chaser's victim."

Chase nodded. "Any chance Lilly saw you go to the barn to meet Hayes?"

"I don't know."

He swore and stopped to pull her around to face him. "You have no idea what you've stumbled into. This family—" He waved a hand through the air, then let out a long exasperated breath before he loosened his grip on her. "I know you want to protect Lilly. It's your nature. But Marni, when it comes to Calloway money, Lilly isn't that much different from Felicia."

"What is it you're trying to tell me?" she asked, pulling free of his hold.

"She's already jealous of your baby. If she thought you wanted her husband—"

"Why would she think that?" Marni cried.

Chase shrugged. "It's not like the woman is rational. If she followed you to the barn—"

"Hayes just wanted to talk about her."

"Or warn you about her?"

Marni hugged herself, realizing that was probably more accurate. What had Hayes said? "I'm just worried that Lilly might—" What had he planned to say?

"Get cleaned up," Chase ordered. She bristled and he softened his tone as he reached to pick straw from her hair. "A hot bath will warm you up. You're shivering. I'll find you some clean clothes. Then we're getting out of here before anything else happens."

Until that moment, Marni hadn't realized she was shaking. She didn't kid herself it was from the cold.

MARNI WENT to her room and removed the maternity form with trembling fingers. For the last twenty-four hours, it had been almost her constant companion. Her body now felt slim. Streamlined. That should have made her happy.

Instead, she felt so strange without "Sam" and tried to laugh at her own foolishness only to find herself in tears.

Hormones. Wearing that silly maternity form had kicked in more than her hormones. Now she had maternal feelings she'd never known she possessed. There had never been a baby. And yet she was keenly aware of a feeling of loss as she stepped into the large clawfoot tub and sank into the bubbles.

A day ago, she couldn't have imagined how her twin could have fallen in love so quickly, so completely. A day ago, she couldn't have imagined how anyone could have fallen in love with Chase Calloway. Now she knew. Marni's heart ached with that knowledge.

DESIRE. It hit Chase the moment he stepped through the adjoining door of their bedrooms and caught the sweet scent of bath crystals. He'd knocked several times, then, worried, he'd used the key to open the door. That's when he heard the sound of water sloshing against the tub. Instantly he could imagine her, shoulder deep in bubbles. Her skin pink and soft. There would be a sprinkling of freckles across her chest above her breasts. Oh, her breasts. He groaned silently. Full, round, the nipples dark and hardening from the room's chill.

He knocked again on the bedroom door. "Marni?" He took a tentative step, balancing on his one crutch, telling himself all the reasons he should wait until she was out of the tub. But he'd brought her clean clothing. And the gentle lap of the water drew him, along with the sweet scent of the bubbles and the mere thought of Marni neck deep in the large, old tub.

The bathroom door was open. At first all he saw was bubbles. Then her head came up out of the water, her shoulders, the tops of her breasts. A sprite, her body wet and slick, her russet hair trailing down her back.

"Marni." It came out a hoarse plea. Desire almost dropped him to his knees.

She looked up, startled, then slid back into the tub until the bubbles were up to her chin.

He moved toward her, wanting to throw himself into the water with her, the need to feel her against him overwhelming. What had this woman done to him in such a short period of time? All he knew was what she was doing to him right now.

"Chase," she whispered, eyes wide as if she could see how badly he wanted her. It was the pleading he saw there that stopped him. Until he could prove to her that he wasn't her twin's lover—

With his free hand, he pulled a towel from the rack and held it out to her, turning his gaze away. "Get dried off," he said, his voice husky. "Please."

She took the towel.

He could hear her drying herself; the sound of the thick, absorbent towel on her skin skittered across his senses like a live electrical wire. "Get dressed." He hadn't meant it to sound so much like an order. "I borrowed these from Felicia," he said, not knowing what to do with the clothes.

He stood for a moment, a war going on inside him. He wanted to see Marni without the maternity form almost as badly as he wanted to hold her. But he couldn't let himself. Even if Marni would have let him.

He dropped the clothing on the small stool by the tub and stalked out of the room, cursing himself for the feelings tormenting him. He threw what little he'd brought here into the suitcase still open in the bottom of the closet and slammed the case shut with a finality that wasn't lost on him. He couldn't see himself ever coming back. This was his father's house, a place as dark and warped as the man himself had been.

Chase felt sick at heart, less over his father's death than his father's life. Jabe had had three sons, three chances. As far as Chase could tell, he'd blown it with all three. No one would grieve his death. Except Chase's mother, if she'd still been alive. She forgave Jabe everything. Jabe had been his mother's one weakness. A weakness that had slowly killed her.

Chase tried to concentrate on the problem at hand. Once Elise McCumber admitted that she and Chase had never been lovers, then Marni and her sister would be safe. The question was: Whose baby was Elise carrying? Someone who'd been driving the ranch truck that day and had used the name Chase Calloway to impress her, the fool.

It would just be a matter of clearing up this misunderstanding.

"I'm ready," Marni said behind him.

He turned to find her standing in the doorway, looking very pregnant. "What the hell are you doing still wearing that?" He couldn't hide his disappointment. Or his concern that she'd continue this charade knowing how dangerous it was.

"I've decided to stay Elise McCumber," she said, lifting her chin with defiance.

"Have you lost your mind?"

"Elise is in danger. You said so yourself. I have to protect her and the baby. Until we can prove she isn't carrying your child."

He stared at the woman before him, her face flushed from her bath, her damp hair hanging in tendrils on the soft whiteness of her neck, her eyes large as a doe's. "You are without a doubt the most exasperating woman I have ever met."

She smiled. "I'll take that as a compliment."

He shook his head as he reached for his suitcase. "You would."

Chapter Twelve

It was dusk by the time they left the ranch in Chase's pickup, the bare cottonwoods stark against the winter sky. Marni had to drive, to Chase's annoyance, because the truck was a stick shift and he couldn't operate the clutch with his leg in a cast.

They left quietly, none of the family around, it seemed, to say goodbye or good riddance. As they pulled away, Marni looked up at the tiny window under the third-floor eave but couldn't tell if Lilly was there watching them leave.

"Is it too late to go to your mother's farm tonight?" Chase asked.

Marni glanced at her watch. It wasn't quite five but already the sky had turned a dusky deep blue. They could be at the farm in a couple of hours. "Are you sure that's what you want to do?"

"Yes." He shot her a look. "I want this over with."

Was he that sure? Or was it just the opposite? Either way, they were about to find out the truth.

They followed Sixteenmile Creek out of the canyon. Walls of snow banked each side of the narrow road as they drove past Maudlow and on into Bozeman.

They stopped at the hospital emergency room and had a doctor check Chase's leg.

"Since you seem intent on walking on it," the doctor

said, "why don't we just get rid of the cast? It's supposed to come off in a couple of days anyway." The X ray showed that the bone had healed nicely.

While she waited for Chase, Marni called the farm from the hospital pay phone. The sheriff had already let Elise know that her twin had been snowed in and was fine. Her mother quickly agreed it would be best not to tell Elise they were on their way to the farm because she was anxious enough as it was.

Marni's second call was to her boutique. Her manager sounded frantic with all the Christmas shoppers. But, Marni had to admit, her crew seemed to be doing fine without her. Better than fine. Sales were up; everything was going smoothly. She felt a swell of pride in her workers.

When she checked at the desk, the nurse said Hayes had regained consciousness and was sleeping. Marni walked away, relieved, but the memory of Lilly's strange reaction to her husband's accident still bothered her.

"Ready?" Chase asked as he came out of the emergency room, walking a little stiffly.

"How does it feel?" Marni asked.

He smiled. "Great. I can't tell you how glad I am to finally get that damned thing off. I want to look in on Hayes, then let's get going."

She nodded, as ready as she was ever going to be.

They drove over Bozeman Pass, a wonderland of snow and ice, then followed the Yellowstone River east from Livingston. The small western towns they passed looked like Christmas villages all decked out in snowcapped eaves, bright with Christmas lights and decorations.

Chase said little on the drive along the river. Marni wondered if he was worrying about the moment when he would meet her sister. She knew he must be grieving the death of his father, no matter how awful Jabe Calloway had been in life. She also knew Chase wasn't happy about her still pretending to be Elise or the fact that he was still involved in her life as long as she was pretending to carry his child.

But that could soon be over. Unless of course he was wrong. Unless Elise was pregnant with his baby.

Marni tried not to think about that as the sky darkened to midnight blue above the whiteness. Stars studded the velvet, each a brilliant sparkling jewel in the night, making Marni think of the three wise men who had followed a star to a manger.

Just as they reached Columbus, the moon rose, a fiery ball of orange over the mountains. Marni looked out into the winter night, unable to appreciate its stark beauty. Too much had happened in the last twenty-four hours and so much was still unresolved.

They turned at Columbus and headed north into wheat country. Once on the snow-covered gravel road, they lost all other traffic. Still Chase kept checking behind them, just as he had since they'd left the ranch.

"You really think someone would try to follow us?" she asked, watching the countryside open up and house lights become few and far between.

He shrugged and kept looking behind them, his mood as dark as the lock of hair that fell onto his forehead.

Marni tried not to think about who might be following them to the farm.

She watched the dark landscape roll by, her thoughts returning to the one thing she couldn't keep from her mind: the moment Elise saw Chase.

CHASE WASN'T SURE what he'd expected as they came over the rise and the pickup's headlights caught on the large old mailbox with McCumber printed on the side.

"Can you stop here?" Marni asked. "I think it would be best if I didn't make an appearance like this." She placed a hand over the maternity form that had become such a part of her in his mind.

He slowed the pickup and came to a stop, the mailbox in his headlights. Someone had tied a big red bow on it. He felt a lump in this throat and looked out at the wheat fields, gold stubble poking up through the snow in the winter moonlight, rather than look at Marni.

"All set," she said.

He glanced at her. She looked small in the dash lights. Small, pretty. And afraid. He wanted to reassure her, but decided nothing he could say would convince either of them right now.

Slowly, he turned the pickup up the long snowy rutted driveway, aiming it between the pine windbreak.

He couldn't help remembering the stories Marni had told about her childhood as he caught sight of the big old three-story farmhouse standing at the end of the lane. The place pulled at him, the same way Marni McCumber had done for the last twenty-four hours.

Marni glanced over at him and must have misread the look on his face. "Having doubts?" she asked.

He wanted to laugh. Doubts? He'd spent thirty-five years growing into the man he was. Now in just one day, this woman had him wondering who he was, what he wanted and just what he was capable of. He doubted everything about himself.

"Let's get this over with," he said.

The farmhouse was everything Calloway Ranch wasn't. Bright, cheerful, inviting. From the moment he stepped onto the porch, he could smell something wonderful cooking inside the house. He passed the worn porch swing and could almost see Marni sitting cross-legged in it against a summer sunset. He started to knock, but Marni opened the door and stuck her head in.

"Anybody home?" she called.

Her question was answered with the frantic patter of feet, shouts and laughter. A half-dozen children, from toddlers to near teens, came flying to the door; several small ones threw themselves into her waiting arms.

"Santa's coming," one of the younger ones proclaimed. "But look at all the presents already under the tree."

Marni smiled back at Chase and pushed her way into the house so he could close the door behind him.

"These are my brothers' children," she said and made the introductions, introducing him as a "friend."

"You're coming for Christmas, aren't you?" one of the older kids said to Marni. "You always come home for Christmas." Home it seemed was this house; each of her brothers had his own house on the family farm but it was the old farmhouse where everyone gathered.

"And it's only four more days," interjected a young excited child.

Marni seemed to hesitate, then smiled broadly. "I wouldn't miss it for the world."

Chase saw Marni blink back tears. He knew how much coming here for Christmas meant to her without ever having to ask. He knew this woman not with his head but his heart. And he wished to hell he didn't. He watched her look around at the Christmas decorations, knowing how much all of this meant to her. Decorations were everywhere, most obviously made by the passel of nieces and nephews now filling the entry hall. Past them, he could see the tree, a large spruce thick with homemade ornaments. Unless he missed his guess, most of them held special memories for Marni.

Chase could imagine Christmas in this house, with this family. He felt those horrible pangs from his childhood when his only wish in life was for this kind of a family, this kind of Christmas. He brushed those thoughts away, trying to keep them where they belonged, with the lonely little boy he'd been. He no longer needed these things, he told himself. His life was just the way he wanted it.

He glanced over at Marni and was shocked by the thought that ricocheted through his head. He missed seeing her pregnant.

MARNI COULD SMELL her mother's famous Christmas cookies baking in the kitchen. "Silent Night" played on the radio and she smiled as she heard her mother begin to sing. The memory of all the other Christmases they'd spent here as a family warmed her the way the fire in the woodstove never could. Now all she had to worry about was this Christmas.

"Come on," her youngest niece cried. "Grandma just got through making fudge. She said we could have some as soon as you got here."

They all clambered toward the kitchen. "Maria, you cut each of the children one piece of fudge," she heard her mother say.

"One?" came the universal cry.

"One," Mary Margaret McCumber said sternly. "Behave while I see to your aunt Marni."

Marni felt her stomach roil, her nerves suddenly strung taut. The moment of truth. She felt as if she might throw up.

She looked at Chase. He stood inside the door, his hands at his side, his face set in stone. She recognized that expression, seen it enough times on his handsome face since yesterday. Stubborn determination. But there was something else about him that caused a fissure of concern to run through her as Mary Margaret McCumber came out of the kitchen. Worry. She read it in his eyes. Was he not as sure as he wanted her to believe? Or was something else bothering him?

Mary Margaret stopped in the middle of the room to dry her hands on her apron, give Chase Calloway the once-over, and a disapproving nod, then turned her gaze on Marni. Her mother was tall with graying blond hair that she kept long and in a no-nonsense braid down her back.

"Your sister" was all her mother said with a wave of her hand down the hall toward the sewing room. With a shake of her head, she turned back to the kitchen. "I have to rescue the fudge. I made pot roast. I saved some for you, so of course you're eating."

Leave it to Mother to think her cooking could solve all

their problems. Marni only wished it could as she led the way to the back of the house and the sewing room.

At the closed door, she hesitated, glancing over her shoulder at Chase to be sure he was still with her. Then she turned the knob and stepped in, leaving Chase in the hallway.

Elise sat in the middle of the bed in the makeshift bedroom, propped up with dozens of pillows, surrounded by books, magazines, videos, a laptop, fax machine and beauty supplies. She looked bored—and very pregnant.

When she spied Marni standing in the doorway, she smiled with an eagerness that made Marni's heart hurt. "You're back. I've been going crazy. Mother—" She waved a hand through the air with no need to continue along those lines; it was a McCumber form of communication all the women in the family understood. "What happened? Why didn't you call? Or at least E-mail or fax me."

Just like El, the E-mail junkie. Just because she spent hours on E-mail with friends, she assumed everyone did. She didn't realize some people didn't even have a computer, let alone a fax machine.

"Didn't Mother tell you the snowstorm knocked out the phone and the electricity?" Marni said.

"Well, yes, but surely there was *something* you could have done. Is Chase all right? You did see him, didn't you? What did he say—"

"I brought him with me," Marni interrupted.

"Here?" Elise cried, picking up the hand mirror from her pile of beauty supplies. "Oh no, I'm a disaster!"

Marni watched her sister primp and felt tears rush her eyes. Her twin had a special beauty that Marni knew was only partially due to the pregnancy. "You look great."

"Really?" El asked.

"Really. Are you ready?" Marni wished *she* were ready for this.

Elise nodded enthusiastically, a hundred-watt smile on her face. Marni moved aside to let Chase enter the room.

MARNI HEARD CHASE step into the doorway. She didn't turn around to look at him. Instead, she watched her sister's face. The smile faded. Elise frowned and seemed to be trying to see past Chase out into the empty hallway.

"What's going on?" El asked. "I thought you said you brought Chase?"

"I did." Marni spun around, thinking he must not be behind her. "This is Chase. Chase Calloway."

Elise shook her head. "Not the Chase Calloway I know."

Thank God, Marni thought as she faced her twin.

"This is not Chase," El repeated.

Marni turned to look at him again. He smiled, letting out a relieved sigh as he raked his fingers through his hair. Marni didn't even mind his I-told-you-so look. Her heart thundered in her ears. Chase hadn't fathered Elise's baby. Just as he'd said. Just as Marni had prayed. She felt such a wave of relief she had to sit down on the edge of Elise's bed.

"What's going on here?" Elise asked, looking confused.

"It's a long story," Marni said. "The good news is that you aren't carrying Chase Calloway's baby."

"Then whose baby am I carrying?" El cried. "Are you sure you went to the Calloway Ranch in the Horseshoe Hills?"

"El, I went to the right ranch. I met the whole family. Believe me, this is Chase Calloway. You're sure he isn't the man who fathered your child?" she asked again.

"Did he tell you he fathered my child?" she asked, shooting him a look.

"Well, no, as a matter of fact he said— Never mind." Marni looked up at Chase. "You're just sure this isn't the man you met last summer?"

"Positive," El said, giving her twin a questioning look. "How many times do I have to say it?"

Marni laughed, and smiled at Chase. Elise and the baby were safe. "El isn't carrying your baby."

"I know," he said, sounding as relieved as she felt.

"But there is a resemblance," she heard El say behind her. Marni swung around to look at her sister.

"A resemblance?" Chase asked, stepping closer.

"Oh yeah, there's definitely a resemblance," El said, taking a closer look. "You look enough like him to be his brother."

Marni felt her heart leap into her throat.

"Why don't you describe your Chase Calloway for us," he suggested as he pulled up a chair beside Elise's bed.

El leaned back against the pillows, her gaze on him. "This is very strange."

If only she knew how strange, Marni thought.

"Tell me about the guy," Chase encouraged. "He definitely used the name Chase Calloway, right?"

El nodded. "It isn't a name you're apt to forget."

Chase smiled at that. "What exactly did he look like?"

"Handsome," Elise said with a smile. "Like you but different." She studied Chase for a moment. "His eyes weren't quite as pale blue. His hair was neater."

Marni suppressed a smile. Chase's hair was its usual rumpled mess. But she realized that she loved it that way. It made her want to run her fingers through it. She shook off such thoughts, suddenly picking up on El's last words.

"And his hair wasn't quite as dark," Elise said.

She had just described both Dayton and Hayes. "Did he have a mustache?" Marni asked.

Elise nodded and laughed. "A cute little one that curled over his lip like a caterpillar." Leave it to Elise to forget that highly significant little detail.

Dayton. Marni's gaze met Chase's.

He shook his head. "Both of my brothers had mustaches last summer."

"You think the man was one of your brothers?" Elise asked. "Why would he lie about his name?"

"Both brothers are...married," Marni said.

El let out a small cry and buried her face in her hands.

"I can't believe this. We were so perfect together. He said he loved me. That he wanted a life with me. He wanted my baby."

"He probably does want your baby," Chase said.

"My God," Marni breathed as the full impact hit her. Elise was pregnant with either Dayton's or Hayes's baby. The first grandchild. And since Jabe didn't change his will— "Oh, Chase."

He nodded. "This definitely complicates things."

"Do you have photographs of your brothers?" El asked.

Chase shook his head. "But we can get them. Meanwhile, is there anything else you can tell us about the man?"

Heavy tears coursed down El's face. She shook her head, no.

MARY MARGARET knocked on the open door, took one look at Elise and narrowed a glare at Chase. "What's she crying about?" she demanded.

Marni jumped to Chase's defense, making her mother raise an eyebrow. "Chase isn't *the* Chase who—" She waved a hand through the air.

Her mother, who'd perfected this form of communication, understood immediately. "Then who in all the saints is?"

"That's what we intend to find out," Chase said, getting to his feet.

"Not until after dinner," her mother announced. "I'll bring you a tray," she told Marni before she could protest. "You can eat with your sister. Chase— That really is your name, isn't it?"

"Yes, ma'am," he replied quickly.

"Chase will eat with me in the kitchen," she ordered. "We have some things to talk about."

THE KITCHEN SMELLED of pot roast and fresh homemade bread. Chase tried not to breathe too deeply. It was a smell he knew better than to become accustomed to. And yet he found himself breathing it in the way a drowning man fights for oxygen.

"You're in love with my daughter?" Mary Margaret asked, catching him completely off guard as she set a plate for him at the kitchen table.

"I've never seen Elise before today," he said quickly.

She gave him an impatient look. "I'm referring to my other daughter, Marni."

He opened his mouth to speak but nothing came out.

"What have you done to her?"

He almost choked. "Nothing. She—"

"She what?" the woman asked, eyeing him intently.

Marni had tried to make him fall for her, that's what. A confirmed bachelor. Worse than that, a man who had no desire to get involved, let alone married. And a man who'd never wanted children. Still didn't. He'd been quite happy. Damned happy. Well, happy enough. Until she came along. "She turned my life upside down," he said truthfully.

Mary Margaret made a disgusted face. "She's in love with you."

"What?"

"Surely you can see that?"

Chase glanced through the open kitchen door back toward the sewing room. It had never dawned on him that Marni might really be in love with him. Sure, she'd pretended she was, but that was when she was pretending to be Elise. And sure, there was some chemical attraction— "I'm not real sure she even likes me."

Mary Margaret shook her head as she began to fill his plate with pot roast, potatoes, carrots, onions and gravy. "These vegetables are from my garden."

He stared down at the food. The woman was mistaken about Marni's feelings. Not that he wanted even to think that it might be true; he was having a hard enough time trying to sort out his own feelings.

"You'd best tell me what kind of trouble my El is in," Mary Margaret said, changing the subject so fast she gave him whiplash.

He started to avoid the truth but she stopped him with a shake of her head. "Don't even bother," she said, then handed him a piece of warm homemade bread, which she'd already lathered with butter. "As I've always told my children, lying to me is a very bad idea."

He nodded, feeling like one of those children and wishing he didn't like the idea so much. He started with his father changing his will and ended with Elise's statement that the man she fell in love with could be his brother, the resemblance was that strong.

Mary Margaret crossed herself, then said, "You'll take care of Marni."

It wasn't a question, but he answered it anyway. "Yes. If she'll let me."

Marni's mother smiled at that. "There is nothing wrong with a headstrong woman."

"If you say so."

"One more thing. Promise me my daughter will be home for Christmas."

He started to tell her he couldn't promise that but she cut him off.

"You bring her home for Christmas," she ordered.

He considered straightening her out on a few things, but decided she'd find out soon enough. Even if her daughter was in love with him, which was ludicrous. He wasn't bringing her home for Christmas. This house, this McCumber lifestyle, was a trap, one he fought to resist. Just the way he fought the idea that he might be falling in love with Marni McCumber.

"Eat," Mary Margaret said. "You're going to need your strength."

"ARE YOU GOING to tell me?" Elise said.

Marni looked up at her twin. "Tell you what?"

"About Chase."

"Yours or mine?" *Mine?* Where had that come from. "The one I brought here?" she quickly amended.

Marni watched El nod and pick at her food, no doubt knowing Mother would eventually make her eat.

"It's complicated," Marni said, not sure what El was getting at.

El made an impatient noise. "Do you think Mother is settling for that line?"

Marni would bet Mary Margaret was forcing every detail out of Chase at this very moment.

She looked at her twin, knowing she had to be honest with her. "It's not good news, El." She told her about Jabe's will and the fortune he'd left the firstborn grandchild. "There's a very good chance you're carrying that child. Because of the large amount of money involved, Chase is worried that—"

"You're saying I might be in danger?"

"I'm afraid so," Marni admitted. Reluctantly, she told her twin about her mishap in the attic, Hayes's accident in the barn and the fire that had destroyed her car. She finished with Jabe's death and Chase's suspicion that his father didn't kill himself.

Elise took it better than Marni had expected.

"But you don't have anything to worry about here at the farm," Marni reassured her. "No one could get past Mother, let alone our brothers."

Elise actually smiled at that, then sobered. "You and Chase are going to try to find my baby's father, aren't you?"

"I don't know about Chase," Marni said, "but I am."

"That means you have to keep pretending to be me, huh?"

El was no fool. "Yes."

"Oh, Marni," she said, pulling her sister into a hug. "I wish I'd never gotten you into this."

El wiped at her tears and straightened, that McCumber

determination back. "I know he loves me. I wish he hadn't lied to me, but I can understand now why he did."

Marni didn't want to believe love could be that blind. It scared her. "You just worry about junior here."

For the first time, Marni laid her hand on her twin's stomach, surprised at how hard it felt. The baby moved and Marni smiled, thrilled to feel the life inside her sister.

"I know it's silly to still make Christmas wishes," El said, placing her hand over Marni's.

Marni smiled, remembering the December nights as girls when they'd stared up at the stars, silently making Christmas wishes on the brightest star overhead. "I don't think it's silly to wish. After all, Christmas is a time of miracles, right?"

El nodded, tears in her eyes.

And Marni promised herself that with or without Chase's help, she'd find the father of her twin's baby and try to give El the happy ending she so desperately wished for. Marni just worried it would take nothing short of a Christmas miracle to make it happen.

Chapter Thirteen

December 22

"Thank you," Marni said as they drove down the driveway the next morning. Chase could see the farmhouse in the rearview mirror and Mary Margaret standing on the porch, her hands knotted in her apron. He didn't have to see her face to know she was worried. So was he.

"For what?" he asked, wondering what Marni could possibly have to thank him for. He'd been cold and abrupt with her most of the morning, dreading going back to Bozeman, hating that she was determined to use herself as bait to draw out the killer, and worse yet, angry with himself because he wasn't about to let her do it alone. Not that he was being chivalrous. Even if she hadn't been in trouble, he wasn't ready to part company. Not yet.

"For taking time to bring me up here."

"I had to prove that I wasn't Elise's lover," he said. "This seemed the fastest way to do it."

Marni nodded. "I should have believed you. I wanted to."

He waved that away. "It should be easy to find out which of my half brothers is. Then hopefully by now the sheriff will have the autopsy back and know that Jabe didn't kill himself, there will be an investigation and—" And what? Did he really believe one of his brothers was a murderer? Someone in that family was, he reminded himself. The same person who'd made attempts on Marni's life?

The only thing he was reasonably sure of was that Elise would be safe with her large family looking after her. He'd met her four brothers, all large and mild-mannered but very protective. Especially of their sisters. He'd come away knowing they wouldn't let any man hurt their sister. Either sister.

Not that he personally had anything to worry about. True, he seemed to have feelings for Marni, but these feelings had come on too quickly, too strongly. He didn't trust them. So he promised himself he was going to take some time to try to make sense out of them before he did anything...rash.

"As soon as they find the murderer, it will be over," he finished. "Meanwhile, your sister's safe."

"At least it's not a concern of yours anymore," Marni said.

He looked over at her. Did she really expect him to walk away now? What kind of man did the woman think he was, anyway? Certainly not the kind a woman like her would fall in love with. Not that he believed she had.

"You can just drop me off at my place."

"So you can wait for the killer to come for you?" he demanded. Did she really think he could distance himself from all this just because he wasn't the father of her twin's baby? True, distance was his specialty. And he had been a jackass all morning.

"This isn't your problem," she said, that chin of hers going airborne.

It was all he could do not to stop the pickup and kiss some sense into her. *Great idea.* "It's my family. It's my problem. And anyway, I can't let you do this alone." He felt her gaze on him. "We're in this together whether you like it or not. You're carrying my baby... At least the world thinks you are. So it only makes sense that you stay at my place." He groaned inwardly at the mere thought.

He'd lain in the narrow twin bed in one of the boys' rooms last night feeling more at home than he ever had anywhere before. Thinking about what Mary Margaret had said about Marni being in love with him. Thinking about the kisses they'd shared, the touches, the looks. Was it possible?

This morning Mary Margaret had taken one glance at him and laughed happily. "You look like you slept with the angels."

He couldn't remember a night when he'd slept more soundly. Nor a breakfast he'd enjoyed more. Noisy, disorganized, utter chaos. He'd sat listening to all the chatter, wishing he and Marni never had to leave the farm. Telling himself that it was because she was safe here and wouldn't be once they went back to Bozeman. But in his heart, he knew it was so much more, more than he wanted to admit. He'd liked the idea that Marni might be, if nothing more, attracted to him. And he'd liked feeling a part of this noisy, boisterous family temporarily.

That's why he had to get out of there. It made him forget how painful loving could be. And for a while he'd forgotten the promise he'd made himself beside his mother's deathbed. He'd seen what his mother's love for Jabe Calloway had brought her, and what his love for his mother had cost him. He'd promised himself he'd never know that kind of pain again because he'd never let himself love anyone that much.

And he'd looked down the table at Marni. Her smile had seized his heart in a death grip and his mood had gone sour. This woman had the ability to do more than just break his heart.

"We're going to do this together," he said. "It's settled. So don't even bother to argue." To his amazement, she didn't.

"You think it's Dayton?" she asked later as they neared the first Bozeman exit.

"Sounds like Dayton. He's had his share of affairs."

"I hate to think he's the man El fell in love with," she said.

"Women fall in love with the wrong man sometimes," he said, thinking of his mother, thinking of Marni, if she was indeed falling for him.

"If it is Dayton, then he has two women pregnant," she said. "Covering his bets, you think?"

He wished he knew. "What I don't understand is why when you showed up at the ranch, one of my brothers didn't react more...strongly. Why didn't one of them say something to you? The real father of the baby must have been shocked when he saw you there."

"Both seemed surprised," Marni said. "But everyone in your family was surprised. You know," she said thoughtfully. "That night after dinner, Hayes was waiting in the alcove on the stairs for either his mother or me. If he hadn't been there—"

He glanced over at her. "What?"

"Oh, Vanessa dropped her scarf on the stairs and I stepped on it and—"

"You almost fell down the stairs?" he demanded.

"I didn't, but I could have if Hayes hadn't been there. He seemed very upset with his mother and said something about it not happening again."

"I wonder what that was about?" Chase said, eyeing Marni. "Why didn't you mention that you'd had a close call on the stairs?"

"I guess it slipped my mind," she said.

He could see there was more. "Did anything else happen I don't know about?"

"Someone came by my room later that night and tried my door."

"You think it was Elise's lover?" Chase asked.

She shrugged. "Surely he would have made some attempt to talk to me while I was at the ranch. He had to know he would be exposed eventually. If he thought I was Elise, he'd have tried to reason with me, don't you think?

And if he realized I was an impostor, he would have confronted me. He couldn't just think this would all blow over.''

Unless he thought Elise would be dead before anyone found out the truth, Chase thought. What was the father of Elise's baby going to do next? he wondered as they drove into Bozeman.

''Bet he was confused when I didn't seem to recognize him and was claiming that you were the father of my child,'' Marni said.

Chase nodded. ''Unless he thought you were trying to get even with him for lying to you. But still, it would seem like he would have come forward. After all, you were seemingly carrying Jabe's first heir and a bundle of money.''

''Maybe he was protecting himself. He didn't want his wife to know, afraid she might leave him. Or—''

Chase looked over at her. ''Or because he was afraid of what she'd do to you?''

''You're thinking of Lilly,'' she said.

He cut her off before she could defend Lilly. ''I wouldn't want to meet either Lilly or Felicia in a dark alley. Especially if they thought I was trying to take something of theirs.''

''Elise didn't even know he was married.''

''Like that would make a big difference to Lilly or Felicia,'' Chase said more sarcastically than he'd meant to. Sometimes Marni was too naive and trusting. He reminded himself that she hadn't grown up the way he had. Nor did she have the Calloways as family.

''More than likely, the reason one of my brothers didn't come forward had nothing to do with his wife,'' Chase said. ''He was probably more concerned about Jabe's reaction. Jabe wouldn't have liked his first grandchild to be born to a son who already had a wife. Worse yet, a pregnant wife, if it turns out to be Dayton.''

''Do you think Jabe would have been so angry he could

have changed back his will before the baby was born?'' Marni asked.

"It's a possibility, or cut that son out entirely."

"The father of El's baby can't be the killer," Marni said firmly as they neared the Bozeman exit and he heard her putting on the maternity form again.

"I hope you're right," Chase said.

The Christmas lights glittered at the stoplights along Main Street—red, gold, blue, green. For a while, Chase had forgotten about Christmas. And the promise Mary Margaret had asked of him. He told himself he'd find the killer before Christmas Day. Not for Mary Margaret. Not for Elise. But for his own selfish reason. He wanted Marni out of this charade. He wanted her safe. He had three days.

Marni's house was what Chase had expected. A cute cottage with a white picket fence, a wide pillared porch with a swing and paned windows with pale green shutters. A dollhouse all decorated for Christmas with lights strung along the eaves and a snowman in the yard complete with carrot nose and an old slouch hat.

"Nice snowman," he said.

"The neighborhood kids and I built him," she said proudly. "I'm surprised it weathered the storm."

Chase held the storm door open while Marni dug out her key. The door swung in to reveal shiny hardwood floors, colorful throw rugs and pretty papered walls, trimmed in oak.

A collection of teddy bears huddled in a large overstuffed chair, bright and cheerful in red and green ribbons and bows. Reindeer drew a sleigh across the mantel over the small fireplace, pulling a cheerful Santa and a bulging bag full of presents.

Everywhere in the room he felt Marni. The decor reflected her strong roots, her good taste, her secure sense of herself, from the handed-down Christmas decorations, the mementos on the shelves, the photographs on the walls, the hand-crocheted tablecloth on the dining-room table. Even the furniture itself.

The place had a homeyness that tugged at the part of him that had yearned for such a house in his youth. He found himself wishing for Marni's childhood, just as he had at breakfast the last two mornings.

He'd so desperately wanted a family, roots, a feeling of belonging somewhere. He and his mother had moved from town to town, living in dark, dingy basement apartments. He'd picked up odd jobs in the neighborhood to help support them, and later had to quit school and work full-time when his mother became so ill.

It wasn't until he was fourteen and his mother realized she was dying that she finally told him about his family. And he'd gotten his wish, he thought bitterly. The Calloway clan. Someone should have warned him to be careful what he wished for.

Well, it was too late to change his childhood, too late to change the man he was. Not even Marni McCumber could do that, he told himself.

Marni took a couple of steps into the room and stopped. "Someone's been here."

Chase glanced quickly around the room, seeing nothing that looked amiss. "Why do you say that?"

She pointed to one of the rugs on the floor. The corner of it had been kicked up.

That was her proof? "You have to be kidding."

She went to the rug and straightened it, then looked around, her gaze coming to a halt as she stared at one of the dining-room walls. "The photograph's missing."

"What photograph?" he asked, his heart suddenly in his throat.

"One of me and Elise."

He moved then, covering the rest of the house. The small neat kitchen and dinette with light pouring in from the many windows. The two upstairs bedrooms. The bathroom.

There were tracks in the backyard coming up the steps

but the snow had blown them in, making them just hollows. When he checked the back door, he found the lock had been jimmied open.

Chapter Fourteen

"Let's get you packed and out of here as quickly as possible," Chase said. "Whoever has the photo must have suspected something before he broke in."

"He still doesn't know which of us is carrying a Calloway baby."

"Not yet. We're going to have to find him before he does. Pack what you'll need for a couple of days," he ordered, anxious to get out of this house.

This house, Marni and that stupid maternity form, her big warm family, everything about the woman made him feel vulnerable, he thought as he followed Marni upstairs.

He stood for a moment in the middle of her bedroom, watching her pull out a suitcase and start putting a few items into it, and realized this room was exactly as he'd thought it would be. What was he doing even thinking about her bedroom? He let out an annoyed growl and headed for the hallway to wait.

"I'm hurrying," she said, misinterpreting his growl.

She packed quickly and efficiently, something he doubted her twin could have done with a dozen people at her beck and call. Although the two sisters looked identical except for their hairstyles, he'd noticed the differences and found himself pleased by them.

There was a strength to Marni that he liked, he realized, standing in the hallway, unable to keep his eyes off her.

He was counting on that strength to get them through the next few days.

As they were leaving the house, a big gray-striped cat hopped down from the fence to snake around Marni's legs. She bent to give it a pat and scold it about staying out of the street.

"Your cat?" he asked, not surprised now that he thought about it. She was the type. Snowman in the yard. A loyal feline waiting at the door each evening after work.

But she shook her head. "My neighbor's. We share. Ivan spends the day with her then comes to wait for me on the porch each night when I get home from the boutique. It's nice. Do you have a pet?"

Chase shook his head. "It wouldn't be fair to an animal since I spend so much time at work." He was used to coming home to an empty house. He liked it fine that way. And the silly cat wasn't even hers. So why did she make him feel bad because he didn't have a pet?

She wasn't the one making him feel bad, he reminded himself. *Marni and her shared cat makes you remember that puppy you found as a kid.* He didn't want to think about the puppy or what had happened to it. He still felt sick, more than twenty-five years later, about the puppy he'd been forced to leave behind.

As he drove down South Willson Avenue, large historic houses glittered with fresh snow and Christmas lights under old-fashioned streetlights. He thought how different his own Bozeman neighborhood was and wondered what Marni would think of it. He knew it would be a test; he just hadn't realized how badly he wanted her to pass.

"I should stop by my boutique, just to be sure everything's all right," Marni said.

Did she really think she could go back to her old life as if nothing had happened? "You can't very well show up at the shop seven months pregnant in the middle of the day without having to do a lot of explaining."

"You're right, I just keep forgetting who I am."

He knew that feeling.

"Chase?"

He glanced over at her, surprised sometimes by the effect just looking at her had on him. "Yes?"

"Do you really think this will be over by Christmas?"

"Yes." He hoped. "Otherwise, Santa will have to find you at my place."

"You're sure that won't be an imposition?" she asked.

An imposition? He wanted to laugh. It would be pure hell to be trapped with her in his small apartment. But he had no choice. He feared for Marni's life as long as she was wearing that maternity form. And whoever wanted Elise out of the way would eventually come for her.

"I must warn you, though," he said. "My place is pretty...basic."

HER FIRST CHRISTMAS away from her family. The thought instantly depressed her. She'd never missed a Christmas at the farm with her family. This year especially she wanted to be at home on Christmas morning.

Chase reached over and took her hand, and she felt a rush of contrition. How could she be thinking about herself at a time like this. Chase had just lost his father. And El's life was in danger. There would be other Christmases.

Marni watched the familiar streets blur by, thinking how different Bozeman looked. But Bozeman hadn't changed; she had. Marni McCumber was a different woman from the one who'd gone to work two days ago with her only care in the world the holiday rush. The last forty-eight hours had changed that. Had changed her. She knew it was more than pretending to be pregnant. More than being in danger, or worrying about her sister.

She glanced at the man beside her. She knew it was Chase and the feelings she had for him. She'd lain in bed last night, looking out at the stars, thinking about Chase. Making her own Christmas wish, one she didn't dare acknowledge now in the daylight.

Marni was surprised when Chase pulled up in front of a
small grocery store in a northside Bozeman neighborhood
that had seen better days. The grocery was one of those
old-fashioned kind before convenience stores. A green
awning hung over the front. The neon sign read simply
Burton's. Chase opened the pickup door to get out.

"Do we need groceries?" Marni asked.

"No, sweetheart, this is home." He sounded offended as
he reached in the back for their suitcases. "I told you it
was basic."

She said nothing as he led her up open wooden stairs to
the second floor over the grocery store. He slipped a key
into the lock, opened the door and reached in to turn on a
light. Then he stood aside to let Marni enter, obviously
waiting for her reaction.

She braced herself, fighting not to let her thoughts show
as she stepped in. The spacious apartment ran the entire
width and length of the store below. Before her was a
sparsely furnished living room with an arched opening into
a kitchen and breakfast nook, both of which were large and
roomy. Through another open door, Marni saw an older
bathroom and past it, what had to be the bedroom, large
and empty except for the double bed sitting like an island
in the middle of the room. As she glanced toward the other
two rooms, she noticed that one seemed to be an office of
sorts, the other empty except for a few boxes of what appeared to be used plumbing and electrical supplies.

What hit Marni was the total lack of anything that told
her about the man who lived here. No mementos. No photographs. Nothing personal. It reminded her of the bedroom
he'd used at the ranch. Except she suspected he didn't live
out of an open suitcase in the bottom of his closet. But it
was possible. And yet, the apartment told her so much
about the man who lived there.

"It's—" She searched for the right word.

"Basic?" he asked.

It fit the picture Jabe had painted of his oldest son. A

man who wouldn't let himself get attached to anything. Especially a woman. "It's you," she said, meeting Chase's gaze.

He looked as if he was almost positive that wasn't a compliment. "You can take the bedroom." He carried her suitcase in and put it on the bed.

The bedroom was no different from the rest of the apartment. Clean, but without any personal touches. If he thought his apartment would push her away, he was wrong. Marni felt herself wanting so desperately to reach out to this man. To nurture him. To love him.

She heard him in the living room rewinding his answering machine and couldn't help overhearing the messages from the calls he'd had. Most sounded like business, she thought as she changed clothes. Then the sheriff's voice came on, saying he had the autopsy results, followed by Vanessa with a short, to-the-point message to let Chase know that the funeral would be at 10:00 a.m. the next morning at Sunset Memorial.

The machine stopped. None of the messages had sounded personal or from a woman. Marni felt more relief than she should have. Then realized a woman was exactly what Chase needed in his life. He just didn't know it yet.

CHASE HURRIEDLY DIALED the sheriff at his home number.

"I've got the autopsy results." Silence.

Chase held his breath.

"You did know Jabe was dying?"

The sheriff could have told him Martians had landed in the Gallatin Valley and he'd have been less surprised. "Dying?"

"The coroner found a large amount of prescription drugs in Jabe's system. Painkillers. He was dying of cancer."

Chase felt his head swim. Flashes of memory. Glimpses of weakness he thought he'd seen in Jabe. The feeling that his father was in trouble long before the first accident.

"That's why he wanted a grandchild so badly," Chase

said, more to himself than the sheriff. It also explained Jabe's one last attempt to get Chase into the family business. Dying of cancer. Just like Chase's mother. The irony of it made him sick.

"Given that," Sheriff Danner continued, "and the other evidence, the powder burns on his right hand, his prints on the .38, no sign of a struggle, his death has been ruled a suicide."

Chase raked his hand through his hair. "You said he had a lot of painkillers in his system. Enough that he couldn't have put up much of a struggle?" he asked, still trying to deal with the fact that his father had been dying.

"Yes, but there's no evidence to support homicide. Maybe the pain of dying was just too much for him. I'm sorry."

Jabe Calloway would have hung on until his very last breath, Chase thought as he replaced the receiver and looked up to find Marni standing in the bedroom doorway—sans the maternity form. Looking…great.

"Do you think you should be without—" He waved his hand through the air but he obviously didn't have the McCumber women's knack for nonverbal communication.

"Without what?" she asked.

"The baby," he said without thinking.

She looked confused.

"The maternity form."

"I know what you're referring to," she said patiently. "You didn't really expect me to wear it all the time, did you?"

He hadn't thought about it, but now that he did, yes, he expected her to wear it. Not that he needed that stupid maternity form between them to keep him away from her. "What if someone stops by?"

She was giving him a strange look that said she thought he was overreacting. "I could put it on before you open the door."

He could tell she thought he was making too big a deal out of this. "Fine." He told her what the sheriff had said.

She stumbled to a chair and sat down, looking shocked. "Chase, I saw your father take some pills."

"When?"

She frowned. "That first day. And again the next, the day he died."

Was it his imagination or was her hair getting blonder each time she washed it? He'd thought it was redder the first time he'd seen her standing in the foyer at Calloway Ranch. The color had struck him somehow as wrong for her. He shook his head, realizing his mind had wandered in a direction he hadn't wanted to go.

Fighting to keep his distance, he headed for the door. "I have to go down to the store. I'll be right downstairs, so don't worry. You'll be safe and I won't be long." He turned and left without looking at her, wondering how he could spend time in that apartment with that woman without— Without what? Going crazy, he assured himself. Nothing more than that.

MARNI WALKED to the front window and looked out into the neighborhood. The houses she could see from the window looked old and in need of repair. She thought of the man who'd rented this apartment and realized how little she knew about Chase. Just like Elise, she reminded herself. They both had fallen in love with mystery men.

What did Chase do for a living? She had no clue. Whatever it was, it had him living in an apartment over a grocery store on a rundown side of town. If he thought that would put her off, he was sadly mistaken. Her own father had been a farmer until his death. He'd taught her that work shaped a person and made them strong and independent as well as gave them a purpose in life.

She smiled as she thought of her father. He'd applauded her when she worked her way through college to get her business degree, then took out a small business loan to open her boutique. He'd lived long enough to see her make a success of the shop and she'd reveled in his pride in her.

Her boutique. Marni called her manager and gave her the number where she could be reached, explaining that something had come up and she wouldn't be in the shop for a few days.

"You had a call earlier. From—just a minute, it's right here—a woman who said her name was Lilly. That's all she left. No number."

"I have her number, thanks," Marni said. "Did she say what she wanted?"

"She sounded a little...strange."

Very diplomatic. "Like she might have finished off a bottle of wine before she called?" Marni asked.

"I'm afraid so."

Long after Marni hung up, she couldn't get Lilly off her mind. Finally she picked up the phone and dialed the ranch. Hilda answered on the second ring. "I'm calling for Lilly."

"She can't be disturbed."

Passed out probably. "Is Vanessa around?"

"Just a moment," Hilda said.

Vanessa came on the line and Marni hoped she hadn't made a mistake by asking for her.

"Yes?" She sounded irritable.

"It's Elise McCumber," she said quickly.

"Yes?" Vanessa's voice got chillier.

"I'm calling about Lilly."

Silence.

"I'm worried about her."

"Lilly is not your concern, Miss McCumber." She hung up, but not before Marni heard another sound on the line. A faint cry. One single word. "Elise."

Marni quickly dialed the ranch again.

"I'm sorry, Lilly isn't taking phone calls," Hilda said.

"Can't I at least leave my number so she can call me?" Marni pleaded.

"I'm sorry. Mrs. Calloway gave specific instructions."

Marni bet she did.

Hilda hung up.

CHASE WALKED IN in time to hear Marni swear and then chastise herself for doing so.

"Something wrong?" he asked.

She spun around, obviously embarrassed at having been caught. But was it for swearing or something to do with the phone call? She hesitated a little too long answering and he decided it was the phone call.

"Just the usual problems at the boutique," she said vaguely.

He nodded, admiring her obvious inability to lie well. Nor did she seem to like doing it, he thought. Just like swearing. "Is it something you have to see to?"

"No, they seem to have everything under control now. I just worry too much."

Yeah, she did. About other people. Not about her boutique. Who was it this time? Her twin? Or someone else?

"I thought I'd make us something to eat, unless you'd like to go out," he said, heading for the kitchen with a bag of groceries under his arm.

"I could help you," she said.

He groaned. Exactly what he needed, the two of them in the kitchen. As large as it was, it wouldn't be large enough. "Sure," he said, telling himself he could be warm and charming and distant at the same time. Hell, who was he kidding? He didn't know how to be warm and charming. It wasn't his nature. And if he couldn't keep his thoughts off her—as well as his hands—he'd have to depend on his nature to keep them apart.

But as he started taking the groceries out of the bag and felt her beside him, he wasn't even sure he could be distant. Or nasty enough. It had worked on other women, but not Marni McCumber. He didn't like the feeling that he was in over his head. And worse yet, Marni knew it.

CHASE SUGGESTED they eat on TV trays in the living room instead of in the breakfast nook. "There's a Jazz basketball game I'd like to see. If you don't mind."

She didn't mind. Not that she didn't realize why they weren't eating in the breakfast nook. And why he wanted the TV on while they ate. Look how he'd been in the kitchen. A man who seemed to have nerves of steel suddenly dropping the can opener, rattling pans, spilling the soup.

Marni had watched as Chase heated a can of tomato soup. She'd offered to help but he'd assured her he was an old hand at soup-heating. She didn't doubt that.

But she'd leaned against the counter and watched him, something that for some reason had made him very nervous. Was it possible she had more effect on him than he wanted to admit?

As she ate her soup and pretended to watch the basketball game on television, she found her thoughts returning to Lilly. Why wouldn't Vanessa let her talk to her? It only deepened Marni's concerns. At least she would get to see Lilly at the funeral tomorrow and make a point of talking to her. Feeling better, Marni turned her attention to her soup, Chase and the game.

Chase seemed relieved when the game ended, the Jazz winning, and the meal officially over.

Marni washed the dishes while Chase put clean sheets on the bed. When she came out of the kitchen, he was making up a bed on the couch.

"I can sleep there," Marni offered.

He shook his head. "It's only temporary."

Subtle, she thought as she thanked him for the bedroom.

"I called the hospital. I guess the whole family is there. I thought we'd go see Hayes during visiting hours. It would be a good time to let the family know you're staying with me." He was also concerned about his half brother, Marni knew. He cared more about that family than he wanted to admit.

He studied her a moment. "You realize what this means. You're making yourself a sitting duck as long as you wear that maternity form. It's not too late to change your mind."

She shook her head. Better she and Sam be the bait than Elise and the baby. "It will just take me a moment to get ready."

BOZEMAN DEACONESS HOSPITAL sat up on a hill overlooking the city. When Chase parked, Marni spotted a new car parked in the lot with the license plate CALOWAY, misspelled obviously to make it fit.

"Vanessa?" Marni asked.

Chase nodded.

"I expected she'd drive something a little more…"

"Pretentious?" he suggested. "She only drives her Mercedes in the summer." He pointed to one of the Calloway Ranch pickups and a small red four-wheel drive with FELICIA plates. "Looks like the whole family's here."

Marni hoped that meant Lilly, as well. She couldn't throw off the bad feeling she had. Nor forget the way Lilly had cried that one single word. "Elise."

They found everyone, Felicia, Dayton, Lilly, Vanessa, Hilda and Cook in Hayes's room. Hayes lay in bed, his head bandaged, his face ashen. Lilly sat in a chair next to him. Marni tried to get her attention but realized it was futile. Lilly appeared to be either highly inebriated or sedated.

Vanessa motioned for Dayton to take them out into the hall. Felicia came along.

"How's Hayes?" Chase asked.

"He seems to be okay. They gave him something to help him sleep," Dayton said. He shot Marni an angry look as if he blamed her for Hayes's accident.

"No memory loss?" Marni asked, thinking of Chase's accident. Would Hayes remember what had happened? Would he remember that Marni wasn't pregnant? But more important, would he remember Elise, *if* he was her lover?

"The docs say he responded to all their questions just fine," Dayton said, eyeing Marni suspiciously. "Why?"

"One Calloway who can't remember is enough," Chase said in answer. "Elise is staying at my place."

Dayton stared at his brother. "You're buying that this is your kid?"

"Yeah, do you have a problem with that?" Chase asked.

Marni felt Dayton's gaze, hot with hate. Was there a chance he thought she *was* Elise? Thought she was only pretending Chase was the father of her baby to get back at him? Or was it just because he thought she carried Jabe Calloway's grandchild, a child who could take the money from his own?

"I can't believe how much this baby has grown," Felicia said, her hand going to her stomach almost on cue.

She did look as though she'd grown overnight, Marni noted. Or maybe it was only the new maternity top that made her look that way.

Felicia linked a hand through Dayton's arm with a possessiveness that surprised Marni. "The doctor is a little worried I might deliver early, all the excitement," Felicia said.

"I suppose Jabe's will hasn't turned up," Chase said pointedly to Dayton.

"I heard you're determined to prove that Father was murdered," Dayton said with no little disgust.

"Yes," Chase said. "I am. Let me know if there's any change with Hayes." He put his arm around Marni's shoulders, his touch warm and reassuring. She reminded herself he was just doing this for show.

They left Felicia and Dayton standing outside Hayes's hospital room door. When Marni looked back, she saw that they appeared to be arguing over something. She wondered what.

"She's hoping she has that baby before yours," Chase said, following her gaze.

Did that explain the way Felicia was acting? Marni felt

a chill. Did Felicia suspect Elise might be carrying her husband's child?

Chase seemed lost in his own thoughts. And from the scowl on his face, they were dark.

"I've been thinking," Marni said as they walked to his pickup.

Chase opened her door for her and gave her a look that said he wasn't sure he wanted to hear what she'd been thinking.

"If Dayton's telling the truth, and he came into the library immediately after the gunshot and there was no one else in the room except Jabe, then the killer was either still in the room or found another way out."

Chase didn't comment as she climbed into the pickup. He closed the passenger door and went around to the other side.

"Everyone was accounted for moments after the shot, so the killer wasn't still in the room," Chase said as he slid in next to her and started the pickup. "And there isn't another way out. Which means Dayton was lying."

"Maybe not. I think I know how the killer got away so quickly," Marni said.

Chase started to drive away from the hospital but stopped to turn and look at her.

"I think that house is a maze of secret stairways and passages," she said, launching into her theory enthusiastically. "Jabe told me it was originally built by a horse thief turned politician. A man like that would need ways to get around the house—and out of the house—without being seen." She took a quick breath, afraid he would think her theory foolish. "I have a feeling there's a passageway into the library."

He studied her but said nothing.

"And that's how the murderer got away, possibly with the will." She waited, but still he said nothing, as if he anticipated what was coming next. "There's one way to find out."

"Go back to the ranch and search for secret passages," Chase said.

"Everyone's at the hospital. It would be the perfect time."

He looked as though he might argue, desperately wanted to argue. "How did I know that's what you were thinking?"

"You do have a key to the house, don't you? It wouldn't be like breaking and entering."

He groaned. "You're going to be the death of me."

She certainly hoped not.

THEY DROVE to the ranch, the sky a dark velvet dusted with starlight. Just as Marni had said, no one was home. Chase used his key and let them in and Marni went right to the spot behind the stairs. She inspected the paneling closely, thinking about the way it opened and trying to remember exactly where Lilly had been standing when she'd unlocked it.

After a few futile attempts, Marni pressed a spot and the door slid open. She turned to find Chase watching, his eyes wide with amazement as he glanced into the passageway.

"How many more of these are there, do you think?" he asked.

Marni shook her head. "I would imagine there's at least one on every level, but I suspect there's more. The house could be a honeycomb of secret passageways. Anyone who knew them could get around without being seen."

"The question is, how many people know about this," he said, glancing up the stairwell.

"Lilly and the person who pushed over the armoire that day in the attic. Maybe more."

"Or maybe just one person," Chase said as he stepped into the stairwell. "How do you close the door?"

"I don't know." Marni started up the stairs behind him, immediately aware of being in the confines of the passageway with Chase.

The door slid closed behind them and Chase stopped with a start.

"There must be a device in one of the stairs," Marni said.

"I hope you're right and there's one that reopens it," Chase said. He pulled a flashlight from his jacket and lit the way as they climbed the stairs, stopping at the first landing to search for other doors.

They found one that opened onto a long narrow tunnel and followed it. At the end of the tunnel was a short flight of stairs that dropped to the first floor and what appeared to be a dead end. But as they neared the wall at the bottom of the stairs, a panel door slid open.

"It's the library," Chase said, shining his flashlight into the room. "Just like you thought."

"That's how the killer got away so fast with the will before Dayton came in."

"Unless Dayton is the killer," Chase said. He looked down at her, his body so close she could feel his heat radiating toward her. For just a moment she thought he might kiss her. She touched her tongue to her upper lip, her heart pounding. He let out a curse. "Come on," he said gruffly. "We don't know how much time we have."

They followed the stairway up, discovering an intricate system of corridors that appeared to run throughout the house and to all the bedrooms.

"Well, we know how the killer could have gotten away," Chase said. "But we haven't narrowed our list of suspects much."

Marni nodded in agreement. "Anyone who knows about the secret passages could have killed Jabe."

"Lilly is still at the top of that list," Chase reminded her as they reached the bottom stairs and the door automatically opened. "As far as we know, she might be the only person in the house who knows about the passageways."

They drove out of the ranch and were past Maudlow, almost to Poison Hollow, when they spotted headlights coming up the road. "We got out just in time," Chase said, sounding relieved.

As they passed the Calloway Ranch truck and Dayton, Marni looked back to see him hit the brakes.

"I think he recognized your truck," she said. "He'll know we were at the house."

Chase nodded. "That might work to our advantage, now that I think about it. If he's our killer, it will make him more nervous. He'll do something stupid."

"And if he's not?" Marni asked, trying not to think about what stupid thing the killer might do.

"Then he'll surely mention it to Vanessa and everyone in the house will know. It's impossible to keep a secret in that house."

Marni wasn't so sure about that. Jabe's killer was still at large. So was the person who wanted her dead.

Chase drove through a fast-food burger joint, and bought them both meals. They ate in the semidarkness of a shopping center, listening to golden oldies on the radio.

Back at the apartment, Chase made a big production out of how tired he was. Marni took the hint and headed for the bedroom. She climbed into bed, wondering about him, wondering about herself. How could she have fallen in love so quickly and with a man who wanted nothing to do with her? More important, what was she going to do about it?

CHASE BALLED UP the pillow and dropped his head onto it, determined Marni McCumber wasn't going to keep him from getting a good night's sleep.

But the ghosts of his past weren't about to let him sleep. He kept thinking about his father dying of cancer and keeping it a secret. Someone knew though. The same person who had filled Jabe full of painkillers and then blown a hole in his head.

No matter what the sheriff said, Jabe Calloway had been murdered. More than two attempts had been made on

Marni's life. And one on Jabe's before that. The question was, Who was behind them?

One of his brothers was the father of Elise's baby. With the will as it was, that baby stood to inherit a huge portion of the Calloway fortune. Not that there wasn't plenty left for the rest of the family. But they were a greedy lot and he had to assume the money was the murderer's motive.

The family knew now that Marni was staying with him. And eventually, one of them would make his or her move. Chase hoped he could figure out which one before that happened. But he was ready nonetheless. Under the couch was his .357, loaded and ready. Meanwhile, he had to find out which brother was Elise's lover.

While down in the grocery store earlier, Chase had called a friend of his, a photographer at the *Bozeman Chronicle*, and asked him if he could dig up shots of Dayton and Hayes Calloway from the file. Both of his brothers had been in the news for one business profile or another.

His friend Doug hadn't asked why, just said he'd have them tomorrow and would be happy to make Chase copies.

Getting the photos was at least a place to start, Chase thought. Not that he thought either of his brothers had tried to kill Marni and his own baby, especially a baby worth a small fortune. Certainly not to keep their wives. Lilly didn't even pretend to care for Hayes. Chase knew Felicia had to be aware of Dayton's many indiscretions. It wasn't as if he tried to keep them secret. No, Chase couldn't see either brother attempting murder to save his marriage.

But he could see either brother killing Jabe. The Calloway boys, himself included, hated their father for a variety of good reasons, Chase thought.

He closed his eyes, searching for sleep, praying for sleep. He groaned as his thoughts went straight to Marni. As much as he'd tried not to, he'd caught a glimpse of her as she'd come out of the bathroom wearing, of all things, a chenille robe. Wrapped modestly around her, covering everything but about two inches of her nightgown, sticking out the bottom of the robe. Flannel.

God, a woman in a flannel nightgown and a grandmother kind of robe and he couldn't get the image off his mind. Nor could he forget the scent of her. Soapy clean. Her face shiny. Her hair brushed and floating around her shoulders. Her feet and ankles bare.

He groaned again, sitting up on the couch to beat his pillow into submission, before he lay back down. Once again he started to tell himself all the reasons why it would never work, the two of them, then he remembered the phone call.

He reached over, picked up the receiver and hit redial. The phone rang and rang. He thought he'd been wrong. Maybe she had called the boutique as she'd indicated earlier. Maybe it was only his suspicious mind that made him think she hadn't wanted him to know whom she'd called.

The phone kept ringing. The boutique would be closed now. No one would answer. He was ready to hang up, feeling bad about suspecting Marni, when the phone quit ringing.

"Hello." The voice of a woman. Awakened from sleep. "May I help you?" Hilda asked.

She'd already helped him, Chase thought, hanging up. Now all he wondered was why Marni had called the ranch and why she felt the need to lie about it.

Lilly. He shook his head and lay down again, with a curse. Why couldn't Marni see that befriending Lilly was a big mistake? Because it was Marni's nature. She saw Lilly as defenseless and in need of an advocate. But Chase wondered just how defenseless Lilly Calloway really was. And if Hayes turned out to be Elise's lover, who knew what Lilly was capable of?

When Marni came out of the bathroom a second time, she wished him a good-night, turned out the light and closed the bedroom door.

He groaned as he heard the springs on the bed squeak as she climbed between the sheets. It was going to be a long night.

Chapter Fifteen

December 23

The next morning, Chase insisted Marni go down to the store for coffee while he made a few phone calls.

She got the impression he hadn't slept well. Also that she made him uncomfortable. She could see that whenever she was around him. And more and more, she hoped it might be because he shared some of her feelings. It made her smile as she took the stairs to the store.

To Marni's surprise the small grocery was nothing as she'd expected. The moment she opened the door she smelled fresh coffee. And something else. Cookies baking. Chocolate chip. Marni stood for a moment, amazed how light and airy the store was. And immaculately clean.

Somewhere behind the neat aisles music played softly. But it was another sound, children giggling, that Marni followed to the back of the store, past rows of canned goods.

"Good morning," a robust woman said from behind the counter and smiled. "You look like a woman who could use a cup of coffee."

"You read my mind," Marni said as the woman handed her a pottery cup filled with a wonderful almondy aroma.

"The store's specialty. You must be new to the neighborhood." She held out her hand. "I'm Angie."

Marni took her hand, thinking how different this little

store was from the chains she'd been in. "Marni Mc-Cumber." Then quickly added, "Just call me Elise. Everyone does."

Angie smiled broadly. "Welcome to Burton's." She motioned to several comfortable-looking chairs set around a small round oak table. Behind the chairs were two bookshelves full of used paperbacks. Sunlight streamed in the windows, making the little setting so inviting Marni was tempted, but she knew Chase would be down any minute and anxious to go. He seemed awfully impatient this morning.

She heard the giggles again. They had an impish quality that drew her deeper into the store. She peeked around a corner into a large open room filled with sunshine, soft couches and chairs and toys. Large colorful animals had been painted on the walls. This room was not only the source of the music but the giggles.

Marni peered over the back of one of the couches to find a half-dozen preschool-age children huddled together amidst a pile of toys, playing a game with a young college-age woman. Whatever the game was, it had the kids in hysterics.

Marni smiled, unable to resist.

"They're having a grand old time today," Angie said. "Here, you'd better try one of these."

She offered Marni a cookie, straight out of the oven. "You run a day care in the back of the grocery," Marni asked as she took a bite of the cookie. "Oh this cookie is...delicious."

Angie smiled. "My own recipe." She looked back at the children. "It's something the owner of the store started. A place where the neighborhood could come not just to buy groceries but to visit, let the kids play for a while and give their moms a break. Some of the mothers in this neighborhood are going back to school, trying to get jobs, trying to better themselves. Burton's just helps them with a little free baby-sitting."

"That's incredible," Marni said, looking around the store.

"It's kind of a haven in an area of the city that's seen better days," Angie said. "Chase says the neighborhood will get better if there's hope. That's what Burton's is. Hope."

"Chase?" Marni asked in surprise. "Chase Calloway *owns* Burton's?"

Angie laughed. "I thought you knew."

She looked around the store, seeing it with different eyes. Chase Calloway never ceased to amaze her. But she wondered if she'd ever get to know the real him or would he always try to hide that from her? That's if he even gave her a chance to get to know him, she reminded herself.

Behind her, Marni heard the door of the store open with the faint tinkle of the bell. She turned, expecting to see Chase. Instead, a young woman came through the door. Two things instantly struck Marni about her. Her long dark hair and her enormous pregnant stomach.

"How are you doing, Raine, dear?" Angie inquired as the woman worked her way back through the rows of groceries.

"I can't wait until I have this baby," Raine said, sounding exhausted. She smiled at Marni, taking in Sam.

Marni was surprised how young the woman was.

"At least finals are over and next semester will be easier," Angie said, totaling up the small amount of groceries the young woman put on the counter.

When Raine reached into her purse to pay, Angie stopped her. "Chase says since you've been volunteering in the back it's his treat today."

The woman looked up, surprised and instantly relieved. "Thank you, Angie. Please tell him when you see him how much I appreciate this."

"Not at all. You just take care of yourself and that baby. And if you need anything, anything at all, Chase says for you to let him know."

"Does Chase take that kind of interest in all his customers?" Marni asked after Raine left.

"That one he worries about. So young. Got herself in a bind. But she'll be fine once she has her baby."

Marni wanted to ask more about Raine, but the bell over the front door tinkled again and this time Chase's broad shoulders filled the doorway. He gave her a curt nod, then retreated outside.

"I'd better get going," Marni said, finishing the wonderful coffee and handing Angie the cup. "What do I owe you?"

Angie shook her head. "No charge for new people in the neighborhood. Just come back soon."

"I will," Marni said, hurrying out to find Chase waiting for her in the pickup. She climbed in, pleasantly surprised to find that he'd let it run and warm up for her.

"That's quite the store you live over," Marni said, glancing back. "Although I do wonder how the owner makes a living, giving away free child care and groceries."

If Chase heard her, he didn't take the bait. She doubted he'd ever volunteer any information about himself.

"I have to check on a couple of jobs," he said, shifting the pickup into gear.

"Jobs?" He had other jobs?

They had only gone a few blocks when Chase pulled up in front of a small rundown house that was in the process of being remodeled. "I'll only be a moment," he said and got out.

Marni watched him through the front window of the house, talking to an older man doing carpentry work inside. A few minutes later, Chase came back to the pickup. He drove a block to another house, this one in even worse repair than the last.

"You're a carpenter?" she asked when she couldn't stand it any longer.

"Would that surprise you?" he asked.

Nothing about him would surprise her. And yet everything did. Especially Burton's. Why had he named it that? she wondered. "I've wondered what you did for a living ever since I found out you didn't work for Calloway Ranches," she said.

Not surprisingly, he didn't respond.

"Shouldn't you be working? I mean, will you lose your job?"

He smiled. "Are you worried that I'll go hungry?"

She laughed. "Not as long as you live over that grocery store. I'm sure the owner would see that you didn't starve until you got on your feet again."

Chase opened his door. "I can take a few days off without being evicted. I'll be right back."

They checked a couple more of Chase's jobs, all in the same neighborhood as his apartment, then Chase took her back to his place where he opened a can of bean with bacon soup and they ate an early lunch in front of the TV.

Marni realized he was using the TV to keep from having to talk to her. She suspected he was using the apartment and the soup to try to send her a message. Only he didn't know how many ball games she could watch, how many cans of soup she could eat. Nor did he know that by pushing her away he only made her more determined to find the Chase he was trying so hard to hide from her. She wasn't just a sucker for people in trouble; she had the patience of Job. She could wait out Chase Calloway, she told herself.

CHASE SAW MARNI gazing out the window wistfully. He glanced around the apartment, suddenly aware of how drab it looked. Certainly no sign that Christmas was only two days away.

He felt almost guilty for the way he'd been behaving. Almost. He was just being himself. Fighting for his life was more like it. *Whatever you say, Scrooge.* He groaned silently. Okay, so maybe he'd been laying it on pretty thick with the canned soup in front of the television, the fast-food burgers in the pickup cab.

He looked at Marni's slim back, her hair golden in the light, and felt a stab of contrition. Marni was trying to save her pregnant twin and what was Chase Calloway doing to help? Not much. He was too busy trying to shore up the walls around his heart.

"I have to run an errand. Just to be safe, would you mind staying with Angie in the store until I get back? I won't be long." He knew he sounded mysterious. "It's a quick job I have to do." He knew she'd understand work if nothing else.

When he came back, he found her in the day-care part of the store, playing a game with the kids. He stood watching her, overwhelmed with emotions that choked him up and made him angry with himself. He'd hoped these ridiculous feelings would go away but, if anything, they seemed to be getting stronger. If he didn't know better, he'd think he was falling in love with this woman.

"Come on," he said after she'd finished the game. "We have to get ready."

She looked up at him, surprised, it seemed, to find him standing there. He suspected she knew what he'd been feeling moments before. Sometimes he felt as if she could see into his heart. That was a frightening thought, when he didn't even know his own mind around her, let alone his heart.

"I got you something," he said as they climbed the stairs. He felt suddenly foolish. What if she read more into the gift than he'd meant her to? He mentally kicked himself for feeling anxious as he opened the door to the apartment for her and watched her face to see her reaction.

MARNI STARED at the hopelessly lopsided Christmas tree standing by the front window.

"It was the only one left in town," Chase said quickly. "I know how you are about Christmas and all…"

Her eyes filled with tears. "It's the most beautiful Christmas tree I've ever seen," she said, turning to look at him.

He smiled, appearing relieved and at the same time embarrassed. "I picked up some lights and I thought—"

"The kids in the day care would make ornaments," she finished for him. "Maybe string some popcorn and cranberries and make a party out of it."

He laughed and nodded. "That's exactly what I thought you'd say."

She flew to him, wrapping her arms around his neck in a hug. "Thank you."

"It's nothing," he said softly as his arms came around her.

Marni stood in the circle of his arms, her arms around his neck, looking up into his gaze.

He drew her closer, his lips coming down on hers. Gentle, tentative, then demanding.

He drew back to look into her eyes. "We'd better get ready for the funeral." And pulled away.

Sunset Memorial Cemetery sat on a wooded hillside overlooking Bozeman. Most days only pine trees and tombstones silhouetted the winter sky. Today hundreds of cars lined the narrow cemetery roads.

"Vanessa loves a spectacle," Chase said in disgust as he parked the pickup. "She's finally found a role she can excel at—Jabe Calloway's grieving widow." He motioned to the camera crews around Vanessa. The widow wore black and appeared to be sniffling into a hankie.

Chase led Marni up the freshly plowed road to stand at the back of the large crowd of mourners. Other camera crews had set up their equipment graveside, anxious to get thirty seconds of the rich, notorious and dead on the nightly news. Chase wondered how many of the mourners were there for the chance to see themselves on TV, how many had come out of morbid curiosity and how many wanted to be sure Jabe Calloway was dead and gone.

One thing Chase knew for sure, none had attended out of friendship. Jabe Calloway had no friends that Chase knew of. Only enemies. And family. And at least one of them was an enemy, too, he thought.

As the service started, Dayton took his place between his mother and wife. Chase watched Felicia and Vanessa scan the crowd furtively from behind their black veils.

"Do you see Lilly?" Marni whispered beside Chase.

Lilly was conspicuously absent. "Vanessa was probably afraid Lilly would embarrass her."

Vanessa had called earlier that morning at the apartment.

"The media will be at the funeral," she'd announced.

"So?" he'd said, still half-asleep and always easily annoyed with Vanessa and her idea of important life matters. He'd also had a long, sleepless night on the couch he didn't even want to think about.

"We must present a united front."

"What the hell does that mean?" Chase asked.

"We must look like a family."

"Well, for that, you're going to have to do a lot more than get everyone to show up at Jabe's funeral," Chase snapped.

"The point is, I want you there."

"That's a first, Vanessa."

A deep sigh. "Can I count on you, Chase, or not?" she asked with somewhat controlled anger.

"Vanessa, there is only one thing you can count on from me. I know someone in this big, happy family murdered my father and made several attempts on Elise McCumber's life. I plan to see that person behind bars."

"Have you lost your mind?" she hissed into the phone, obviously afraid the hired help might overhear. "The coroner ruled it a suicide and Elise— Really, Chase, she staged those accidents, any fool can see that. The only problem was, one of them went awry and now Hayes is in the hospital."

Chase swore. "That's ridiculous. Elise could have been

killed that day in the barn if I hadn't gotten there when I did.''

''But she wasn't and my Hayes was almost killed,'' Vanessa said, her voice pure ice. ''I don't understand why you, of all people, believe anything that woman says. Unless you *are* the father of her baby.''

He gritted his teeth. ''You might as well hear it from me, Vanessa. Elise is carrying a Calloway baby.''

''The family will demand a paternity test. Imagine the bad publicity if it gets out.''

He wanted to laugh. ''Vanessa, imagine the bad publicity when someone in the family goes down for murder. And it will happen. I'll see to that.''

Chase could hear the anger as hard and brittle as Vanessa Calloway herself. ''Keep throwing around that kind of talk and I'll have the family lawyer slap you with a suit so fast it will make your head swim.''

''Truth is an absolute defense, Vanessa.''

Vanessa had slammed down the phone.

''So much for that big, happy family,'' Chase had said and hung up.

A breeze whispered through the pines now, sending snow showering down as the pastor began to speak, referring to Jabe Calloway in glowing terms. Chase felt ill and wished he hadn't come. Vanessa would be furious that he hadn't arrived on time anyway. And even more angry that he hadn't stood with the ''family.'' That made him feel a little better.

All Chase could think about was getting photographs of his half brothers and sending them to Marni's twin. He wanted the mystery of Elise McCumber's lover solved as quickly as possible. Then he would find the person who killed Jabe and made attempts on Marni's life.

MARNI SEARCHED the crowd for Lilly, hoping Chase was wrong. Worry stole through her when she realized Lilly hadn't made the funeral. Something was terribly wrong.

Marni felt it more strongly this morning. Lilly had looked so out of it at the hospital last night.

A car came speeding up the road, sending snow flying into the air. A murmur moved through the crowd as the car came to an abrupt stop and the driver's door slammed open.

"What the hell?" Chase said beside her.

Marni stared at the mourners, wondering what the commotion was about but unable to see the car and who had arrived in it.

Then she heard Lilly's voice calling Vanessa's name as she moved through the crowd. The reverend halted in mid-sentence and everyone turned as Lilly burst through the mourners, almost falling onto the casket.

"Lilly." Vanessa's voice carried across the cold cemetery. So did her obvious shock and disbelief.

Lilly stood smiling at her mother-in-law. Two things instantly struck Marni as odd. One was Lilly's inebriated state, considering she'd obviously just driven in from the ranch. The second was the scarf she had on. She wore basic funeral black, except for the bright multicolored scarf around her neck. Even from this distance, Marni recognized it as the scarf Vanessa had been wearing the first night she'd met her. It was the same scarf Marni had slipped on on the stairs.

Vanessa staggered. Dayton reached for her but she dropped too quickly.

"My God, she's fainted," Marni heard someone cry.

Suddenly the crowd obscured both Vanessa's fallen form and the rest of the family.

"I don't believe this," Chase said, shaking his head.

By the time Vanessa had been revived and the crowd moved back to let the funeral service continue, Lilly and her car were gone. And Marni wondered how a woman that drunk could get away that quickly. She remembered the look that she'd seen pass between Vanessa and Lilly.

"Something's wrong," she told Chase as the service

broke up. He hurriedly ushered her to the pickup to avoid
a pack of media bearing down on them.

"You're just starting to notice that?" Chase asked as he
pulled away before a camera crew could reach them.

"There's something going on between Vanessa and
Lilly," Marni said, recalling the scene they'd just witnessed. "How did Lilly disappear so fast?"

"Maybe Dayton got her out of there before she could
cause any more trouble," Chase suggested.

"I still think Lilly is in some kind of trouble, more trouble than just her drinking."

Chase sighed as he pulled over a few blocks from the
cemetery and turned to Marni. "Look, I know you see Lilly
as the underdog here, but you could be wrong, Marni. Lilly
looked like she could take care of herself at the funeral,
whatever all that was about."

"Lilly tried to reach me at the boutique. She left a message, but when I called her back at the ranch, Hilda
wouldn't let me talk to her. Chase, I heard her on the line
a moment before I was cut off. She only said one word."

"Help?"

Marni gave him an impatient look. "Elise."

"Elise?" he asked skeptically.

"It was the way she said it."

"Lilly's been in trouble for years, Marni. When she's
drinking, she doesn't even know what she's doing."

"I just have this bad feeling."

"So do I. The only difference is, my bad feeling says
Lilly might be a murderer."

Marni chewed at her lower lip for a moment. "You really think I could be that wrong about her?"

"I don't want to take any chances." He raked a hand
through his hair. "Look, Marni, I admire your compassion.
I even admire you putting yourself on the line for your
sister. I don't mean to sound callous but Lilly isn't our
problem. Our problem is finding out which of my brothers

is the father of Elise's baby. And you seem to have forgotten that someone wants you dead."

"There haven't been any more attempts," Marni said.

"Right, and maybe there won't be." He didn't sound as if he believed that any more than she did. "Look, I have a friend getting photos of Dayton and Hayes to show Elise. We should be able to pick them up."

"Elise has a fax machine at the farm," Marni said, anxious to get this over with. "And I have one at the boutique."

THEY DROVE to the boutique after picking up the pictures and parked in the alley. Marni had called her manager to let her know they would be coming.

Marni noticed barricades going up downtown and suddenly realized why. "I'd completely forgotten. The Christmas Stroll is tonight," she said, a little sad she wouldn't be at the boutique. It was the busiest night of the year, but also one of the most fun. She always baked Christmas cookies and made hot apple cider to give away. It was the last big event before Christmas, one that brought the town together in the true spirit of the holiday.

"There's next Christmas," Chase said, reading her thoughts.

Next Christmas? "This one isn't over yet," Marni said, thinking of her Christmas wish.

"What do you want for Christmas?" Chase asked, surprising her.

She glanced over at him. "Why are you asking me that?"

He shrugged. "I just wondered."

"You're afraid we aren't going to get this thing solved by Christmas, aren't you?"

"Maybe I just wanted to get you something," he said softly. "It looks a little bare under the tree. If there's something you really want, I wish you'd tell me." When she didn't say anything, he got out.

Tears filled Marni's eyes and she felt so choked up she didn't dare speak as she followed him. Snowflakes began to lazily fall from the heavens and she breathed in the cold air, intensely aware of the man walking beside her. Oh yes, there was something she really wanted. She'd made her Christmas wish that night at the farm, staring up at the stars. Hastily she wiped her tears and looked over at Chase. "I'll think about it."

Marni unlocked the back door and stepped into the small, neat office. The door into the boutique was closed but Marni could hear the sound of shoppers in the next room.

She shrugged off her coat and mittens, then took the two photographs Chase handed her. She dialed the number at the farm and told Elise what she planned to do.

"One of them has to be my Chase, huh," Elise said.

"Yes," Marni agreed. "Call me here at the boutique on the private line and let me know which one." She hung up.

Putting the first photo facedown in the fax machine, Marni dialed the number at the farm again and hit start. Slowly the photo of Dayton rolled through the machine. Then the one of Hayes.

Marni glanced at Chase. He looked as nervous as she felt. The phone rang, making her jump. She picked up the receiver on the first ring.

"That's him," El cried, sounding close to tears.

Marni shot a glance at Chase. "Which one? The first photo or the second?"

"The second," Elise cried. "Who is he?"

"Chase's half brother Hayes."

"He's the one in the hospital?"

"Yes, but he's doing fine."

Elise began to cry. "And he's married?"

"Yes."

"Oh, Marni, I don't understand. I just don't understand."

"Neither do I, but we'll find out. Meanwhile, listen to me, you have to think of the baby."

"He loves me," El cried. "He loves our baby. I know he does." She hung up.

Marni replaced the receiver and looked over at Chase again, stunned. "I'm so surprised. I thought it would be Dayton. Not Hayes." And yet, hadn't she found it impossible to believe her sister could ever fall for a man like Dayton? "How could Hayes do this to my sister?"

"I have to admit it surprises me," Chase said. "But there's history there you don't know about."

"What kind of history?" Marni asked.

"When he married Lilly it was because he thought she was pregnant with his child. When the baby was born, there were complications. That's when Hayes discovered he wasn't the father. It was no secret, not even to him, that Lilly had been in love with someone else and married Hayes on the rebound. Then when the baby died, Lilly had a breakdown of sorts."

"How horrible for Lilly. And Hayes."

"I don't think they ever had much of a marriage," Chase said.

"Then why did he stay with her?"

Chase shook his head. The noise in the shop grew louder. "I guess we'll have to ask him."

CHASE PUSHED OPEN the door to Hayes's hospital room for Marni. Hayes saw her, sat up in surprise and quickly lay back. "You're not Elise."

"No," Marni said. "I'm her twin, Marni McCumber."

"But Elise is why we're here," Chase said, closing the door behind him as he approached his brother's bed.

Hayes closed his eyes for a moment. "I can explain."

"There is only one thing I need to know," Marni said. "Do you love my sister?"

Hayes looked over at her for a moment, then smiled. "You look so much like her. When I saw you at the house— I guess I don't have to tell you what a shock that was. Especially to find out Elise was pregnant."

"You didn't know?" she asked in surprise.

"How could I? The last time we'd talked was August and I'd been so...foolish. I thought that's why you were pretending Chase was the father of your baby."

"Why did you use *my* name?" Chase demanded, trying to hold in the anger he felt. For all they knew, it had been Hayes who'd tried to kill Marni.

"I guess I wanted to be you," Hayes said. "Unencumbered. Elise was the first woman I'd met who—" He looked away, his face reddening. "I'm sorry I involved you in this, Chase. I never thought it would go past an innocent lunch."

"You never answered my question," Marni reminded him.

Hayes met her gaze. "Do I love Elise? Oh God yes. When I saw you at the ranch and thought you were Elise, I knew you had to be carrying my baby. I was overjoyed. Just the thought of us having a baby together—"

"You came to my room that night," Marni said.

He nodded. "I had to see you. To try to explain. To tell you how happy I was about the baby. And to warn you about Lilly. She'd found out about us."

"Excuse me," Chase interrupted. "You're telling us Lilly knows about you and Elise?"

"She has for months. She was so angry—"

"I would imagine she was," Chase said. "What did you think was going to happen?"

"You don't understand," Hayes said. "I've wanted a divorce for years. But I couldn't."

"Because Jabe would have disapproved," Chase said with disgust. "And Vanessa would have thrown a fit that you might want to soil the family name with Lilly's dirty laundry, because I'll bet Lilly wouldn't have gone quietly."

"I didn't care. Not about any of that. Do you really think what Father and Mother thought would make me stay in a loveless marriage? Especially after I'd met Elise? Do you really think I'm that shallow?"

Chase looked at Hayes. Yeah, that's exactly what he'd thought. Shallow and spineless.

"Lilly told me if I ever left her, she'd kill herself. I believed her."

"Lilly needs help, professional help," Marni said.

"Don't you think I tried to get it for her?" Hayes cried. "Vanessa and Jabe wouldn't hear of it. I went behind their backs and set up an appointment for Lilly. She refused to go and told Vanessa. Now Lilly has made herself a prisoner in that house with Vanessa as warden."

"Surely there is some way to make Lilly see that she needs help," Marni said.

"Right now, I'm more worried about Elise," Hayes said. "Is she all right? And the baby?"

Marni nodded.

"Someone's trying to kill Marni because they think she's Elise and carrying a Calloway baby," Chase said. "Want to tell us what you know about that?"

"I was afraid of this," Hayes said, his expression pained. "I've never seen Lilly so...upset. That's why I sent that note for you to meet me in the barn," he said to Marni. "I wanted to warn you about Lilly. Then I realized you weren't Elise."

"Someone had fixed the latch on Wind Chaser's stall so it wouldn't lock," Chase said. "Marni says she smelled Lilly's perfume just before the accident. It wasn't the first accident, either."

Hayes looked sick. "I talked to Lilly this morning. She says she wants a divorce. I don't think she'll bother you or Elise again."

"If she's the one who tried to hurt me," Marni said. "I don't think she was."

"Marni is a little too trusting," Chase said, shaking his head.

"I'm not going back to the ranch," Hayes said. "I've been thinking about leaving the family business for some

time. Now with Father gone, there's nothing stopping me.''
He addressed Marni. ''When can I see Elise?''

''Not until the killer is behind bars,'' Chase said.

''You don't think I would harm Elise and my baby, do
you?'' he asked Chase angrily.

''We don't want to lead anyone to Elise,'' Chase said,
realizing he did trust Hayes.

''Find this guy,'' Hayes said emotionally. ''Don't let
anything happen to Elise and my baby, please, Chase.''

Chase took his brother's hand and squeezed it. Maybe
there was more to Hayes Calloway than he'd thought all
these years.

Chapter Sixteen

As Marni and Chase left the hospital it started to snow.
They drove toward town and the Christmas Stroll. Christmas music played as musicians roamed through the crowds
filling the barricaded streets. Marni rolled down her window as Chase drove slowly along one of the open streets,
dodging shoppers, street performers and vendors.

The smell of roasted chestnuts, hot apple cider and pep-
permint sticks wafted through the air. A theatrical group
from *The Nutcracker* danced on a street corner. A group of
singing Santas moved through the crowds in a wave of
bright red.

Shoppers roamed in and out of the stores, their arms
filled with packages as overhead, Christmas lights glittered
in the falling snow and bundled-up children waited in line
to sit on a real Santa's broad lap and tell him their last-
minute Christmas wishes.

"I'm sorry about your Christmas," Chase said.

"It's not so bad. Who knows, maybe by Christmas Eve
there'll be a happy ending." She turned to see Chase's
profile, his jaw set, his expression one of stubborn determination. "For Hayes and Elise and their baby," she added
hastily.

He didn't comment, just wound his way back to
Burton's, parked in the dark shadows of the store, but
didn't get out. Instead he sat, staring out into the darkness.

There weren't a lot of Christmas decorations on the houses in this part of town. Nor many streetlights.

He raked a hand through his hair. "Maybe you should go to the farm until this is over."

"You think the killer will eventually come after me here, don't you?" Marni asked quietly.

He nodded and glanced out his side window. Snow had begun to pile up on the windshield, obscuring the darkness.

"I'm not leaving you," she said.

He shook his head. "Staying with me could be the biggest mistake of your life."

She doubted he was talking about the killer who was after her. "I'm willing to take my chances."

He turned to look at her. The tension in the pickup cab arced between them like an electrical short. She met his gaze, feeling the heat of it warm her skin. She knew if he ever let himself go—

"You don't understand," he said, his voice so filled with anguish it was all she could do not to pull him into her arms.

"My childhood wasn't like yours. You have no idea what it was like."

"Tell me," she whispered.

He leaned his forearms over the steering wheel, his gaze still directed into the darkness. "I didn't have a home, just a series of rented apartments, some little more than shacks." The words seemed to come with great difficulty. She knew how hard it must be for him to tell her and her heart broke for him.

"We kept on the move, my mother living in fear that Jabe would find out she hadn't had the abortion, that he'd come and steal me away from her, and all the time she was dying of a broken heart because he didn't come after her."

She didn't speak, just waited as the snow fell silently outside the pickup.

"I used to desperately want what other kids had," he went on. "A home. A family. Someone who loved me and took care of me. My mother was dying of a broken heart from the time I was born and finally from cancer. She wasn't there emotionally most of the time nor physically at the end.''

The windows began to fog over, the cold to creep in around the doors. Marni hugged Sam as she watched Chase struggle with words to describe his childhood, his pain.

''My mother taught me not to get attached to anything or anyone. About the time I made friends, we moved. What was horrible was that she never stopped loving him, couldn't seem to stop no matter what he'd done to her. I watched her love him and saw that love kill her long before the cancer did and I promised myself I would never love like that, certainly never that stupidly, that blindly.''

Marni stared at his profile, a dark silhouette in the pickup cab, finally understanding why Chase had fought his feelings for her so hard.

He turned to look at her. ''For thirty-five years I've managed to keep that promise to myself.''

She could see the pleading in his eyes. The last thing he wanted was to fall in love with her.

''The Christmas Stroll must be breaking up,'' he said, glancing past her.

Marni could still hear faint Christmas music in the distance. A group of people passed in front of the store, their laughter carrying on the night air. Just a few blocks away she knew the police would be removing barricades as street cleaners came in to sweep up the last of the Christmas Stroll.

The air suddenly felt colder in the pickup; the night darker as she felt Chase pull away from her and yet not move a muscle. Snow fell harder, covering the windshield.

''We better go in,'' he said, sounding as though that was the last thing he wanted to do.

Marni opened her door and stepped out, her hand going to Sam, a connection to Chase, although a tentative one. As she stepped from the pickup into the pool of darkness beside the grocery store, she heard a sound and turned. He came out of the blackness under the stairs to the apartment. At first he was only a movement. Then a flash of white beard against the red of his costume. Santa Claus. Under the stairs?

He rushed at her, knocking her off balance. She fell back into the side of the pickup as her purse was wrenched from her grasp. A cry escaped her lips. She heard Chase slam his door and take off running past her after the mugger.

Santa sprinted across the street to the alley, her purse under his arm, with Chase in hot pursuit.

Marni leaned against the truck, her legs trembling, her pulse a drum inside her head. The sound of them running died away into the night. Cold and darkness closed in. Snowflakes fell in a white sheet of silence, cocooning her. She suddenly felt incredibly alone.

Chase. She had only a moment to fear for him before she heard it. Movement. Followed by an unerring icy awareness that the sound had come from under the wooden stairs. In the black hole of blackness beneath them. The same place the Santa mugger had hidden.

She looked but could see nothing, falling snow and night cloaking whatever hid there, as she felt for the door handle behind her, thinking she might have a chance to get inside the pickup before—

Something emerged from under the stairs, furtive, menacing, seizing her as effectively as hands around her throat.

She froze for that split second. Unable to move. To speak. To breathe. Something too large, too odd-shaped to be human moved quickly through the snow and darkness. And she knew it was coming for her.

CHASE SPRINTED after the mugger, his leg aching with the slamming movement. It was an ache he ignored. Cold anger fueled his body. He closed the distance between himself and the Santa. A mugger in Bozeman. In his neighborhood. He'd only heard of such a thing here one other time.

Santa had almost reached the end of the alley. A little closer and Chase could grab the guy's red suit. The mugger turned and Chase saw the eyes looking out of the white fake beard.

The memory came back in a sharp fast burst. Chase felt a jolt. A clear shot of memory. The truck barreling down on him and his father. The sound of the engine wound up. Streetlights reflecting off the windshield. The feel of the air, cold. The smell of snow. And the face behind the truck's steering wheel. Chase let out an oath as he saw the driver's face—the same face as the Santa in front of him.

Just then the Santa mugger flung Marni's purse hard at Chase's head. Chase didn't see it coming, didn't even know what it was until it hit him in the face, momentarily blinding him. It slowed him just enough. The Santa rounded the corner, ducked between two parked cars and disappeared into a crowd of people returning from the Stroll.

Chase stopped, leaning over to catch his breath, the memory still sharp and clear. The face of the hit-and-run driver. The face of the Santa. A man who used to work for Calloway Ranches. Monte Decker.

MARNI FUMBLED for the door handle, found it and pulled. Too late. The huge object came out of the snowstorm at her. Marni looked up it in surprise and confusion, shocked by its size, by its face. *Good God, it was the Nutcracker.* The giant toy threw itself at her, slamming her against the pickup, knocking the breath from her lungs as it tried to pin her there.

She struggled against its superior strength and size. The pressure lessened for just a moment and she thought it would run off. Then she realized that wasn't what it had in mind.

A hysterical scream jammed in her throat as she saw what it pulled from inside its costume and now held in its gloved hand. The knife blade glittered silver in the snowfall as it lunged at her.

Marni screamed.

CHASE HAD JUST bent down to pick up Marni's purse from the snow when he heard her scream.

He ran, the pain in his leg, the fire in his lungs, forgotten. Through the falling snow he could make out a shape. Huge. Misshapen. It stood over something lying on the ground beside his pickup.

My God! Marni. He didn't realize until later that he yelled. A shriek filled with anguish and fear. A war cry.

The strange figure scurried away into the snow and darkness behind the store. Chase flung himself to his knees in the snow at Marni's side and pulled her to him, feeling her warm blood soak through his mittens.

"Marni," he cried, a silent prayer racing through his head. Please, God, don't let her die.

"Chase," she whispered.

He heard a door open across the street. "Get an ambulance," he yelled. "Hurry."

She turned away, though she was embarrassing to try to see that was her maternity form. She had an...

Chapter Seventeen

Chase paced the floor of the hospital waiting room, too anxious to sit. He couldn't believe he'd been so stupid as to let a mugger trick him and draw him away from Marni so the killer could get that close to her. He cursed his stupidity, paced and prayed. When the doctor finally stuck his head out from the emergency room, Chase nearly pounced on him.

"Is she all right?" he demanded. "Tell me she's all right."

"She's fine," the doctor said quickly. "The wound is superficial. The maternity form she was wearing saved her from serious injury. She was very lucky."

"Can I take her home?" Chase asked, forgetting that just hours ago he hadn't wanted to be in the apartment with her, hadn't trusted himself.

"She's as anxious as you are to get out of here," the doctor told him. "I assume you've already talked with the police."

Chase nodded. The police had an APB out for Monte Decker and his unknown accomplice. "They've questioned Marni?"

"I believe they want her to make a formal statement later," the doctor said and pushed open the emergency-room door.

Chase saw Marni sitting on one of the gurneys, a white

bandage showing through the slash in her maternity top. In the trash was her maternity form. She saw him and got to her feet, a tentative smile on her face. He shrugged off his coat as he walked toward her.

"Just a flesh wound," she said, sounding as relieved as he felt.

He draped his coat over her shoulders. "Let's get out of here. I called us a cab."

The cab was waiting outside the hospital when they came out. Chase opened the door for her and slid in beside her. He put his arm around her, not surprised how natural it felt when she curled against him.

"Are you cold?" he asked, feeling her tremble as the cab pulled away.

She shook her head, but still he pulled her closer.

"No reason to be cold," he said, holding her, looking out into the darkness, still filled with rage at the person who'd done this to her. "Or afraid. I called the ranch and told them you lost your baby. You're safe now." He hoped.

MARNI SNUGGLED against him, needing the feel of his arm around her, his warmth soaking into her. She felt as if Sam had been real. Had been her child. And Chase's.

Chase carried her up the stairs, against her protests, and into the bedroom where he placed her on the bed with the greatest of care. He stood for a moment as if he didn't know what to do.

"Chase," she said quietly when he started to leave.

He turned to look at her, his gaze locking with hers. "It's late," he said, but didn't move, didn't stop staring into her eyes. "It, wouldn't work."

Her heart began to pound in anticipation. "What wouldn't work?" she whispered, hoping they were talking about the same thing and that he was dead wrong.

"If we made love it wouldn't change anything."

She started to tell him that she didn't care, but he cut her off.

"Making love to you would be a huge mistake," he said, moving closer. "I'd regret it. But worse, you'd regret it."

"I'd never regret it."

He shook his head. "You know when you look at me like that, what it does to me?"

"No," she answered truthfully. She only knew what his look did to her.

"And those nightclothes of yours…"

"My nightclothes?" she asked in surprise. Surely he wasn't talking about her flannel nightgown and chenille robe?

"Do you have any idea how sexy you look in them?"

She laughed, having no idea what he was talking about.

"Oh, yeah," he said, brushing a lock of her hair back from her face as he sat down on the edge of the bed next to her. "And when you sit there like that, all innocent, wide-eyed and trusting—" He let out a sigh as he brushed his bare knuckles across the skin of her cheek. "You're asking too much, Marni."

"What am I asking, Chase?" she whispered, her heart pounding at the look in his eyes.

"You're asking me to surrender my heart. I can't do it. That's what I've been trying to tell you from the moment we met."

"Not surrender," Marni said, bringing his fingers to her lips. "Just open it a little."

He cupped her face in his hands. "When I'm around you, I want to open myself up to you." He drew her to him. "Your mouth makes me crazy to kiss you. And when I look into your eyes—" He kissed her, his lips, his tongue, seeking, searching, demanding.

She gave herself to him, opening her lips to let him inside to explore, to lay claim to her. He took her mouth with an intimacy that both shocked and excited her.

She wrapped her arms around his neck and kissed him back, wanting to give as much as to receive. She hoped enthusiasm would make up for her lack of experience.

He pulled back to look into her face. "If we do this, it won't be making love," he said softly.

She smiled. "I want you, Chase. I've never wanted anyone like I want you."

She watched him unbutton her top and slide it off her shoulders to expose the jogging bra she wore underneath. She wished she were the kind of woman who wore skimpy, lacy underthings.

But to her surprise, he let out a sigh of pleasure. She followed his gaze to her breasts, and saw that her nipples strained against the stretchy material of the bra. He ran a thumb over one taut nipple, making her shudder.

He kissed her again, this time with a fever that sent her pulse skyrocketing. She felt his hands cup her bottom and she let out a sigh of pleasure of her own.

He pulled back to look at her, his blue eyes dark and serious. "I don't want to hurt you."

"You won't hurt me," she said, not sure if they were talking about her flesh wound or her heart. Then she did something totally out of character. She drew the bra over her head, exposing her bare breasts to his eyes, to his mouth, to his hands.

She felt a jolt, the tremor centering deep inside her as he tasted, touched and teased her nipples into hard, aching nubs. "Please, Chase," she pleaded, reaching for the buttons of his shirt, fumbling them open until she could lay her palms against the silken hardness of his chest. She could feel his heart hammering beneath her hands. She slid his shirt over his broad shoulders to let it drop behind him.

They sat like that for a long moment. Breathing, hearts pounding, just looking at each other. "Stop me now, Marni."

She shook her head. "I can't do that."

He slid off the bed to pull her to her feet. She melted against the warm strength of him as he tugged off her jeans. He smiled as he watched her fumble with the buttons of his jeans, then reached down to help her. As he slid out of them, out of everything, she felt his maleness against her. For one moment, she felt a sudden panic. Then she looked into his eyes and her heart filled with such love for him, she told herself nothing mattered but this moment.

She drew him down for a kiss, surprised at herself and a little embarrassed. Amusement flickered in his blue gaze. He lifted her into his arms and took her to the bed.

"Marni," he whispered as he lowered her to the mattress and lay down beside her. He ran his fingers across her lips, down her throat, over her breast. His eyes followed his fingers, then flicked back to meet her gaze when she moaned softly. "I want you so much it hurts."

She nodded, feeling her shyness come back as he pulled off her panties. To her surprise, he bent down to kiss the aching spot between her thighs. She cried out with pleasure.

"Please, Chase," she pleaded again, needing to feel him deep within her.

He slid back up her body, now slick with a fine sheen of perspiration.

"Marni, you have done this before, haven't you?" he said, looking into her eyes.

She kissed him in answer. He touched her and she opened to him, feeling both pressure and pleasure. Then he was inside her and she thought she might explode with all the sensations.

He took her with such gentleness, with slow, loving concern. And the sensations soared as high as the mountain peaks that circled the valley, as high as her hopes. Breathlessly, she held tight to him, letting him take her with him, knowing no matter what he'd said, he was making love to her.

LONG AFTER he'd felt the tremors in her subside, he held her, the heat of their bodies still melding them together as he imprinted the sensation of her skin in his mind.

He moved away from her slowly. Pushing himself up on

one elbow, he looked down into her face, shocked by the feelings inside him.

Tears ran down her cheeks. She licked at them as they touched her lips. And smiled up at him.

"Why didn't you tell me?" he demanded, more angry with himself than her. He should never had made love to her. He thought he'd known the risk he was taking with his heart. He'd been dead wrong.

"It doesn't matter."

"Like hell it doesn't. You know I would never have made love to you if I'd known."

She smiled as she looked up at him. "Yes, I know."

He swung off the bed and pulled on his jeans, feeling too naked, too vulnerable. What had made him think he could do this and not feel anything? Even if this hadn't been her first time....

"Chase," she said, touching his bare back. "I don't regret it. I'll never regret it."

He looked at her, all the anger running out of him at the sight of her. "Why me, Marni?"

She took his hand and pulled him down onto the bed. He felt himself lean toward her kiss, unable to resist. He let himself enjoy her lips against his, her bare breasts brushing against his bare chest.

When she pulled back, he looked into her eyes and quit lying to himself. Those feelings he had for this woman. He couldn't keep telling himself they weren't love. Love.

He swore softly under his breath as he let her coax him back into the bed. He lay with her, still wearing his jeans as if they were protective armor. She snuggled into the crook of his arm and he pulled her to him. He could feel her breath on his chest. His heart ached just beneath the spot.

"I love you, Chase," she whispered.

"Go to sleep," he said as he pulled her to him. "We have a big day tomorrow."

Chapter Eighteen

Christmas Eve

Marni woke to warmth—and pounding. She opened her eyes, her first sensation Chase's body spooned around hers, his arms still holding her. She snuggled against him, breathing in the scent of him, memorizing again the feel of him. Then the pounding broke through her pleasant haze.

"Chase," Marni said, sitting up a little.

He didn't open his eyes, just pulled her closer against him. "Mmm, Marni."

"Chase, there's someone at the door."

He sat up then, blinking away sleep. "Don't move." He jumped up to pull on his jeans and hurried to the door.

"Raine," she heard Chase say in surprise.

"It's the baby," Raine cried. "I have to get to the hospital but my car won't start...."

"Don't worry," Chase said. "We'll get you there. Sit down. Let me get dressed. It won't take a moment."

Marni flew out of bed, searching frantically for her clothing. She was half-dressed when Chase came back into the room.

"One of the neighbors, a college student, she's—"

"Having a baby. I heard. Give me your keys and I'll start the pickup."

Chase tossed her the keys. "She looks scared."

Marni smiled, realizing that he was hoping she'd help with Raine. "You know me," she said.

He smiled back. "Yeah, I do."

When she came out of the bedroom, Raine was perched on the edge of the couch, leaning back, holding her swollen stomach in obvious pain.

"Has your water broken yet?" Marni asked, going to the young woman.

Raine shook her head. Marni took her hand and smiled. "I'm Marni McCumber. Everything is going to be fine."

"I remember you from the store yesterday." She frowned. "Weren't you pregnant though?"

"It's a long story," Marni said. "How far apart are your contractions?"

"I don't know. I just woke up to all this pain and I knew it was the baby coming."

Marni waited until Raine got through her next contraction before she said, "I'm going to start the truck. I've watched my sisters-in-law do this a half-dozen times. There's nothing to it."

Raine smiled. "Right."

Marni had the pickup running and warming up as Chase brought Raine down the stairs. Marni slid over to the middle to let Raine into the passenger side. Chase got behind the wheel and drove through the deserted early-morning streets. He talked, telling stories about house building, of all things. Marni doubted Raine was listening but Marni loved Chase's attempt to distract the young woman from her contractions, which were steadily getting closer together.

Once at the hospital, Raine was rushed to a birthing room, while Chase filled out forms. When he finished, he asked if he could do anything to help with her bill.

"It's been paid by the adoptive parents," the woman said.

"She's giving her baby up for adoption?" Marni asked in surprise as they moved to a waiting area.

"She's unmarried, has just started college and only has a part-time job that barely supports her, let alone her and a baby," Chase said.

"What about the baby's father?"

"He's not much older than she is and not ready for this kind of responsibility, emotionally or financially," Chase said. "Raine knows she's too young to be a single mother. It wouldn't be fair to her or her baby."

"Tell me about Burton's," she said as they sat down to wait.

He shrugged. "There isn't much to tell."

"I doubt that. You own Burton's. You're a carpenter. Why do I think there's more to it than that?"

"I never lied to you, Marni," he said seriously. "I am a carpenter, although I don't do much of the work myself anymore. I own Burton's. Actually six."

"Six Burton's? Why did you name them Burton's?"

"It was my mother's name. Charlotte Burton. It was my name for fourteen years." He glanced away. "I started the stores because of her. I'd like to think our lives might have been different if there'd been a Burton's in the neighborhoods we lived in when I was a kid. If there'd been someplace my mother could have found hope."

Marni reached over and took his hand and squeezed it, tears in her eyes. "And you're a carpenter?"

"I buy old houses and fix them up and—"

"Give them away," she said, getting the picture.

Chase laughed as he met her gaze, seemingly pleased that she understood. "Jabe insisted I acknowledge him as my father. He forced his name on me and his money, dumping large sums into my account on my birthdays. I took his name. I refused to spend his money. I was working on a house for an elderly couple in the neighborhood, and I realized how many more houses I would be able to repair with Jabe's money. How many more Burton's I could open. When I told him what I was doing with his money, he almost had a coronary."

"But he kept giving you money each birthday?"

"Yeah, he did. Maybe he had a heart, after all." Chase stopped talking and looked away.

"You loved him," she said. "That's nothing to be ashamed of."

"I hated him, too," Chase said.

A nurse came down the hall toward them. "Excuse me," she said. "Your friend asked if you both would mind coming to the birthing room. I think she could use some reassurance."

They found Raine in pain, but more scared than anything else, Marni thought.

"The contractions, they're getting so close together," Raine cried as Marni took her hand.

"That's good," Marni said. "That means it's almost over. I'll help you breathe through them."

Chase had gone to the other side of the bed. He pressed a cool cloth to Raine's forehead and Marni was struck with a vision of him tending his sick mother. The man who came up with Burton's, a little hope for the neighborhood. Marni felt such a rush of love for him.

An hour later, Raine delivered a tiny baby girl. Marni saw the infant come into the world. It captured her heart with its bright eyes, head of dark straight hair and tiny button of a nose.

But it was Chase's reaction that touched her the most. He stared at the infant for a long moment, then looked up at Marni, eyes misty. A surprise, from a man who never wanted a baby of his own.

THEY WERE in Raine's room, when Chase heard his name called over the paging system. He picked up the phone, surprised to hear the sheriff's voice on the other end of the line. "I thought you might be at the hospital visiting your brother," the sheriff said without preamble. "We've picked up Monte Decker."

Chase let out a sigh of relief and smiled over at Marni.

She looked questioningly at him. "The sheriff's got your Santa mugger," he mouthed to Marni. "Did he tell you who he's working for?" Chase asked the sheriff.

"No, he says he's not talking until he gets a lawyer. But after we arrested him, we got a warrant and searched his apartment in Willow Creek."

Chase felt his heart pick up a beat.

"We found a photograph, probably the one you told us about that was missing from Marni McCumber's residence. She's an identical twin, right?"

"Monte had the photo," Chase said, trying to figure out what that meant, other than the fact that Decker had been the one who broke into Marni's house. "What about his accomplice, the person who attacked Marni?"

"We don't have anything yet, but when Monte made his one phone call, he called Calloway Ranch."

BY THE TIME they left Raine in her private room, Marni was glad to see that the young woman seemed confident that her decision to give up the baby was the right one.

"I just want my little girl to have a good home with two loving parents," she said. "Thank you for being here with me."

Marni left, thinking about that adorable baby girl in the nursery. She wondered if Chase was also thinking about the birth. It had been the first she'd ever witnessed and recalling it still moved her to tears, the miracle of it.

"Excuse me," a woman called out as they passed the front desk. "Mr. Calloway?"

"Yes?" Chase said, stepping over to the desk.

"I thought I should let someone in the family know. Your brother, Hayes Calloway. I'm afraid he checked himself out of the hospital a little while ago. Against his doctor's orders."

"You'd better call the farm and warn your family," Chase said as they headed out of the hospital.

"You think that's where he's headed?" Marni asked in

surprise. "But how—" She stopped, realizing that she'd foolishly told the whole family all about the farm at breakfast a few days ago. It would be fairly easy for any of them to find the McCumber farm. "Oh, Chase."

"Don't worry, your brothers can handle it, not that I think Hayes is a risk. I'm sure he just wants to make sure for himself that Elise and the baby are all right. I'd do the same thing if I were him."

She looked at Chase. He would, she thought, more drawn to this man as each day passed, more in love with him.

Chase was unlocking the pickup when Dayton drove up and rolled down his window.

"Did you hear?" he cried.

Was he referring to Hayes leaving the hospital or had something else happened? Marni wondered with dread. Something to do with Lilly.

"Felicia had her baby." Dayton pulled into the parking place next to theirs and got out with a bouquet of roses in one hand and cigars in the other.

"Is the baby all right?" Marni asked. She thought about what Chase had said about Felicia's determination to have the baby before Elise.

"Oh, yeah," Dayton said. "It's a baby girl. Small, but doing fine, the doctor says." He stared at Marni. "Don't tell me you delivered yours, too?"

"There was an accident," Chase said solemnly. "She lost it."

Marni watched Dayton's expression, saw the relief and wondered if he'd been the person in the Nutcracker costume.

"That's too bad," Dayton said as he shoved a cigar into Chase's pocket and started toward the hospital.

"Not exactly Mr. Sensitive, is he?" Chase commented.

"I guess you can't expect him to be brokenhearted under the circumstances," Marni whispered back.

"Hey," Dayton called to them. "You're coming up to

see her, aren't you? Candy Cane Calloway. What do you
think of that for a name?''

Marni doubted Dayton would want to know what she
thought. "We should probably go see the baby," she said
to Chase, although she could tell by his expression that he
wasn't wild about the idea.

"Candy Cane Calloway," Dayton repeated as the three
of them entered the hospital. "Great name for a kid who's
going to be loaded with dough."

When they reached the nursery, they looked through the
window and saw that the Calloway baby's bassinet was
empty. "She must be with Felicia," Dayton said, sounding
a little worried.

CHASE DIDN'T WANT to think about Felicia and Dayton as
parents. It frightened him more than thinking of himself as
one. And it was something he'd thought about since Marni
McCumber had turned up on his doorstep claiming to be
pregnant with his child. After witnessing Raine's daughter's birth, he couldn't get it out of his head.

When they walked into Felicia's room, the nurse was
handing Felicia her baby.

"It isn't going to spit up on me again, is it?" Felicia
asked, awkwardly taking the baby.

"Babies do that," the nurse said.

Chase watched Felicia accept the warm bottle from the
nurse and poke it at the baby's mouth. Any doubts he had
about what kind of mother Felicia would make were
quickly answered.

The baby began to cry. "Here," she said, calling after
the nurse. "Do something with her."

"It's your baby, Mrs. Calloway," the nurse said and
closed the door behind her.

"We're going to get a nanny," Dayton said to no one
in particular.

"Dayton!" Felicia cried, holding the blanket-wrapped
baby out to him.

"Don't look at me," he said in horror.

Marni stepped to Felicia's bedside and took the wriggling, crying infant from her. She held the baby to her breast and rocked it gently, cooing softly. The infant hushed after a moment, something not lost on Chase.

Chase watched, mesmerized by the sight. He felt a strong tug on his heartstrings; Marni looked so right with a baby in her arms.

She smiled as she peeked into the blanket. Then let out a cry. Chase rushed to her side to see what was wrong.

"Is something wrong with my baby?" Felicia demanded.

Marni stood staring down at the baby, her eyes wide. "This baby—"

Chase looked down at the infant in her arms and swore. Marni hadn't been the only person pretending to be pregnant. His gaze flicked up to settle on Dayton.

"What's wrong?" Dayton demanded.

"This isn't your baby," Chase said.

"Of course it is."

Chase shook his head. "You'd do anything for money, wouldn't you, Dayton? Even buy a baby and try to pass it off as your own."

"Get the hell out of here," Dayton cried, sounding tougher than he looked. "You have no right to—"

"I have every right," Chase said, advancing on his half brother. "I was there when this baby came into the world."

"What's going on in here?" the nurse demanded from the doorway.

"Could you take the baby back to the nursery?" Chase asked.

"Oh, Dayton," Felicia wailed. "I told you this wasn't going to work."

The nurse took a moment to assess the situation, then lifted the baby from Marni's arms. Chase saw how hard it was for Marni to give her up and wanted to bury his fist in Dayton's face.

"You're a liar, Dayton," Chase said through gritted teeth

the moment the nurse left with the baby. "You just proved that. I've thought from the beginning that you killed Jabe. I didn't understand why. But I do now."

"You're wrong," Dayton said, holding up his hands. "I didn't kill the old man. All I did was adopt a baby. There's no law against that."

"You don't think trying to pass off this baby as your own to collect the inheritance is illegal?" Chase asked. "You knew Raine would deliver before Elise, you knew she was small and so was her baby. You figured you could pass off the infant as premature because of that. And it might have worked, if we hadn't been at that particular baby's birth."

"All right, maybe I was wrong but—"

"You had motive and opportunity to kill Jabe. You couldn't let him change his will back because you already had this baby scam going." But because of that, Chase realized Dayton had no reason to want Marni dead. He knew Raine would give birth first.

"I tried to talk him out of leaving his money to the first kid," Dayton cried. "He wouldn't listen. He was so determined to have a grandchild, preferably yours. And then when this—" he waved a hand in Marni's direction "—woman showed up seven months pregnant— What choice did I have? Let you get the money? But I didn't kill Father. I *couldn't* kill Father."

Dayton looked at Marni then Chase. "So what's the big deal? Neither of us wins. You don't have a baby and neither do I. That means half of the old man's riches gets divided equally among the three of us, right? With half to Mother."

Chase wasn't about to tell Dayton that a Calloway baby would be born soon. Let him be surprised when Elise and Hayes's baby inherited the money. By then, Chase had hoped Dayton would be behind bars for the murder of Jabe Calloway. Now he wasn't so sure.

"Oh, Chase," Marni cried the moment they left Felicia's room. She threw herself into his arms. He held her tightly.

"Don't worry, the baby will be fine," Chase said. "We'll find someone else to adopt her. The baby is a little jaundiced, so she has to stay in the nursery for a few days anyway. By the time she's ready to leave, we'll have adoptive parents for her."

Marni nodded into his shoulder. "Just the thought of Dayton and Felicia—"

"I know. Let's get out of here."

"Where are we going?" she asked once they were in the pickup and headed down Highland Boulevard toward town.

"To lunch," he said, smiling over at her, hoping food would make them both feel better. "A late lunch, or an early dinner," he said, surprised to find it was late afternoon. "My stomach's growling," he lied. He just wanted out of the hospital and to be alone with Marni. But not back at the apartment. Not yet, anyway. "The sheriff can wait. We'll stop on the way and call the farm and warn them about Hayes."

She looked worried. "Everything's going to be all right now," he assured her, praying that was true.

By now his family would have heard that Marni was no longer pregnant, he told himself. That should make her safe. He shoved away that little voice in his head that argued the killer was still at large and as long as he was, neither Marni nor Elise were safe.

"Lunch," he said. They'd have lunch, then he'd figure out what to do about the news the sheriff had given him.

"Lunch, huh?" she said, smiling back at him. "Let me guess? A can of soup, crackers and another ball game?"

"All right, I admit I was trying to keep you at a distance."

She laughed. "Do you think I didn't know that? Too bad I like canned soup and ball games on TV, huh?"

His look caressed her face. "I admit it didn't work."

She shook her head, no it didn't. "Are you sorry?"

His gaze turned so serious it scared her. "Only if I end up hurting you."

She heard the pain in his voice. "You won't," she said, sliding over to snuggle against him. "About that lunch, what exactly did you have in mind?"

He watched her, often surprised by what he saw. A freshness, a wholesomeness and yet a passionate, interesting, compassionate woman. Marni McCumber saw the good in everybody. What did she see in him? he wondered. What if she was wrong about him?

"No soup, no ball game, no crackers," he said, heading out of town.

She laughed when he pulled up in front of Guadalupe's Mexican restaurant. And seemed pleased when he asked for a back booth with candlelight, and ordered them both chile rellenos and kissed her the moment the waiter left the table.

"Mmm," Marni said. "What did you have in mind for dessert?"

"We need to talk," Chase said seriously.

The waiter returned and put a bowl of salsa and chips in front of them and two tall beers. Marni took a sip of beer.

"Everything's happened so fast," he said, knowing how lame that sounded. "Marni, I don't know how I feel about some…things."

"About me, isn't that what you mean?" she asked quietly.

"No, I know how I feel about you, dammit. I'm just having a hard time seeing myself married."

"Who said anything about marriage?" she asked, a catch in her voice.

He wanted to laugh. "Marni, you're the marrying kind." She started to interrupt, probably to argue that she wasn't, but he stopped her. "I'm not sure about marriage, let alone kids. And don't tell me you don't want babies. I saw how you were with Raine's baby girl."

Marni touched her cheek to brush away a tear. "Pretending to be pregnant with your baby made me realize that I do want a baby." She looked into his eyes. "I want your baby, Chase. But I'll wait as long as it takes."

"That's what I'm trying to tell you, Marni. I'm not sure I can give you that. Ever."

The waiter brought their food and Chase mentally kicked himself for killing both of their appetites. His timing was amazing but he'd felt he needed to be truthful with her. He cared too much about her not to be.

He changed the subject, telling her what the sheriff had told him about the photo and Monte Decker's phone call.

"Someone at that house hired him," Chase said. He added, "Monte and Lilly were friends when he worked for Calloway Ranch. Maybe even lovers. Lilly knew about Elise and Hayes. Hayes said himself she was furious. When you add in her drinking problem—"

"What if Lilly doesn't drink as much as everyone thinks she does?" Marni asked. "What if she's just pretending to be unstable?"

He found himself staring at her in disbelief. "Why would Lilly do that?"

"She said something to me about being safe as long as they didn't know she knew what was going on."

"That shows how stable she is," he said.

"Look how she was at the funeral."

"Exactly."

"Don't you think it's amazing," Marni said, "that she was capable of driving all the way from the ranch if she was as drunk as she seemed? I just feel like there's more going on with her than we know."

"There is," he said, trying to keep his voice down. "She knows about Elise and Hayes and she thinks you're Elise. Isn't that enough?"

"She knew about Elise and Hayes when I was at the ranch and she thought I was Elise," Marni said. "Remember the day she gave me the baby booties? She said then that she should hate me but that I wasn't the one to blame."

He raked his hand through his hair. "Marni, for all we know she had just tried to kill you in the attic. She came back to see if she'd succeeded and must have heard the two of us talking by the toppled armoire. So she snatched the booties and gave them to you to sucker you in."

Marni started to argue but he cut her off. "What if Lilly's dangerous as hell? What if she's behind all these accidents? After her baby died, she blamed everyone. She was convinced for a while that Vanessa had purposely killed it." He sighed. "I didn't tell you this, but Lilly had an accident during her pregnancy. She fell down the stairs. She blamed Vanessa. Said Vanessa somehow...tripped her. Then later, when the baby died—"

"No wonder there doesn't seem to be any love lost between Lilly and Vanessa," Marni said thoughtfully. "If Lilly really believes Vanessa purposely tripped her— That's what Hayes meant about it not happening again. I just wonder what that scene was about at the funeral. It seemed so...strange."

"The point is," he continued, "Lilly has a lot of bitterness in her. She hated Jabe. Not that I blame her. When it came out that her baby wasn't Hayes's, Jabe threatened to throw her out on the street."

"You don't really think she killed Jabe?" Marni asked in surprise.

"Jabe had so many enemies in that house, who knows. But Lilly was definitely one of them. And let's face it, Jabe's guard was already down because of the painkillers. Lilly would have seemed so harmless to Jabe. He might not have realized she put painkillers into his drink. A woman could have helped Jabe pull the trigger after the amount of painkillers he'd ingested."

When Monte Decker confessed, would he link Lilly to his crimes? Dayton? Or someone Chase was overlooking?

They finished their meal and Chase ordered them both flan for dessert.

"Your father mentioned that you're a Jane Austen fan," Marni said out of the blue.

"I used to read Austen to my mother when she wasn't feeling well. She never got tired of hearing *Pride and Prejudice*."

Marni reached across the table, smiling as she took his hand and squeezed it. "You never cease to amaze me, Chase Calloway."

He saw the love in her eyes, unconditional, and said the words that had filled his head and his heart for days. "I love you, Marni."

The words instantly brought tears to her eyes. Her smile widened. "Do you believe in Christmas wishes?" she asked.

His heart gave a leap and he realized with a start what day it was. Christmas Eve. And he hadn't gotten Marni anything for Christmas.

"Surely you wished for more than that," he said. "I wanted to buy you something special."

"Chase," she said, meeting his loving gaze with one of her own. "Telling me that you love me is the best, most special Christmas present you could have given me."

As they left the restaurant, Chase found himself wanting to give her any and everything she wished for. But could he give her the one thing he knew she wanted more than anything on earth?

They started across the road to his pickup and Chase heard a sound that made his blood freeze solid.

A car, engine revved to the max. As it bore down on them, Chase felt that split second feeling of déjà vu.

Chase grabbed Marni and flung them both into the snow-filled barrow pit beside the road. The car sped past, the wheels so close Chase could hear them throwing up chunks of ice. The car rounded the corner and was gone.

"Are you all right?" Chase cried, getting to his feet.

She nodded as he helped her up. She looked shaken but unhurt. "What about you?"

He nodded, too, relief filling him that she was all right.

"Hold me?" she said, stepping into his arms.

He wrapped his arms around her and they stood that way for a long time.

"Don't you think we'd better call the sheriff?" she said, pulling back to look at him.

"Did you see the person driving the car?"

She shook her head.

All he'd seen was a dark car. He hadn't seen the driver this time. He glanced toward the restaurant. The road was empty, the curtains drawn behind the windows.

He'd wanted to believe that Marni was safe. Monte Decker was in jail. As far as the family knew, Elise McCumber had lost her baby. So why had someone just tried to run them down?

Maybe it had nothing to do with Jabe Calloway's first-born grandchild. Maybe it was much more personal. Lilly still had reason to hate Marni even if Marni was no longer pregnant. And Dayton had reason to hate them both. Or maybe the hit-and-run hadn't even been for Marni. Maybe it had been someone who didn't want him to find out who killed Jabe Calloway.

AFTER THEY'D GIVEN their statements to Sheriff Danner, Chase drove back to the apartment, trying to form a plan. Monte Decker wasn't talking yet, the sheriff said. And it was Christmas Eve. But more important, Marni was still in danger.

He heard her filling the tub, the sweet rich scent of the vanilla bubble bath he'd bought for her at the store filling the air.

He went to stand in the open doorway and watch her undress, reveling in the sight.

She smiled at him as she climbed into the tub. "Did you want to join me?"

Yes. He ached to join her. But he wanted her safe even more than he wanted to make love to her.

He could no longer stand the thought of her risking her life further. Every instinct in him fought to protect her, to rush her to safety, but he knew no place would be safe until the killer was caught.

He raked a hand through his hair and looked at her. "I want this over with."

"So do I."

He stepped to the tub and she pulled him down for a kiss. He smiled at her as he straightened, his love for her overpowering every emotion. "Give me a second and I'll join you."

He headed toward the kitchen for two glasses and a bottle of wine.

That's when he noticed for the first time the light flashing on the answering machine. For just an instant, he almost ignored it. But it might be the sheriff with good news. He hit play.

"Elise." A woman's voice, slurred with either booze or emotion. "I know who killed Jabe." Chase cursed silently. Lilly's voice. "I have proof. I also have Jabe's will, the one he wrote the day he died. But they're never going to let me leave here alive. They keep me doped up. If they knew I was calling you now—" A sound in the background. "Oh, I should have known it would be you—" A thud. Something heavy hit the floor. The phone bounced on the hardwood. Someone picked it up before it could bounce again. Silence. Then they hung up.

Chase looked up to see Marni standing in the bathroom doorway in only a towel. He took one look at her face and knew they were going back to the ranch.

Chapter Nineteen

They drove through the moonless night, the stars distant, the sky a black hood. Marni sat on the bench seat beside Chase, staring out the window at the ice-glazed highway, her heart a fierce thunder in her chest.

Not far out of Dry Creek, the pavement turned to snow-pack. Christmas lights disappeared with the farmhouses. Soon there was nothing but rolling snow-covered hills and sagebrush, rocky bluffs and creek bottom. And eventually, she thought, Calloway Ranch. And Lilly.

Marni felt Chase's trepidation. Someone in this family still wanted one or both of them dead. Tonight's near hit-and-run proved that. Was Lilly behind it as Chase thought? Or was she in just as much trouble—or more—than they were?

They'd tried to call the ranch but the phone was off the hook.

"You know this could be a fool's errand," Chase had said before they left the apartment.

"Even you're worried about Lilly," she said, looking over at him as she picked up her coat.

Now he drove the pickup, the headlights probing the darkness ahead, the tires busting through the occasional drift where the snow had blown across the country road.

As they followed the creek, the dark silhouette of the mountains disappeared, snow filled the sky, obliterating everything, giving Marni the impression of driving into a bottomless pit.

They crossed the narrow bridge. Marni could feel Chase's tension, as strong as her own. Through the snowfall, she saw Calloway Ranch, a dark beast that seemed to hunker in the storm, waiting for something. Or someone.

"This house gives me the creeps," Marni said, more to herself than Chase as he parked the pickup in the yard. A single light shone in the house. Unless Marni missed her guess, it was coming from Jabe's library.

"I guess I don't need to tell you I don't like this," Chase said. "But I wasn't about to leave you at the apartment alone." He had insisted on calling the sheriff before they'd left; a deputy was supposed to meet them out here. But there was no sheriff's car parked with the other cars in front of the house.

"We should wait for the deputy," Chase said.

"It might be too late by the time he gets here." It might already be too late.

Chase let out a low curse as he opened the glove box and pulled out a flashlight. He shoved it into his jacket pocket next to his .357 in the holster under his arm, then reached across the seat to take Marni's hand in his. He gave it a quick squeeze before he opened his door.

They walked up the steps to the porch, their breaths white clouds in front of their faces. Chase knocked. Silence and snow enveloped them and the house. He tried the door. It opened to his touch and he looked over at Marni, and frowned.

"This feels too easy," he whispered.

"Lilly might have left it open for us," Marni said.

Chase didn't look relieved by that thought. Were they walking into a trap? Was this something Lilly had planned all along, sucking in Marni just as Chase suspected?

They stepped into the foyer. Light spilled out of the open door of the library. And the sound of voices, several raised

n anger. Vanessa's and Dayton's voices. They were shout-
ng, so it wasn't surprising they hadn't heard Chase knock.

The two stood facing each other in front of the fire. Fel-
cia sat in a chair off to the side, a wineglass in her hand,
a sour look on her face.

"What is this, a falling-out among thieves?" Chase said
from the doorway.

The three turned in surprise.

"What are you doing here?" Dayton demanded.

"We came to see Lilly," Marni said.

"Whatever for?" Felicia laughed and took another drink.

"Haven't you caused enough trouble for one day?" Vanessa snapped. She swept across the room to the liquor
cabinet, tossed in several ice cubes, then splashed bourbon
into her glass.

"So you heard about Dayton's little baby scam," Chase
said. "Or were you in on it from the beginning?"

Vanessa shot him a withering look. "I most certainly
was not. But what choice did he have under the circumstances?" Her cheeks were flushed, her hair not quite as
perfect as it usually was. She'd discarded her widow black
for a jewel-tone dress that fit like an expensive glove.

"The choices we make are what life's all about, don't
you think, Vanessa?" Chase said, settling his gaze on Day-
on. Dayton squirmed.

"Chase is convinced that I killed Father," Dayton
whined to his mother.

Vanessa looked shocked. Marni watched her, surprised
at how nervous she seemed. "Why in God's name would
Dayton do that?"

"To keep Jabe from changing his will back," Chase said
calmly. "For the money."

"Where is Lilly?" Marni asked, growing more worried
by the minute. Something felt wrong, horribly wrong.

The ice in Vanessa's drink rattled. "She should be down
any moment. To open Christmas presents."

"I think we'd better go look for her," Chase said.

"Good luck," Felicia said. "Who knows where the little waif is hiding."

Marni knew Felicia was right. If Lilly didn't want to be found, they'd never find her in this house. But if she was in trouble somewhere—

"Lilly is fine," Vanessa said with obvious aggravation. "I don't know why you're so concerned with her, why you're so concerned with my family." Her gaze came to rest on Marni's flat stomach. "There seems to be no reason for it."

"Lilly's probably passed out somewhere," Dayton said with disgust as he plopped into a chair.

"We got a strange phone call from her," Chase said. "She said she knew who killed Jabe. She also said she has Jabe's will, the one he wrote just before he died. The call was interrupted and we think she might have met with an accident, Calloway style."

Vanessa put down her glass a little too hard. "That's ridiculous," she said, splashing more bourbon into the glass before moving back to the fire. "Lilly's fine. And all this talk of another will is just holding up probate. I'm sick of it. I need money to run this place, and Lilly—" Vanessa stopped, her face contorted in anger. "Jabe didn't write another will."

"Yes he did," came a voice.

Vanessa dropped the glass in her hand as Lilly's muffled voice echoed through the room. The glass hit the hardwood floor, shattering as the door to the secret passageway opened at the corner of the bookshelf by the fireplace and Lilly stumbled into the room.

At first Marni thought she was drunk, then she saw the blood. It had run down her face from a gash in her left temple, staining the pale pink dress she wore.

Marni and Chase both stepped toward her but Lilly motioned for them to stay back with a hand that held a gun. In her other hand was the scarf Lilly had worn to the funeral, Vanessa's scarf.

"You know there's a will because Jabe told you all about it," Lilly said to Vanessa. "I heard everything from in there." She pointed at the open doorway to the passageway.

"Lilly, you're hurt," Marni cried, staring into Lilly's dirt-smudged face. My God, where had the woman been?

Lilly waved the pistol to hold everyone back. "Vanessa tried to kill me. Then she hid my body in the wall when she heard Dayton and Felicia come home."

"She's drunk," Vanessa said, her voice unsteady. "She probably fell down."

"Yes," Lilly said, glaring at her mother-in-law. "Just like I fell down the stairs when I was pregnant. You knew it wasn't Hayes's baby, didn't you? You even tried to kill Elise McCumber."

"She's babbling," Vanessa said. "And bleeding all over the floor. Dayton, why don't you get Lilly something to calm her down."

Lilly swung the pistol around and aimed it at Dayton. "You aren't going to keep me drugged up anymore, you aren't going to make me think I'm crazy anymore, either. I know what you've been doing. You put my nursery furniture in that room. You put that doll in my baby's crib. And the tape recorder. You did that and then you made it look like I did. You tried to make me think I was losing my mind."

Marni felt sick at the hate she heard in Lilly's voice. And the fear. My God, Marni thought, Lilly still wasn't sure she hadn't done all those things.

"I don't know anything about a room or a tape recorder," Vanessa said, shaking her head at Lilly.

"Liar!" Lilly screamed, pointing the pistol at her. "I know what you're capable of. I heard Jabe tell you he was cutting your sons out of the will and leaving everything to Chase, the only son he could trust."

Marni saw that Vanessa had gone as stone-cold white as the snow outside; her look said she *could* kill Lilly.

"You got him a drink and tried to reason with him, but

he wouldn't listen," Lilly continued, hatred in her eyes. "I saw you put the pills in the drink. I waited, just like you did. Then I saw you put the gun to his head and pull the trigger. And I have proof." She held out the scarf. "You used your scarf to hold the gun. You got Jabe's blood on it."

Marni stared at the scarf in Lilly's hand. Even from where she stood, she could see the dark red stain on it.

"Probably her own blood," Dayton said, coming to his mother's defense, but not sounding very convincing. He got to his feet, looking as if he might bolt from the room at any moment.

"Everyone saw your reaction at the funeral when I showed up wearing this scarf," Lilly said to Vanessa. "You hid the scarf after you killed Jabe, but I saw where."

Vanessa hadn't moved. She stood, visibly trembling, her face ashen, a look of horror in her eyes. "A scarf with blood on it. What does that prove? No one will believe anything you say, Lilly. Not the word of a lush."

"I have the will, Vanessa," Lilly said, smiling at the older woman. "You were afraid I had it and I was going to tell someone, weren't you? That's why you tried to kill me when you overhead me call Marni."

Marni? Marni shot Lilly a look. How did Lilly know her real name? Had she figured it out when she'd seen the photograph of the two sisters? The photo Monte Decker had taken when he broke into Marni's house.

Marni felt sick. Maybe Chase had been right all along. Maybe Lilly had killed Jabe, had made those attempts on Marni's life, had staged this whole thing to get even with Vanessa for the accident on the stairs that she believed had caused her baby to die.

"You thought Jabe hadn't written the new will yet, but then you started to suspect that he had," Lilly said as she edged her way over to the bookshelf. "If I had the scarf, maybe I had the will, huh?"

"What does this new will say?" Felicia asked.

Lilly swayed slightly as if weak from her loss of blood. Marni felt Chase tense beside her. She placed a hand on his arm in warning. Lilly seemed a little unsteady on her feet, but she was still armed and still seemed capable of shooting anyone who moved toward her.

Lilly dropped the scarf on the couch and pulled out a book, one of the Jane Austen books that Marni suspected had belonged to Lottie Burton. Of course that would be where Jabe would hide the will. Lilly opened the book and removed a folded sheet of paper with writing on it.

Vanessa moved more quickly than Marni had thought possible. She leaped forward and snatched the paper from Lilly's hand and tossed it into the fireplace before anyone could react. The flames devoured the sheet instantly.

Lilly let the hand holding the pistol drop to her side. She looked tired, but sober, even sane. "You just implicated yourself, Vanessa. In front of witnesses. You didn't really think that was the actual will?"

Vanessa turned slowly to glare at Lilly, her face twisted in rage.

"Jabe lied to you, Vanessa," Lilly said calmly. "He didn't cut your sons out of his will. He was just angry and taking it out on you. Instead, he did what he'd promised Chase he would, amended his will to leave half of his estate to you, and the rest equally divided among his three sons. Too bad you won't get your share now."

Lilly must have anticipated Vanessa's next move. Just as Vanessa lunged at her, Lilly stepped into the secret passageway.

Chase grabbed for Vanessa, but not quickly enough. Dayton jumped between them, shoving Chase aside. Chase stumbled back into a chair, righting himself just as Vanessa disappeared after Lilly into the walls of the house. Dayton sprang after them; the panel door closed before Chase could reach it.

He swore and turned to race from the library toward the other entrance under the stairs with Marni at his heels. Felicia hadn't moved. She sat watching with a bored look on her face, her drink still in her hand.

Marni rushed to the paneling and quickly opened the door under the stairs. Chase pulled the flashlight from his pocket and started up the steps. Marni followed. They'd gone only a few steps when a gunshot thundered above them and a scream echoed through the inner walls of the house. Another gunshot boomed. Then silence.

Chase swore and pulled the .357 from his holster. "Stay right behind me."

They followed the stairway up, in the direction of a faint sound overhead, until they reached the attic. Marni wasn't surprised to find the door open.

The smell of old furniture and dust mingled with Lilly's scent, gardenia. And Marni realized that Lilly hadn't been wearing perfume in the library. So why did the attic smell of it? She felt a chill as they stepped deeper into the walls of antique furniture.

The beam of Chase's flashlight skittered across the floor, across the massive furniture, then back to a tallboy a few feet away. The light lingered on a corner of an old oak buffet. A piece of clothing had caught on the rough edge. The torn cloth was pale pink.

Marni hung close to Chase as he stepped around the buffet and stopped abruptly. She heard him curse. Looking down, she saw Dayton Calloway lying sprawled on the floor in a pool of blood.

"Oh God, Chase," Marni cried.

He pulled her to him for a moment, holding her with his free arm. "Do you hear that?" he whispered.

Marni felt a chill as she listened. The tape recorder of the baby crying. Lilly's baby. And Vanessa's voice as she tried to soothe the child.

Cautiously they stepped around Dayton, around the toppled armoire and edged their way toward the nursery. Marni could hear the sound of the baby crying softly and Vanessa's voice growing more impatient. Then another sound. The squeak of a rocker, rocking back and forth, back and forth. It made her blood run cold.

The door to the nursery stood open. Marni could see Lilly sitting in the rocker by the window, holding something in her arms, crying softly. Where was the gun? And where was Vanessa?

"Oh God," Marni heard Chase say.

Off to their right, sitting on the floor, her back against the wall, was Vanessa. She stared straight ahead, a look of horror on her face, her hands clutching her chest, blood seeping out through her fingers. Chase looked back at Lilly, still rocking, her gaze at the window.

"She still has the gun," Marni cried.

"Stay here." Chase bent to enter the room. Marni watched as he carefully neared the rocker. "It's over, Lilly," he said in the same tone he talked to the horses. Gentle. Soft. Caring. It brought tears to Marni's eyes.

Lilly looked up at him and smiled. "I took the will from the book and stitched it inside the doll," she said, unfolding the blanket to reveal the worn rag doll.

"Where is the gun, Lilly?" Chase asked.

She glanced back past Chase, then raised her hand slowly to point at Marni. Marni frowned, momentarily confused. Then she felt two strong arms grab her from behind and felt the cold steel of the gun's barrel against her temple.

"You're right, Chase," Dayton said. "It's over and you lose."

Chapter Twenty

Chase turned slowly, feeling the weight of the gun in his hand, realization weighing down his heart. Dayton stood, the wound in his side still bleeding but a smile on his face and a pistol pointed at Marni's head. Behind Chase Lilly continued to rock as if oblivious to what was happening. Or maybe she just didn't care anymore. From in the crib came the sound of the baby again, whimpering softly.

"Nice trick, huh?" Dayton said. "Thought I was dead." He shook his head at his brother. "And Father thought you were the smart one, the special one."

"Is that what this is all about?" Chase demanded.

"I got so sick of hearing about Chase, how wonderful he was, how worthless Hayes and I were," Dayton said angrily.

"Jabe was a fool. But Marni doesn't have anything to do with this. Let her go. This is between you and me now."

Dayton laughed. "Marni has everything to do with it."

Chase had been so sure Lilly was the culprit. "You were the one who tried to kill her. You hired Monte Decker." The steady movement of the rocker almost drowned out the soft crying sound of a baby coming from the crib. "You tried to run Marni and me down earlier."

Dayton smiled. "That was foolish. This is so much better. Everyone will think it was Lilly, poor sick, drunk Lilly. Killed her whole family. Except for Dayton Calloway. Only wounded, he managed to get away and call for help. I'll be a hero. A very rich hero.''

Lord, Chase thought. The man had shot himself. Chase knew now exactly what he was dealing with. His fear level rocketed upward. He met Marni's gaze, silently promising her he'd do whatever he had to, even if it meant giving his own life.

She shook her head, tears flooding her eyes. ''I love you,'' she mouthed.

''Drop the gun, Chase,'' Dayton said angrily. ''You're just sappy enough to try something stupid.''

''What do I have to lose?'' Chase asked, holding tight to the .357 in his hand. ''You plan to kill us all anyway. Maybe I'll kill you before you kill me.''

''Maybe,'' Dayton said, looking a little worried. ''But then you'll have to see Marni's brains blown all over this attic. If you drop the gun, I'll kill you first and spare you that.''

Yeah, Chase just bet he would. But still, he had little choice. He lowered the pistol to the floor, praying that Dayton would slip up and give him just one small chance. That's all he'd need.

''Very good,'' Dayton said. ''Now kick the gun into the corner and come on out of there. You too Lilly.''

Behind him, Chase heard the rocking stop and Lilly rise slowly from the chair. ''You did this, didn't you?'' Lilly said, looking over at the crib. ''To make me look crazy.''

''You are crazy,'' Dayton said. ''You just didn't know how crazy you were until I helped you find out. Crying over that rag doll, listening all the time to that tape with your dead baby crying on it.''

Chase bent to come out of the room and Dayton stepped back, pulling Marni with him. Lilly followed, clutching the rag doll still wrapped in its blanket.

''You should listen to the tape,'' Lilly said to Marni. ''I'm not the one who's crazy. I wasn't the one who killed my baby.''

Lilly advanced on Dayton and Marni, the doll in her arms.

"Get back, you stupid woman," Dayton cried.

Lilly didn't seem to hear him. "See, Dayton," she said as she pulled back the baby blanket. "See what you've done."

Chase watched Lilly, his pulse thundering in his ears. Lilly would either get them all killed or—

Lilly grabbed the doll from the blanket with one hand, thrusting it into Dayton's face at the same time she thrust with the other hand, the hand still hidden in the baby blanket.

Dayton recoiled at the sight of the worn rag doll. But not quickly enough because he couldn't drag Marni with him. Lilly went in from the side, driving the knitting needles into his side. Dayton screamed.

Chase sprung, throwing himself at the gun in Dayton's hand. Dayton got off only one shot. But it went wild as Chase knocked the gun away. The sound thundered through the attic.

Chase pushed Marni aside, driving his fist into Dayton's face. Dayton fell back, the knitting needles still stuck in his side, agony in his features as he hit the floor hard. He reached for the gun lying between him and Vanessa but she reached it first. She lifted the gun, pointing it at Dayton.

"You don't understand, Mother," Dayton cried. "If you went to prison for Father's murder— The bad publicity. But if you were killed by Lilly—"

The gun wavered in Vanessa's hand as she stared at her son, her favorite son, the spoiled one. She let her arm drop. Marni quickly picked up the pistol and handed it to Chase.

From inside the nursery, he could hear the baby crying loudly now on the tape. Then Vanessa's angry voice. "All we need is another bastard in the family." The baby's crying stopped abruptly. The tape ended.

Epilogue

*Christmas Eve
One year later*

Marni smiled as snow began to fall the moment they turned onto the road to the farm.

"You're going to get your white Christmas," Chase said as he reached across the seat to squeeze Marni's hand. "I know how you love Christmas."

Had it only been a year ago that she'd made a Christmas wish on a star in this same winter sky? She glanced at Chase, realizing she'd gotten more than she could have ever wished for.

"Oh, Chase, I can hardly wait." She took his hand and placed it on her swollen stomach. "Feel that?" she asked and saw his eyes widen. "That's your son."

He smiled at his wife, his gaze filled with love. "Our son." In the car seat behind them, their daughter let out a cry of delight as she spied the falling snow. "Jingle Bells" came on the radio and Chase began to sing along to Laramie Burton Calloway's delight. She clapped her hands, laughing at the faces her daddy made at her in the rearview mirror.

Ahead, the bright Christmas lights of the large old farmhouse glittered brightly. Marni felt her heart race with excitement and sheer happiness at the sight. So much had happened in the past year, but they were finally coming home for Christmas. It didn't seem possible that so much good could come out of so much pain.

Elise had given birth to a beautiful baby girl, Elizabeth Marni Calloway, in early February, just days after Hayes's divorce was final. By Valentine's Day, Elise and Hayes were married. Hayes doted on both mother and daughter.

Lilly had spent some time in a private hospital out of state, then had enrolled in business school. The last Marni heard from her, she was thinking of opening her own business. A knitting shop. She'd met a man in her weekly therapy group. Like her, he'd lost a child.

Monte Decker had confessed that Dayton hired him to run down Jabe Calloway and later to lure Chase away from Marni on the night of the Christmas Stroll. Dayton swore he'd only wanted Monte to frighten his father—not hurt him. As for Marni, Dayton finally admitted that he'd been behind Marni's accidents, including the knife attack outside Burton's. It hadn't been anything personal, he'd said. He just couldn't let her give birth to the first grandchild of Jabe Calloway.

From the beginning, he'd planned to implicate Lilly. He knew she often hid in the tiny room off the attic, mourning the loss of her baby. He'd made it into a nursery after Marni arrived at Calloway Ranch looking seven months pregnant and claiming to be carrying Chase's baby.

Dayton had bragged that the tape recorder in the crib had been a stroke of genius. He'd stumbled across the tapes in Lilly's room and realized that right after her baby was born she'd left a tape recorder going in the nursery at night, afraid for her child since the family had found out the baby wasn't a real Calloway.

Her paranoia had paid off for Dayton. Once he'd started playing the tapes, Lilly had gotten much worse, believing Vanessa had killed her baby. The truth was, the baby had died of sudden infant death syndrome. But Lilly had convinced herself Vanessa was to blame. That obsession only made Lilly look all the more guilty of Dayton's crimes.

Dayton had hired Monte Decker because he knew of Monte's relationship with Lilly. Monte hadn't known Dayton was planning to frame Lilly. It had been Monte who'd told Lilly that Elise had an identical twin named Marni McCumber. When Hayes left the hospital, Lilly had known he'd gone to meet Elise and that the woman she knew had to be Marni.

Shooting his mother that night in the attic had been an accident, Dayton claimed. Dayton still felt bad about it, he said.

After he'd pleaded guilty, the judge sentenced him to forty years without parole at Deer Lodge, the Montana state prison. The last Marni heard, he was making horsehair key chains and still blaming what had happened to him on bad luck.

Vanessa died the night of the shooting. The blood on her scarf turned out to be Jabe's just as Lilly had said. Lilly's testimony convinced the sheriff to change Jabe Calloway's death from suicide to murder.

Felicia Calloway fled the state and the scandal. The last Marni heard, she'd changed her name and was dating a computer business tycoon.

With Jabe's will from inside Lilly's rag doll, Hayes and Chase inherited the entire Calloway estate. Hayes moved back to the ranch and took over for his father. At one point he thought about tearing down the house, but when he and Elise got married, she talked him out of it.

"Wait until you see what I can do with this place," she'd told him. Hayes and Elise and their baby girl brought happiness to the old house, something it had never known. Elise replaced the darkness inside with light and brought all the original antiques down from the attic. And with her dramatic style, she threw parties that brought laughter into the house, chasing away the ghosts.

Last year, Chase and Marni arrived at the farm just as

the sun came up on Christmas Day, just in time to watch the kids open their presents.

The happy clamor of the McCumber clan helped ease the horror they'd both just lived through.

Later that day, after the family had scattered, Marni had found Chase standing before the Christmas tree. She'd come up behind him and put her cheek against his back as she wrapped her arms around him.

"Are you all right?" she'd asked softly.

She felt him nod.

"There's two things I need to ask you," he said, turning around to face her.

She held her breath.

"I never thought I'd ever say these words but, Marni, you've made me realize how much was missing from my life," he said quietly. "I can't imagine life without you now. Nor do I want to." He took her hands in his, his blue-eyed gaze searched her face. "Will you marry me?"

"Oh, Chase," she cried, throwing herself into his arms. "I can't imagine my life without you, either."

He laughed and held her tightly to him. "I was hoping you'd say that. But does that mean yes?"

"Yes, oh yes," she cried, pulling back to look into his face. "But you said you had two questions to ask me."

He nodded. "I couldn't ask you to marry me unless I was ready to have a baby, Marni. You and babies, they just seem to go together. I can't wait to get you pregnant."

She laughed. "Chase, you've made my every Christmas wish come true."

"Except one," he said solemnly. "There's one more wish I'd like to grant you, Marni McCumber."

She'd looked into his handsome face, her heart pounding. Could he mean what she thought he did? Her eyes filled with tears. "You don't mean—"

"What would you say to us adopting Raine's baby?"

Marni had burst into tears, amazing for a woman who seldom used to cry before. "Oh, Chase," was all she got out. Her Christmas wish had come true beyond her wildest dreams.

Now, as Chase pulled up in front of the farmhouse, Marni saw the Christmas-tree lights blinking at the front window. She got out of the car to the sound of Christmas carols as the front door burst open and her family spilled out onto the porch to welcome them.

Marni blamed her tears on hormones as she watched Chase lift their daughter from her car seat, and the three of them headed into the welcoming arms of the McCumber family.

Finally, Chase had found a home and a family. And Marni had found a happiness and contentment she'd never dreamed possible. She smiled as she thought of all the Christmases they would spend in this old farmhouse.

But just as she started up the walk, something caught her eye. She looked upward, catching the glitter of stars poking through the clouds and snowfall. Tears filled her eyes as she thought of her father. For years as a young girl her only Christmas wish was that her father could be with them for Christmas.

Now Marni gazed up at the stars shining through a break in the clouds. Snowflakes tumbled down, touching her face lightly. And she knew he'd always been there, every Christmas. Just as he was this one.

"Are you all right?" Chase asked from the porch, concern in his voice.

Marni shifted her gaze to her husband and daughter. Her hand went to the son she'd give birth to before the new year. "Oh, yes," she said, smiling as she walked up the steps to join them. "Oh, yes."

Ring in the New Year with

New Year's Resolution:

FAMILY

This heartwarming collection of three contemporary stories rings in the New Year with babies, families and the best of holiday romance.

Add a dash of romance to your holiday celebrations with this exciting new collection, featuring bestselling authors **Barbara Bretton, Anne McAllister** and **Leandra Logan.**

Available in December,
wherever Harlequin books are sold.

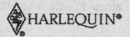

HARLEQUIN®

HARLEQUIN®

INTRIGUE®

Seven Sins

Seven men and women

**Seven flaws that keep them from safety...
from love...from their destiny...**

**Seven chances to win it all...
or lose everything...**

Patricia Rosemoor and Harlequin Intrigue bring you
Seven Sins—a new series based on heroes and heroines
with fatal flaws...and the courage to rise above them.

Join us for the first two books:

#439 BEFORE THE FALL
coming in October 1997

#451 AFTER THE DARK
coming in January 1998

And watch for more SEVEN SINS books in the months to
come—only from Patricia Rosemoor and Harlequin Intrigue!

Look us up on-line at: http://www.romance.net   SS1097

DEBBIE MACOMBER

invites you to the

HEART OF TEXAS

Join Debbie Macomber as she brings you the lives
and loves of the folks in the ranching community
of Promise, Texas.

If you loved Midnight Sons—don't miss
Heart of Texas! A brand-new six-book series
from Debbie Macomber.

Available in February 1998
at your favorite retail store.

Heart of Texas by Debbie Macomber

Lonesome Cowboy	February '98
Texas Two-Step	March '98
Caroline's Child	April '98
Dr. Texas	May '98
Nell's Cowboy	June '98
Lone Star Baby	July '98

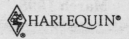

HARLEQUIN®

HPHRT1

Harlequin Women Know Romance When They See It.

And they'll see it on **ROMANCE CLASSICS**, the new 24-hour TV channel devoted to romantic movies and original programs like the special **Romantically Speaking—Harlequin™ Goes Prime Time**.

Romantically Speaking—Harlequin™ Goes Prime Time introduces you to many of your favorite romance authors in a program developed exclusively for Harlequin® readers.

Watch for **Romantically Speaking—Harlequin™ Goes Prime Time** beginning in the summer of 1997.

If you're not receiving ROMANCE CLASSICS, call your local cable operator or satellite provider and ask for it today!

Escape to the network of your dreams.

See Ingrid Bergman and Gregory Peck in *Spellbound* on Romance Classics.

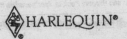